THE MODERN LIBRARY

of the World's Best Books

THE FALL

&

EXILE AND
THE KINGDOM

THE FALL

&

EXILE AND
THE KINGDOM

Albert Camus

Translated from the French by
JUSTIN O'BRIEN

The Modern Library / New York

The Fall © Copyright 1956 by Alfred A. Knopf, Inc.
Originally published in French as *La Chute*.
Copyright 1956 by Librairie Gallimard.

Exile and the Kingdom © Copyright 1957, 1958
by Alfred A. Knopf, Inc.

Originally published in French as *L'Exil et le Royaume*.
© 1957 Librairie Gallimard.

THE MODERN LIBRARY
is published by
RANDOM HOUSE, INC.

BENNETT CERF   DONALD S. KLOPFER

MANUFACTURED IN THE UNITED STATES OF AMERICA

THE FALL

Some were dreadfully insulted, and quite seriously, to have held up as a model such an immoral character as A Hero of Our Time; *others shrewdly noticed that the author had portrayed himself and his acquaintances. . . .* A Hero of Our Time, *gentlemen, is in fact a portrait, but not of an individual; it is the aggregate of the vices of our whole generation in their fullest expression.* LERMONTOV

May I, *monsieur*, offer my services without running the risk of intruding? I fear you may not be able to make yourself understood by the worthy ape who presides over the fate of this establishment. In fact, he speaks nothing but Dutch. Unless you authorize me to plead your case, he will not guess that you want gin. There, I dare hope he understood me; that nod must mean that he yields to my arguments. He is taking steps; indeed, he is making haste with prudent deliberation. You are lucky; he didn't grunt. When he refuses to serve someone, he merely grunts. No one insists. Being master of one's moods is the privilege of the larger animals. Now I shall withdraw, *monsieur*, happy to have been of help to you. Thank you; I'd accept if I were sure of not being a nuisance. You are too kind. Then I shall bring my glass over beside yours.

You are right. His silence is deafening. It's the silence of the primeval forest, heavy with threats. At times I am amazed by his obstinacy in snubbing

3

civilized languages. His business consists in entertaining sailors of all nationalities in this Amsterdam bar, which for that matter he named—no one knows why—*Mexico City*. With such duties wouldn't you think there might be some fear that his ignorance would be awkward? Fancy the Cro-Magnon man lodged in the Tower of Babel! He would certainly feel out of his element. Yet this one is not aware of his exile; he goes his own sweet way and nothing touches him. One of the rare sentences I have ever heard from his mouth proclaimed that you could take it or leave it. What did one have to take or leave? Doubtless our friend himself. I confess I am drawn by such creatures who are all of a piece. Anyone who has considerably meditated on man, by profession or vocation, is led to feel nostalgia for the primates. They at least don't have any ulterior motives.

Our host, to tell the truth, has some, although he harbors them deep within him. As a result of not understanding what is said in his presence, he has adopted a distrustful disposition. Whence that look of touchy dignity as if he at least suspected that all is not perfect among men. That disposition makes it less easy to discuss anything with him that does not concern his business. Notice, for instance, on the back wall above his head that empty rectangle marking the place where a picture has been taken down. Indeed, there *was* a picture there, and a particularly interesting one, a real masterpiece. Well, I was present when the master of the house received it and when he gave it up. In both cases he did so with the same distrust, after weeks of rumination. In that regard you must admit that society has somewhat spoiled the frank simplicity of his nature.

Mind you, I am not judging him. I consider his distrust justified and should be inclined to share it if, as you see, my communicative nature were not opposed to this. I am talkative, alas, and make friends easily. Although I know how to keep my distance, I seize any and every opportunity. When I used to live in France, were I to meet an intelligent man I immediately sought his company. If that be foolish . . . Ah, I see you smile at that use of the subjunctive. I confess my weakness for that mood and for fine speech in general. A weakness that I criticize in myself, believe me. I am well aware that an addiction to silk underwear does not necessarily imply that one's feet are dirty. Nonetheless, style, like sheer silk, too often hides eczema. My consolation is to tell myself that, after all, those who murder the language are not pure either. Why yes, let's have another gin.

Are you staying long in Amsterdam? A beautiful city, isn't it? Fascinating? There's an adjective I haven't heard in some time. Not since leaving Paris, in fact, years ago. But the heart has its own memory and I have forgotten nothing of our beautiful capital, nor of its quays. Paris is a real *trompe-l'œil*, a magnificent stage-setting inhabited by four million silhouettes. Nearly five million at the last census? Why, they must have multiplied. And that wouldn't surprise me. It always seemed to me that our fellow citizens had two passions: ideas and fornication. Without rhyme or reason, so to speak. Still, let us take care not to condemn them; they are not the only ones, for all Europe is in the same boat. I sometimes think of what future historians will say of us. A single sentence will suffice for modern man: he fornicated and read the

6

papers. After that vigorous definition, the subject will be, if I may say so, exhausted.

Oh, not the Dutch; they are much less modern! They have time—just look at them. What do they do? Well, these gentlemen over here live off the labors of those ladies over there. All of them, moreover, both male and female, are very middle-class creatures who have come here, as usual, out of mythomania or stupidity. Through too much or too little imagination, in short. From time to time, these gentlemen indulge in a little knife- or revolver-play, but don't get the idea that they're keen on it. Their role calls for it, that's all, and they are dying of fright as they shoot it out. Nevertheless, I find them more moral than the others, those who kill in the bosom of the family by attrition. Haven't you noticed that our society is organized for this kind of liquidation? You have heard, of course, of those tiny fish in the rivers of Brazil that attack the unwary swimmer by thousands and with swift little nibbles clean him up in a few minutes, leaving only an immaculate skeleton? Well, that's what their organization is. "Do you want a good clean

7

life? Like everybody else?" You say yes, of course.
How can one say no? "O.K. You'll be cleaned up.
Here's a job, a family, and organized leisure activities." And the little teeth attack the flesh, right
down to the bone. But I am unjust. I shouldn't say
their organization. It is *ours*, after all: it's a question of which will clean up the other.

Here is our gin at last. To your prosperity.
Yes, the ape opened his mouth to call me doctor.
In these countries everyone is a doctor, or a professor. They like showing respect, out of kindness
and out of modesty. Among them, at least, spitefulness is not a national institution. Besides, I am
not a doctor. If you want to know, I was a lawyer
before coming here. Now, I am a judge-penitent.

But allow me to introduce myself: Jean-Baptiste Clamence, at your service. Pleased to know
you. You are in business, no doubt? In a way? Excellent reply! Judicious too: in all things we are
merely "in a way." Now, allow me to play the detective. You are my age in a way, with the sophisticated eye of the man in his forties who has seen
everything, in a way; you are well dressed in a
way, that is as people are in our country; and your

hands are smooth. Hence a bourgeois, in a way! But a cultured bourgeois! Smiling at the use of the subjunctive, in fact, proves your culture twice over because you recognize it to begin with and then because you feel superior to it. Lastly, I amuse you. And be it said without vanity, this implies in you a certain open-mindedness. Consequently you are in a way . . . But no matter. Professions interest me less than sects. Allow me to ask you two questions and don't answer if you consider them indiscreet. Do you have any possessions? Some? Good. Have you shared them with the poor? No? Then you are what I call a Sadducee. If you are not familiar with the Scriptures, I admit that this won't help you. But it does help you? So you know the Scriptures? Decidedly, you interest me.

As for me . . . Well, judge for yourself. By my stature, my shoulders, and this face that I have often been told was shy, I rather look like a rugby player, don't I? But if I am judged by my conversation I have to be granted a little subtlety. The camel that provided the hair for my overcoat was probably mangy; yet my nails are manicured. I, too, am sophisticated, and yet I confide in you without caution on the sole basis of your looks. Finally, despite my good manners and my fine speech, I frequent sailors' bars in the Zeedijk. Come on, give up. My profession is double, that's all, like the human being. I have already told you, I am a judge-penitent. Only one thing is simple in my case: I possess nothing. Yes, I was rich. No, I shared nothing with the poor. What does that prove? That I, too, was a Sadducee . . . Oh, do you hear the foghorns in the harbor? There'll be fog tonight on the Zuider Zee.

You're leaving already? Forgive me for having perhaps detained you. No, I beg you; I won't let you pay. I am at home at *Mexico City* and have been particularly pleased to receive you here. I shall certainly be here tomorrow, as I am every evening, and I shall be pleased to accept your invitation. Your way back? . . . Well . . . But if you don't have any objection, the easiest thing would be for me to accompany you as far as the harbor. Thence, by going around the Jewish quarter you'll find those fine avenues with their parade of streetcars full of flowers and thundering sounds. Your hotel is on one of them, the Damrak. You first, please. I live in the Jewish quarter or what was called so until our Hitlerian brethren made room. What a cleanup! Seventy-five thousand Jews deported or assassinated; that's real vacuum-cleaning. I admire that diligence, that methodical patience! When one has no character one *has* to apply a method. Here it did wonders incontrovertibly, and I am living on the site of one of the greatest crimes in history. Perhaps that's what helps me to understand the ape and his distrust. Thus I can struggle against my natural inclination carrying me toward fraternizing. When I see a new face, something in me sounds the alarm. "Slow! Danger!" Even when the attraction is strongest, I am on my guard.

Do you know that in my little village, during a punitive operation, a German officer courteously asked an old woman to please choose which of her two sons would be shot as a hostage? Choose!— can you imagine that? That one? No, this one. And see him go. Let's not dwell on it, but believe me, *monsieur*, any surprise is possible. I knew a pure heart who rejected distrust. He was a pacifist and libertarian and loved all humanity and the animals

11

The Fall

with an equal love. An exceptional soul, that's certain. Well, during the last wars of religion in Europe he had retired to the country. He had written on his threshold: "Wherever you come from, come in and be welcome." Who do you think answered that noble invitation? The militia, who made themselves at home and disemboweled him.

Oh, pardon, *madame!* But she didn't understand a word of it anyway. All these people, eh? out so late despite this rain which hasn't let up for days. Fortunately there is gin, the sole glimmer of light in this darkness. Do you feel the golden, copper-colored light it kindles in you? I like walking through the city of an evening in the warmth of gin. I walk for nights on end, I dream or talk to myself interminably. Yes, like this evening—and I fear making your head swim somewhat. Thank you, you are most courteous. But it's the overflow; as soon as I open my mouth, sentences start to flow. Besides, this country inspires me. I like these people swarming on the sidewalks, wedged into a little space of houses and canals, hemmed in by fogs, cold lands, and the sea steaming like a wet wash. I like them, for they are double. They are here and elsewhere.

Yes, indeed! From hearing their heavy tread on the damp pavement, from seeing them move heavily between their shops full of gilded herrings and jewels the color of dead leaves, you probably think they are here this evening? You are like everybody else; you take these good people for a tribe of syndics and merchants counting their gold crowns with their chances of eternal life, whose only lyricism consists in occasionally, without doffing their broad-brimmed hats, taking anatomy lessons? You are wrong. They walk along with us, to be sure, and yet see where their heads are: in that fog compounded of neon, gin, and mint emanating from the shop signs above them. Holland is a dream, *monsieur*, a dream of gold and smoke —smokier by day, more gilded by night. And night and day that dream is peopled with Lohengrins like these, dreamily riding their black bicycles with high handle-bars, funereal swans constantly drifting throughout the whole land, around the seas, along the canals. Their heads in their copper-colored clouds, they dream; they cycle in circles; they pray, somnambulists in the fog's gilded incense; they have ceased to be here. They have gone thousands of miles away, toward Java, the distant isle. They pray to those grimacing gods of Indonesia with which they have decorated all their shopwindows and which at this moment are floating aimlessly above us before alighting, like sumptuous monkeys, on the signs and stepped roofs to remind these homesick colonials that Holland is not only the Europe of merchants but also the sea, the sea that leads to Cipango and to those islands where men die mad and happy.

But I am letting myself go! I am pleading a case! Forgive me. Habit, *monsieur*, vocation, also the desire to make you fully understand this city, and the heart of things! For we are at the heart of things here. Have you noticed that Amsterdam's concentric canals resemble the circles of hell? The middle-class hell, of course, peopled with bad dreams. When one comes from the outside, as one gradually goes through those circles, life—and hence its crimes—becomes denser, darker. Here, we are in the last circle. The circle of the . . .

14

Ah, you know that? By heaven, you become harder to classify. But you understand then why I can say that the center of things is here although we stand at the tip of the continent. A sensitive man grasps such oddities. In any case, the newspaper readers and the fornicators can go no further. They come from the four corners of Europe and stop facing the inner sea, on the drab strand. They listen to the foghorns, vainly try to make out the silhouettes of boats in the fog, then turn back over the canals and go home through the rain. Chilled to the bone, they come and ask in all languages for gin at *Mexico City*. There I wait for them.

Till tomorrow, then, *monsieur et cher compatriote*. No, you will easily find your way now: I'll leave you near this bridge. I never cross a bridge at night. It's the result of a vow. Suppose, after all, that someone should jump in the water. One of two things—either you do likewise to fish him out and, in cold weather, you run a great risk! Or you forsake him there and suppressed dives sometimes leave one strangely aching. Good night. What? Those ladies behind those windows? Dream, *monsieur*, cheap dream, a trip to the Indies! Those persons perfume themselves with spices. You go in, they draw the curtains, and the navigation begins. The gods come down onto the naked bodies and the islands are set adrift, lost souls crowned with the tousled hair of palm trees in the wind. Try it.

WHAT is a judge-penitent? Ah, I intrigued you with that business. I meant no harm by it, believe me, and I can explain myself more clearly. In a way, that even belongs to my official duties. But first I must set forth a certain number of facts that will help you to understand my story.

A few years ago I was a lawyer in Paris and, indeed, a rather well-known lawyer. Of course, I didn't tell you my real name. I had a specialty: noble cases. Widows and orphans, as the saying goes —I don't know why, because there are improper widows and ferocious orphans. Yet it was enough for me to sniff the slightest scent of victim on a defendant for me to swing into action. And what action! A real tornado! My heart was on my sleeve. You would really have thought that justice slept with me every night. I am sure you would have admired the rightness of my tone, the appropriateness of my emotion, the persuasion and warmth, the restrained indignation of my speeches before the court. Nature favored me as to my physique, and the noble attitude comes effortlessly. Furthermore, I was buoyed up by two sincere feelings: the satisfaction of being on the right side of the bar and an instinctive scorn for judges in general. That scorn, after all, wasn't perhaps so instinctive. I know now that it had its reasons. But, seen from the outside, it looked rather like a passion. It can't be denied that, for the moment at least, we have to have judges, don't we? However, I could not understand how a man could offer himself to perform such a surprising function. I accepted the fact because I saw it, but rather as I accepted locusts. With this difference: that the invasions of those Orthoptera never brought me a sou whereas I earned my living by carrying on a dialogue with people I scorned.

But, after all, I was on the right side; that was enough to satisfy my conscience. The feeling of the law, the satisfaction of being right, the joy of self-esteem, *cher monsieur*, are powerful incentives for keeping us upright or keeping us moving forward. On the other hand, if you deprive men of them, you transform them into dogs frothing with rage. How many crimes committed merely because their authors could not endure being wrong! I once knew a manufacturer who had a perfect wife, admired by all, and yet he deceived her. That man was literally furious to be in the wrong, to be blocked from receiving, or granting himself, a certificate of virtue. The more virtues his wife manifested, the more vexed he became. Eventually, living in the wrong became unbearable to him. What do you think he did then? He gave up deceiving her? Not at all. He killed her. That is how I entered into relations with him.

My situation was more enviable. Not only did I run no risk of joining the criminal camp (in particular I had no chance of killing my wife, being a bachelor), but I even took up their defense, on the sole condition that they should be noble murderers, as others are noble savages. The very manner in which I conducted that defense gave me great satisfactions. I was truly above reproach in my professional life. I never accepted a bribe, it goes without saying, and I never stooped either to any shady proceedings. And—this is even rarer—I never deigned to flatter any journalist to get him on my side, nor any civil servant whose friendship might be useful to me. I even had the luck of see-ing the Legion of Honor offered to me two or three times and of being able to refuse it with a dis-creet dignity in which I found my true reward. Fi-nally, I never charged the poor a fee and never boasted of it. Don't think for a moment, *cher monsieur*, that I am bragging. I take no credit for this. The avidity which in our society substitutes for ambition has always made me laugh. I was aim-ing higher; you will see that the expression is exact in my case.

But you can already imagine my satisfaction. I enjoyed my own nature to the fullest, and we all know that there lies happiness, although, to soothe one another mutually, we occasionally pretend to condemn such joys as selfishness. At least I enjoyed that part of my nature which reacted so appropri-ately to the widow and orphan that eventually, through exercise, it came to dominate my whole life. For instance, I loved to help blind people cross streets. From as far away as I could see a cane hesi-tating on the edge of a sidewalk, I would rush for-ward, sometimes only a second ahead of another charitable hand already outstretched, snatch the blind person from any solicitude but mine, and lead him gently but firmly along the crosswalk among the traffic obstacles toward the refuge of the other sidewalk, where we would separate with a mutual emotion. In the same way, I always enjoyed giving directions in the street, obliging with a light, lending a hand to heavy pushcarts, pushing a stranded car, buying a paper from the Salvation Army lass or flowers from the old peddler, though I knew she stole them from the Montparnasse cemetery. I also liked—and this is harder to say—I liked to give alms. A very Christian friend of mine admitted that one's initial feeling on seeing a beggar approach one's house is unpleasant. Well, with me it was worse: I used to exult. But let's not dwell on this.

Let us speak rather of my courtesy. It was famous and unquestionable. Indeed, good manners provided me with great delights. If I had the luck, certain mornings, to give up my seat in the bus or subway to someone who obviously deserved it, to pick up some object an old lady had dropped and return it to her with a smile I knew well, or merely to forfeit my taxi to someone in a greater hurry than I, it was a red-letter day. I even rejoiced, I

21

must admit, those days when the transport system being on strike I had a chance to load into my car at the bus stops some of my unfortunate fellow citizens unable to get home. Giving up my seat in the theater to allow a couple to sit together, hoisting a girl's suitcases onto the rack in a train—these were all deeds I performed more often than others because I paid more attention to the opportunities and was better able to relish the pleasure they give.

Consequently I was considered generous, and so I was. I gave a great deal in public and in private. But far from suffering when I had to give up an object or a sum of money, I derived constant pleasures from this—among them a sort of melancholy which occasionally rose within me at the thought of the sterility of those gifts and the probable ingratitude that would follow. I even took such pleasure in giving that I hated to be obliged to do so. Exactitude in money matters bored me to death and I conformed ungraciously. I had to be the master of my liberalities.

These are just little touches but they will help you grasp the constant delights I experienced in my life, and especially in my profession. Being stopped in the corridor of the law courts by the wife of a defendant you represented out of justice or pity alone—I mean without charge—hearing that woman whisper that nothing, no, nothing could ever repay what you had done for them, replying that it was quite natural, that anyone would have done as much, even offering some financial help to tide over the bad days ahead, then—in order to cut the effusions short and preserve their proper resonance—kissing the hand of a poor woman and breaking away—believe me, *cher monsieur*, this is achieving more than the vulgar ambitious man and rising to that supreme summit where virtue is its own reward.

Let's pause on these heights. Now you understand what I meant when I spoke of aiming higher. I was talking, it so happens, of those supreme summits, the only places I can really live. Yes, I have never felt comfortable except in lofty places. Even in the details of daily life, I needed to feel *above*. I preferred the bus to the subway, open carriages to taxis, terraces to closed-in places. An enthusiast for sport planes in which one's head is in the open, on boats I was the eternal pacer of the top deck.

In the mountains I used to flee the deep valleys for the passes and plateaus; I was the man of the mesas at least. If fate had forced me to choose between work at a lathe or as a roofer, don't worry, I'd have chosen the roofs and become acquainted with dizziness. Coalbins, ships' holds, undergrounds, grottoes, pits were repulsive to me. I had even developed a special loathing for speleologists, who had the nerve to fill the front page of our newspapers, and whose records nauseated me. Striving to reach elevation minus eight hundred at the risk of getting one's head caught in a rocky funnel (a siphon, as those fools say!) seemed to me the exploit of perverted or traumatized characters. There was something criminal underlying it.

A natural balcony fifteen hundred feet above a sea still visible bathed in sunlight, on the other hand, was the place where I could breathe most freely, especially if I were alone, well above the human ants. I could readily understand why sermons, decisive preachings, and fire miracles took place on accessible heights. In my opinion no one meditated in cellars or prison cells (unless they were situated in a tower with a broad view); one just became moldy. And I could understand that man who, having entered holy orders, gave up the frock because his cell, instead of overlooking a vast landscape as he expected, looked out on a wall. Rest assured that as far as I was concerned I did not grow moldy. At every hour of the day, within myself and among others, I would scale the heights and light conspicuous fires, and a joyful greeting would rise toward me. Thus at least I took pleasure in life and in my own excellence.

My profession satisfied most happily that vocation for summits. It cleansed me of all bitterness toward my neighbor, whom I always obligated without ever owing him anything. It set me above the judge whom I judged in turn, above the defendant whom I forced to gratitude. Just weigh this, *cher monsieur*, I lived with impunity. I was concerned in no judgment; I was not on the floor of the courtroom, but somewhere in the flies like those gods that are brought down by machinery from time to time to transfigure the action and give it its meaning. After all, living aloft is still the only way of being seen and hailed by the largest number.

Besides, some of my good criminals had killed in obedience to the same feeling. Reading the newspapers afterward, in the sorry condition in which they then were, doubtless brought them a sort of unhappy compensation. Like many men, they had no longer been able to endure anonymity, and that impatience had contributed to leading them to unfortunate extremities. To achieve notoriety it is enough, after all, to kill one's concierge. Unhappily, this is usually an ephemeral reputation, so many concierges are there who deserve and receive the knife. Crime constantly monopolizes the headlines, but the criminal appears there only fugitively, to be replaced at once. In short, such brief triumphs cost too dear. Defending our unfortunate aspirants after a reputation amounted, on the other hand, to becoming really well known, at the same time and in the same places, but by more economical means. Consequently this encouraged me to making more meritorious efforts so that they would pay as little as possible. What they were paying they were doing so to some extent in my place. The indignation, talent, and emotion I expended on them washed away, in return, any debt

I might feel toward them. The judges punished and the defendants expiated, while I, free of any duty, shielded from judgment as from penalty, I freely held sway bathed in a light as of Eden.

Indeed, wasn't that Eden, *cher monsieur:* no intermediary between life and me? Such was my life. I never had to learn how to live. In that regard, I already knew everything at birth. Some people's problem is to protect themselves from men or at least to come to terms with them. In my case, the understanding was already established. Familiar when it was appropriate, silent when necessary, capable of a free and easy manner as readily as of dignity, I was always in harmony. Hence my popularity was great and my successes in society innumerable. I was acceptable in appearance; I revealed myself to be both a tireless dancer and an unobtrusively learned man; I managed to love simultaneously—and this is not easy—women and justice; I indulged in sports and the fine arts—in short, I'll not go on for fear you might suspect me of self-flattery. But just imagine, I beg you, a man at the height of his powers, in perfect health, generously gifted, skilled in bodily exercises as in those

27

of the mind, neither rich nor poor, sleeping well, and fundamentally pleased with himself without showing this otherwise than by a felicitous sociability. You will readily see how I can speak, without immodesty, of a successful life.

Yes, few creatures were more natural than I. I was altogether in harmony with life, fitting into it from top to bottom without rejecting any of its ironies, its grandeur, or its servitude. In particular the flesh, matter, the physical in short, which disconcerts or discourages so many men in love or in solitude, without enslaving me, brought me steady joys. I was made to have a body. Whence that harmony in me, that relaxed mastery that people felt, even to telling me sometimes that it helped them in life. Hence my company was in demand. Often, for instance, people thought they had met me before. Life, its creatures and its gifts, offered themselves to me, and I accepted such marks of homage with a kindly pride. To tell the truth, just from being so fully and simply a man, I looked upon myself as something of a superman.

I was of respectable but humble birth (my father was an officer), and yet, certain mornings, let me confess it humbly, I felt like a king's son, or a burning bush. It was not a matter, mind you, of the certainty I had of being more intelligent than everyone else. Besides, such certainty is of no consequence because so many imbeciles share it. No, as a result of being showered with blessings, I felt, I hesitate to admit, marked out. Personally marked out, among all, for that long and uninterrupted success. This, after all, was a result of my modesty. I refused to attribute that success to my own merits and could not believe that the conjunction in a single person of such different and such extreme virtues was the result of chance alone. This is why in my happy life I felt somehow that that happiness was authorized by some higher decree. When I add that I had no religion you can see even better how extraordinary that conviction was. Whether ordinary or not, it served for some time to raise me above the daily routine and I literally soared for a period of years, for which, to tell the truth, I still long in my heart of hearts. I soared until the evening when . . . But no, that's another matter and it must be forgotten. Anyway, I am perhaps exaggerating. I was at ease in everything, to be sure, but at the same time satisfied with nothing. Each joy made me desire another. I went from festivity to festivity. On occasion I danced for nights on end, ever madder about people and life. At times, late on those nights when the dancing, the slight intoxication, my wild enthusiasm, everyone's violent unrestraint would fill me with a tired and overwhelmed rapture, it would seem to me—at the breaking point of fatigue and for a second's flash —that at last I understood the secret of creatures and of the world. But my fatigue would disappear the next day, and with it the secret; I would rush forth anew. I ran on like that, always heaped with favors, never satiated, without knowing where to stop, until the day—until the evening rather when the music stopped and the lights went out. The gay party at which I had been so happy . . . But allow me to call on our friend the primate. Nod your head to thank him and, above all, drink up with me, I need your understanding.

I see that that declaration amazes you. Have you never suddenly needed understanding, help, friendship? Yes, of course. I have learned to be satisfied with understanding. It is found more readily and, besides, it's not binding. "I beg you to believe in my sympathetic understanding" in the inner discourse always precedes immediately "and now, let's turn to other matters." It's a board chairman's emotion; it comes cheap, after catastrophes. Friendship is less simple. It is long and hard to obtain, but when one has it there's no getting rid of it; one simply has to cope with it. Don't think for a minute that your friends will telephone you every evening, as they ought to, in order to find out if this doesn't happen to be the evening when you are deciding to commit suicide, or simply whether you don't need company, whether you are not in a mood to go out. No, don't worry, they'll ring up the evening you are not alone, when life is beautiful. As for suicide, they would be more likely to push you to it, by virtue of what you owe to yourself, according to them. May heaven protect us, *cher monsieur*, from being set on a pedestal by our friends! Those whose duty is to love us—I mean relatives and connections (what an expression!)— are another matter. They find the right word, all right, and it hits the bull's-eye; they telephone as if shooting a rifle. And they know how to aim. Oh, the Bazaines!

What? What evening? I'll get to it, be patient with me. In a certain way I *am* sticking to my subject with all that about friends and connections. You see, I've heard of a man whose friend had been imprisoned and who slept on the floor of his room every night in order not to enjoy a comfort of which his friend had been deprived. Who, *cher monsieur*, will sleep on the floor for us? Whether I am capable of it myself? Look, I'd like to be and I shall be. Yes, we shall all be capable of it one day, and that will be salvation. But it's not easy, for friendship is absent-minded or at least unavailing. It is incapable of achieving what it wants. Maybe, after all, it doesn't want it enough? Maybe we don't love life enough? Have you noticed that death alone awakens our feelings? How we love the friends who have just left us? How we admire those of our teachers who have ceased to speak, their mouths filled with earth! Then the expression of admiration springs forth naturally, that admiration they were perhaps expecting from us all their lives. But do you know why we are always more just and more generous toward the dead? The reason is simple. With them there is no obligation. They leave us free and we can take our time, fit the testimonial in between a cocktail party and a nice little mistress, in our spare time, in short. If they forced us to anything, it would be to remembering, and we have a short memory. No, it is the recently dead we love among our friends, the painful dead, our emotion, ourselves after all!

For instance, I had a friend I generally avoided. He rather bored me, and, besides, he was something of a moralist. But when he was on his deathbed, I was there—don't worry. I never missed a day. He died satisfied with me, holding both my hands. A woman who used to chase after me, and in vain, had the good sense to die young. What room in my heart at once! And when, in addition, it's a suicide! Lord, what a delightful commotion! One's telephone rings, one's heart overflows, and the intentionally short sentences yet heavy with implications, one's restrained suffering and even, yes, a bit of self-accusation!

That's the way man is, *cher monsieur*. He has

33

two faces: he can't love without self-love. Notice your neighbors if perchance a death takes place in the building. They were asleep in their little routine and suddenly, for example, the concierge dies. At once they awake, bestir themselves, get the details, commiserate. A newly dead man and the show begins at last. They need tragedy, don't you know; it's their little transcendence, their *apéritif*. Moreover, is it mere chance that I should speak of a concierge? I had one, really ill favored, malice incarnate, a monster of insignificance and rancor, who would have discouraged a Franciscan. I had even given up speaking to him, but by his mere existence he compromised my customary contentedness. He died and I went to his funeral. Can you tell me why?

Anyway, the two days preceding the ceremony were full of interest. The concierge's wife was ill, lying in the single room, and near her the coffin had been set on sawhorses. Everyone had to get his mail himself. You opened the door, said *"Bonjour, madame,"* listened to her praise of the dear departed as she pointed to him, and took your mail. Nothing very amusing about that. And yet the whole building passed through her room, which stank of carbolic acid. And the tenants didn't send their servants either; they came themselves to take advantage of the unexpected attraction. The servants did too, of course, but on the sly. The day of the funeral, the coffin was too big for the door. "O my dearie," the wife said from her bed with a surprise at once delighted and grieved, "how big he was!" "Don't worry, *madame*," replied the funeral director, "we'll get him through edgewise, and upright." He was got through upright and then laid down again, and I was the only one (with a former cabaret doorman who, I gathered, used to drink his Pernod every evening with the departed) to go as far as the cemetery and strew flowers on a coffin of astounding luxury. Then I paid a visit to the concierge's wife to receive her thanks expressed as by a great tragedienne. Tell me, what was the reason for all that? None, except the *apéritif*.

I likewise buried an old fellow member of the Lawyers' Guild. A clerk to whom no one paid attention, but I always shook his hand. Where I worked I used to shake everyone's hand, moreover, being doubly sure to miss no one. Without much effort, such cordial simplicity won me the popularity so necessary to my contentment. For the funeral of our clerk the President of the Guild had not gone out of his way. But I did, and on the eve of a trip, as was amply pointed out. It so happened that I knew my presence would be noticed and favorably commented on. Hence, you see, not even the snow that was falling that day made me withdraw.

What? I'm getting to it, never fear; besides, I have never left it. But let me first point out that my concierge's wife, who had gone to such an outlay for the crucifix, heavy oak, and silver handles in order to get the most out of her emotion, had shacked up a month later with an overdressed yokel proud of his singing voice. He used to beat her; frightful screams could be heard and immediately afterward he would open the window and give forth with his favorite song: "Women, how pretty you are!" "All the *same!*" the neighbors would say. All the same what? I ask you. All right, appearances were against the baritone, and against the concierge's wife, too. But nothing proves that they were not in love. And nothing proves either that she did not love her husband. Moreover, when the yokel took flight, his voice and arm exhausted, she —that faithful wife—resumed her praises of the departed. After all, I know of others who have appearances on their side and are no more faithful or sincere. I knew a man who gave twenty years of his life to a scatterbrained woman, sacrificing everything to her, his friendships, his work, the very respectability of his life, and who one evening recognized that he had never loved her. He had been bored, that's all, bored like most people. Hence he had made himself out of whole cloth a life full of complications and drama. Something must happen—and that explains most human commitments. Something must happen, even loveless slavery, even war or death. Hurray then for funerals!

But I at least didn't have that excuse. I was not bored because I was riding on the crest of the wave. On the evening I am speaking about I can say that I was even less bored than ever. And yet . . . You see, *cher monsieur*, it was a fine autumn evening, still warm in town and already damp over

37

the Seine. Night was falling; the sky, still bright in the west, was darkening; the street lamps were glowing dimly. I was walking up the quays of the Left Bank toward the Pont des Arts. The river was gleaming between the stalls of the secondhand booksellers. There were but few people on the quays; Paris was already at dinner. I was treading on the dusty yellow leaves that still recalled summer. Gradually the sky was filling with stars that could be seen for a moment after leaving one street lamp and heading toward another. I enjoyed the return of silence, the evening's mildness, the emptiness of Paris. I was happy. The day had been good: a blind man, the reduced sentence I had hoped for, a cordial handclasp from my client, a few liberalities, and in the afternoon, a brilliant improvisation in the company of several friends on the hardheartedness of our governing class and the hypocrisy of our leaders.

I had gone up on the Pont des Arts, deserted at that hour, to look at the river that could hardly be made out now night had come. Facing the statue of the Vert-Galant, I dominated the island. I felt rising within me a vast feeling of power and—I don't know how to express it—of completion, which cheered my heart. I straightened up and was about to light a cigarette, the cigarette of satisfaction, when, at that very moment, a laugh burst out behind me. Taken by surprise, I suddenly wheeled around; there was no one there. I stepped to the railing; no barge or boat. I turned back toward the island and, again, heard the laughter behind me, a little farther off as if it were going downstream. I stood there motionless. The sound of the laughter was decreasing, but I could still hear it distinctly behind me, come from nowhere unless from the water. At the same time I was aware of the rapid beating of my heart. Please don't misunderstand me; there was nothing mysterious about that laugh; it was a good, hearty, almost friendly laugh, which re-established the proper proportions. Soon I heard nothing more, anyway. I returned to the quays, went up the rue Dauphine, bought some cigarettes I didn't need at all. I was dazed and had trouble breathing. That evening I rang up a friend, who wasn't at home. I was hesitating about going out when, suddenly, I heard laughter under my windows. I opened them. On the sidewalk, in fact, some youths were loudly saying good night. I shrugged my shoulders as I closed the windows; after all, I had a brief to study. I went into the bathroom to drink a glass of water. My reflection was smiling in the mirror, but it seemed to me that my smile was double. . . .

What? Forgive me, I was thinking of something else. I'll see you again tomorrow, probably. Tomorrow, yes, that's right. No, no, I can't stay. Besides, I am called in consultation by that brown bear of a man you see over there. A decent fellow, for sure, whom the police are meanly persecuting out of sheer perversity. You think he looks like a killer? Rest assured that his actions conform to his looks. He burgles likewise, and you will be surprised to learn that that cave man is specialized in the art trade. In Holland everyone is a specialist in paintings and in tulips. This one, with his modest mien, is the author of the most famous theft of a painting. Which one? I may tell you. Don't be surprised at my knowledge. Although I am a judge-penitent, I have my side line here: I am the legal counselor of these good people. I studied the laws of the country and built up a clientele in this quarter where diplomas are not required. It wasn't easy, but I inspire confidence, don't I? I have a good, hearty laugh and an energetic handshake, and those are trump cards. Besides, I settled a few difficult cases, out of self-interest to begin with and later out of conviction. If pimps and thieves were invariably sentenced, all decent people would get to thinking they themselves were constantly innocent, *cher monsieur*. And in my opinion—all right, all right, I'm coming!—that's what must be avoided above all. Otherwise, everything would be just a joke.

Really, *mon cher compatriote*, I am grateful to you for your curiosity. However, there is nothing extraordinary about my story. Since you are interested, I'll tell you that I thought a little about that laugh, for a few days, then forgot about it. Once in a great while, I seemed to hear it within me. But most of the time, without making any effort, I thought of other things.

Yet I must admit that I ceased to walk along the Paris quays. When I would ride along them in a car or bus, a sort of silence would descend on me. I was waiting, I believe. But I would cross the Seine, nothing would happen, and I would breathe again. I also had some health problems at that time. Nothing definite, a dejection perhaps, a sort of difficulty in recovering my good spirits. I saw doctors, who gave me stimulants. I was alternately stimulated and depressed. Life became less easy for me: when the body is sad the heart languishes. It seemed to me that I was half unlearning what I had never learned and yet knew so well—how to live. Yes, I think it was probably then that everything began.

But this evening I don't feel quite up to snuff either. I even find trouble expressing myself. I'm not talking so well, it seems to me, and my words are less assured. Probably the weather. It's hard to breathe; the air is so heavy it weighs on one's chest. Would you object, *mon cher compatriote*, to going out and walking in the town a little? Thank you.

How beautiful the canals are this evening! I like the breath of stagnant waters, the smell of dead leaves soaking in the canal and the funereal scent rising from the barges loaded with flowers. No, no, there's nothing morbid about such a taste, I assure you. On the contrary, it's deliberate with me. The truth is that I force myself to admire these canals. What I like most in the world is Sicily, you see, and especially from the top of Etna, in the sunlight, provided I dominate the island and the sea. Java, too, but at the time of the trade winds. Yes, I went there in my youth. In a general way, I like all islands. It is easier to dominate them.

Charming house, isn't it? The two heads you see up there are heads of Negro slaves. A shop sign. The house belonged to a slave dealer. Oh, they weren't squeamish in those days! They had assurance; they announced: "You see, I'm a man of substance; I'm in the slave trade; I deal in black flesh." Can you imagine anyone today making it known publicly that such is his business? What a scandal! I can hear my Parisian colleagues right now. They are adamant on the subject; they wouldn't hesitate to launch two or three manifestoes, maybe even more! And on reflection, I'd add my signature to theirs. Slavery?—certainly not, we are against it! That we should be forced to establish it at home or in our factories—well, that's natural; but boasting about it, that's the limit!

I am well aware that one can't get along without domineering or being served. Every man needs slaves as he needs fresh air. Commanding is breathing—you agree with me? And even the most destitute manage to breathe. The lowest man in the social scale still has his wife or his child. If he's unmarried, a dog. The essential thing, after all, is being able to get angry with someone who has no

44

right to talk back. "One doesn't talk back to one's father"—you know the expression? In one way it is very odd. To whom should one talk back in this world if not to what one loves? In another way, it is convincing. Somebody has to have the last word. Otherwise, every reason can be answered with another one and there would never be an end to it. Power, on the other hand, settles everything. It took time, but we finally realized that. For instance, you must have noticed that our old Europe at last philosophizes in the right way. We no longer say as in simple times: "This is the way I think. What are your objections?" We have become lucid. For the dialogue we have substituted the communiqué: "This is the truth," we say. "You can discuss it as much as you want; we aren't interested. But in a few years there'll be the police who will show you we are right."

Ah, this dear old planet! All is clear now. We know ourselves; we now know of what we are capable. Just take me, to change examples if not subjects, I have always wanted to be served with a smile. If the maid looked sad, she poisoned my days. She had a right not to be cheerful, to be

45

sure. But I told myself that it was better for her to perform her service with a laugh than with tears. In fact, it was better for me. Yet, without boasting, my reasoning was not altogether idiotic. Likewise, I always refused to eat in Chinese restaurants. Why? Because Orientals when they are silent and in the presence of whites often look scornful. Naturally they keep that look when serving. How then can you enjoy the glazed chicken? And, above all, how can you look at them and think you are right?

Just between us, slavery, preferably with a smile, is inevitable then. But we must not admit it. Isn't it better that whoever cannot do without having slaves should call them free men? For the principle to begin with, and, secondly, not to drive them to despair. We owe them that compensation, don't we? In that way, they will continue to smile and we shall maintain our good conscience. Otherwise, we'd be obliged to reconsider our opinion of ourselves; we'd go mad with suffering, or even become modest—for everything would be possible. Consequently, no shop signs, and this one is shocking. Besides, if everyone told all, displayed his true profession and identity, we shouldn't know which way to turn! Imagine the visiting cards: Dupont, jittery philosopher, or Christian landowner, or adulterous humanist—indeed, there's a wide choice. But it would be hell! Yes, hell must be like that: streets filled with shop signs and no way of explaining one-self. One is classified once and for all.

You, for instance, *mon cher compatriote*, stop and think of what your sign would be. You are silent? Well, you'll tell me later on. I know mine in any case: a double face, a charming Janus, and above it the motto of the house: "Don't rely on it." On my cards: "Jean-Baptiste Clamence, play actor." Why, shortly after the evening I told you about, I discovered something. When I would leave a blind man on the sidewalk to which I had convoyed him, I used to tip my hat to him. Obviously the hat tipping wasn't intended for him, since he couldn't see it. To whom was it addressed? To the public. After playing my part, I would take the bow. Not bad, eh? Another day during the same period, to a motorist who was thanking me for helping him, I replied that no one would have done as much. I meant, of course, anyone. But that unfortunate slip weighed heavy on me. For modesty, really, I took the cake.

I have to admit it humbly, *mon cher compatriote*, I was always bursting with vanity. I, I, I is the refrain of my whole life, which could be heard in everything I said. I could never talk without boasting, especially if I did so with that shattering discretion that was my specialty. It is quite true that I always lived free and powerful. I simply felt released in regard to all for the excellent reason that I recognized no equals. I always considered myself more intelligent than everyone else, as I've told you, but also more sensitive and more skillful, a crack shot, an incomparable driver, a better lover. Even in the fields in which it was easy for me to verify my inferiority—like tennis, for instance, in which I was but a passable partner—it was hard for me not to think that, with a little time for practice, I would surpass the best players. I admitted only superiorities in me and this explained my good will and serenity. When I was concerned with others, I was so out of pure condescension, in utter freedom, and all the credit went to me: my self-esteem would go up a degree.

Along with a few other truths, I discovered these facts little by little in the period following the evening I told you about. Not all at once nor very clearly. First I had to recover my memory. By gradual degrees I saw more clearly, I learned a little of what I knew. Until then I had always been aided by an extraordinary ability to forget. I used to forget everything, beginning with my resolutions. Fundamentally, nothing mattered. War, suicide, love, poverty got my attention, of course, when circumstances forced me, but a courteous, superficial attention. At times, I would pretend to get excited about some cause foreign to my daily life. But basically I didn't really take part in it except, of course, when my freedom was thwarted. How can I express it? Everything slid off—yes, just rolled off me.

In the interest of fairness, it should be said that sometimes my forgetfulness was praiseworthy. You have noticed that there are people whose religion consists in forgiving all offenses, and who do in fact forgive them but never forget them? I wasn't good enough to forgive offenses, but eventually I always forgot them. And the man who thought I hated him couldn't get over seeing me tip my hat to him with a smile. According to his nature, he would then admire my nobility of character or scorn my ill breeding without realizing that my reason was simpler: I had forgotten his very name. The same infirmity that often made me indifferent or ungrateful in such cases made me magnanimous.

I lived consequently without any other continuity than that, from day to day, of I, I, I. From day to day women, from day to day virtue or vice, from day to day, like dogs—but every day myself secure at my post. Thus I progressed on the surface of life, in the realm of words as it were, never in reality. All those books barely read, those friends barely loved, those cities barely visited, those women barely possessed! I went through the gestures out of boredom or absent-mindedness. Then came human beings; they wanted to cling, but there was nothing to cling to, and that was unfortunate —for them. As for me, I forgot. I never remembered anything but myself.

Gradually, however, my memory returned. Or rather, I returned to it, and in it I found the recollection that was awaiting me. But before telling you of it, allow me, *mon cher compatriote*, to give you a few examples (they will be useful to you, I am sure) of what I discovered in the course of my exploration.

One day in my car when I was slow in making a getaway at the green light while our patient fellow citizens immediately began honking furiously behind me, I suddenly remembered another occasion set in similar circumstances. A motorcycle ridden by a spare little man wearing spectacles and plus fours had gone around me and planted itself in front of me at the red light. As he came to a stop the little man had stalled his motor and was vainly striving to revive it. When the light changed, I asked him with my usual courtesy to take his motorcycle out of my way so I might pass. The little man was getting irritable over his wheezy motor. Hence he replied, according to the rules of Parisian courtesy, that I could go climb a tree. I insisted, still polite, but with a slight shade of impatience in my voice. I was immediately told that in any case I could go straight to hell. Meanwhile several horns began to be heard behind me. With

51

greater firmness I begged my interlocutor to be polite and to realize that he was blocking traffic. The irascible character, probably exasperated by the now evident ill will of his motor, informed me that if I wanted what he called a thorough dusting off he would gladly give it to me. Such cynicism filled me with a healthy rage and I got out of my car with the intention of thrashing this coarse individual. I don't think I am cowardly (but what doesn't one think!); I was a head taller than my adversary and my muscles have always been reliable. I still believe the dusting off would have been received rather than given. But I had hardly set foot on the pavement when from the gathering crowd a man stepped forth, rushed at me, assured me that I was the lowest of the low and that he would not allow me to strike a man who had a motorcycle between his legs and hence was at a disadvantage. I turned toward this musketeer and, in truth, didn't even see him. Indeed, hardly had I turned my head when, almost simultaneously, I heard the motorcycle begin popping again and received a violent blow on the ear. Before I had the time to register what had happened, the motorcycle rode away. Dazed, I mechanically walked toward d'Artagnan when, at the same moment, an exasperated concert of horns rose from the now considerable line of vehicles. The light was changing to green. Then, still somewhat bewildered, instead of giving a drubbing to the idiot who had addressed me, I docilely returned to my car and drove off. As I passed, the idiot greeted me with a "poor dope" that I still recall.

A totally insignificant story, in your opinion? Probably. Still it took me some time to forget it, and that's what counts. Yet I had excuses. I had let myself be beaten without replying, but I could not be accused of cowardice. Taken by surprise, addressed from both sides, I had mixed everything up and the horns had put the finishing touch to my embarrassment. Yet I was unhappy about this as if I had violated the code of honor. I could see myself getting back into my car without a reaction, under the ironic gaze of a crowd especially delighted because, as I recall, I was wearing a very elegant blue suit. I could hear the "poor dope" which, in spite of everything, struck me as justified. In short, I had collapsed in public. As a result of a series of circumstances, to be sure, but there are always circumstances. As an afterthought I clearly saw what I should have done. I saw myself felling d'Artagnan with a good hook to the jaw, getting back into my car, pursuing the monkey who had struck me, overtaking him, jamming his machine against the curb, taking him aside, and giving him the licking he had fully deserved. With a few variants, I ran off this little film a hundred times in my imagination. But it was too late, and for several days I chewed a bitter resentment.

Why, it's raining again. Let's stop, shall we, under this portico? Good. Where was I? Oh, yes, honor! Well, when I recovered the recollection of that episode, I realized what it meant. After all, my dream had not stood up to facts. I had dreamed —this was now clear—of being a complete man who managed to make himself respected in his person as well as in his profession. Half Cerdan, half de Gaulle, if you will. In short, I wanted to dominate in all things. This is why I assumed the manner, made a particular point of displaying my physical skill rather than my intellectual gifts. But after having been struck in public without reacting, it was no longer possible for me to cherish that fine picture of myself. If I had been the friend of truth and intelligence I claimed to be, what would that episode have mattered to me? It was already forgotten by those who had witnessed it. I'd have barely accused myself of having got angry over nothing and also, having got angry, of not having managed to face up to the consequences of my anger, for want of presence of mind. Instead of that, I was eager to get my revenge, to strike and conquer. As if my true desire were not to be the most intelligent or most generous creature on earth, but only to beat anyone I wanted, to be the stronger, in short, and in the most elementary way. The truth is that every intelligent man, as you know, dreams of being a gangster and of ruling over society by force alone. As it is not so easy as the detective novels might lead one to believe, one generally relies on politics and joins the cruelest party. What does it matter, after all, if by humiliating one's mind one succeeds in dominating everyone? I discovered in myself sweet dreams of oppression.

I learned at least that I was on the side of the

guilty, the accused, only in exactly so far as their crime caused me no harm. Their guilt made me eloquent because I was not its victim. When I was threatened, I became not only a judge in turn but even more: an irascible master who wanted, regardless of all laws, to strike down the offender and get him on his knees. After that, *mon cher compatriote*, it is very hard to continue seriously believing one has a vocation for justice and is the predestined defender of the widow and orphan.

Since the rain is coming down harder and we have the time, may I impart to you another discovery I made, soon after, in my memory? Let's sit down on this bench out of the rain. For centuries pipe smokers have been watching the same rain falling on the same canal. What I have to tell you is a bit more difficult. This time it concerns a woman. To begin with, you must know that I always succeeded with women—and without much effort. I don't say succeed in making them happy or even in making myself happy through them. No, simply succeed. I used to achieve my ends just about whenever I wanted. I was considered to have charm. Fancy that! You know what charm is: a way of getting the answer yes without having asked any clear question. And that was true of me at the time. Does that surprise you? Come now, don't deny it. With the face I now have, that's quite natural. Alas, after a certain age every man is responsible for his face. Mine . . . But what matter? It's a fact—I was considered to have charm and I took advantage of it.

Without calculation, however; I was in good faith, or almost. My relationship with women was natural, free, easy, as the saying goes. No guile in it except that obvious guile which they look upon as a homage. I loved them, according to the hallowed expression, which amounts to saying that I never loved any of them. I always considered misogyny vulgar and stupid, and almost all the women I have known seemed to me better than I. Nevertheless, setting them so high, I made use of them more often than I served them. How can one make it out?

Of course, true love is exceptional—two or three times a century, more or less. The rest of the time there is vanity or boredom. As for me, in any case I was not the Portuguese Nun. I am not hard-hearted; far from it—full of pity on the contrary and with a ready tear to boot. Only, my emotional impulses always turn toward me, my feelings of pity concern me. It is not true, after all, that I never loved. I conceived at least one great love in my life, of which I was always the object. From that point of view, after the inevitable hardships of youth, I was early focused: sensuality alone dominated my love life. I looked merely for objects of pleasure and conquest. Moreover, I was aided in this by my constitution: nature had been generous with me. I was considerably proud of this and derived many satisfactions therefrom—without my knowing now whether they were physical or based on prestige. Of course you will say that I am boasting again. I shan't deny it and I am hardly proud of doing so, for here I am boasting of what is true.

In any case, my sensuality (to limit myself to it) was so real that even for a ten-minute adventure I'd have disowned father and mother, even were I to regret it bitterly. Indeed—*especially* for a ten-minute adventure and even more so if I were sure it was to have no sequel. I had principles, to be sure, such as that the wife of a friend is sacred.

But I simply ceased quite sincerely, a few days before, to feel any friendship for the husband. Maybe I ought not to call this sensuality? Sensuality is not repulsive. Let's be indulgent and use the word infirmity, a sort of congenital inability to see in love anything but the physical. That infirmity, after all, was convenient. Combined with my faculty for forgetting, it favored my freedom. At the same time, through a certain appearance of inaccessibility and unshakable independence it gave me, it provided the opportunity for new successes. As a result of not being romantic, I gave romance something to work on. Our feminine friends have in common with Bonaparte the belief that they can succeed where everyone else has failed.

In this exchange, moreover, I satisfied something in addition to my sensuality: my passion for gambling. I loved in women my partners in a certain game, which had at least the taste of innocence. You see, I can't endure being bored and appreciate only diversions in life. Any society, however brilliant, soon crushes me whereas I have never been bored with the women I liked. It hurts me to confess it, but I'd have given ten conversations with

Einstein for an initial rendezvous with a pretty chorus girl. It's true that at the tenth rendezvous I was longing for Einstein or a serious book. In short, I was never concerned with the major problems except in the intervals between my little excesses. And how often, standing on the sidewalk involved in a passionate discussion with friends, I lost the thread of the argument being developed because a devastating woman was crossing the street at that very moment.

Hence I played the game. I knew they didn't like one to reveal one's purpose too quickly. First, there had to be conversation, fond attentions, as they say. I wasn't worried about speeches, being a lawyer, nor about glances, having been an amateur actor during my military service. I often changed parts, but it was always the same play. For instance, the scene of the incomprehensible attraction, of the "mysterious something," of the "it's unreasonable, I certainly didn't want to be attracted, I was even tired of love, etc. . . ." always worked, though it is one of the oldest in the repertory. There was also the gambit of the mysterious happiness no other woman has ever given you; it may be a blind alley—indeed, it surely is (for one cannot protect oneself too much)—but it just happens to be unique. Above all, I had perfected a little speech which was always well received and which, I am sure, you will applaud. The essential part of that act lay in the assertion, painful and resigned, that I was nothing, that it was not worth getting involved with me, that my life was elsewhere and not related to everyday happiness—a happiness that maybe I should have preferred to anything, but there you were, it was too late. As to the reasons behind this decisive lateness, I maintained secrecy, knowing that it is always better to go to bed with a mystery. In a way, moreover, I believed what I said; I was living my part. It is not surprising that my partners likewise began to "tread the boards" enthusiastically. The most sensitive among them tried to understand me, and that effort led them to melancholy surrenders. The others, satisfied to note that I was respecting the rules of the game and had the tactfulness to talk before acting, progressed without delay to the realities. This meant I had won—and twice over, since, besides the desire I felt for them, I was satisfying the love I bore myself by verifying each time my special powers.

This is so true that even if some among them provided but slight pleasure, I nevertheless tried to resume relations with them, at long intervals, helped doubtless by that strange desire kindled by absence and a suddenly recovered complicity, but also to verify the fact that our ties still held and that it was my privilege alone to tighten them. Sometimes I went so far as to make them swear not to give themselves to any other man, in order to quiet my worries once and for all on that score. My heart, however, played no part in that worry, nor even my imagination. A certain type of pretension was in fact so personified in me that it was hard for me to imagine, despite the facts, that a woman who had once been mine could ever belong to another. But the oath they swore to me liberated me while it bound them. As soon as I knew they would never belong to anyone, I could make up my mind to break off—which otherwise was almost always impossible for me. As far as they were concerned, I had proved my point once and for all and assured my power for a long time. Strange, isn't it? But that's the way it was, *mon cher compatriote*. Some cry: "Love me!" Others: "Don't love me!" But a certain genus, the worst and most unhappy, cries: "Don't love me and be faithful to me!"

Except that the proof is never definitive, after all; one has to begin again with each new person. As a result of beginning over and over again, one gets in the habit. Soon the speech comes without thinking and the reflex follows; and one day you find yourself taking without really desiring. Believe me, for certain men at least, not taking what one doesn't desire is the hardest thing in the world.

This is what happened eventually and there's no point in telling you who she was except that, without really stirring me, she had attracted me by her passive, avid manner. Frankly, it was a shabby experience, as I should have expected. But I never had any complexes and soon forgot the person, whom I didn't see again. I thought she hadn't noticed anything and didn't even imagine she could have an opinion. Besides, in my eyes her passive manner cut her off from the world. A few weeks later, however, I learned that she had related my deficiencies to a third person. At once I felt as if I had been somewhat deceived; she wasn't so passive as I had thought and she didn't lack judgment. Then I shrugged my shoulders and pretended to laugh. I even laughed outright; clearly the incident was unimportant. If there is any realm in which modesty ought to be the rule, isn't it sex with all the un-foreseeable there is in it? But no, each of us tries to show up to advantage, even in solitude. Despite having shrugged my shoulders, what was my be-havior in fact? I saw that woman again a little later and did everything necessary to charm her and really take her back. It was not very difficult, for *they* don't like either to end on a failure. From that moment onward, without really intending it, I began, in fact, to mortify her in every way. I would give her up and take her back, force her to give herself at inappropriate times and in inappro-priate places, treat her so brutally, in every regard, that eventually I attached myself to her as I imagine the jailer is bound to his prisoner. And this kept up till the day when, in the violent disorder of painful and constrained pleasure, she paid a tribute aloud to what was enslaving her. That very day I began to move away from her. I have forgotten her since.

I'll agree with you, despite your polite silence, that that adventure is not very pretty. But just think of your life, *mon cher compatriote!* Search your memory and perhaps you will find some similar story that you'll tell me later on. In my case, when that business came to mind, I again began to laugh. But it was another kind of laugh, rather like the one I had heard on the Pont des Arts. I was laughing at my speeches and my pleadings in court. Even more at my court pleading than at my speeches to women. To them, at least, I did not lie much. Instinct spoke clearly, without subterfuges, in my attitude. The act of love, for instance, is a confession. Selfishness screams aloud, vanity shows off, or else true generosity reveals itself. Ultimately in that regrettable story, even more than in my other affairs, I had been more outspoken than I thought; I had declared who I was and how I could live. Despite appearances, I was therefore more worthy in my private life—even when (one might say: especially when) I behaved as I have told you

65

—than in my great professional flights about innocence and justice. At least, seeing myself act with
others, I couldn't deceive myself as to the truth
of my nature. No man is a hypocrite in his pleasures—have I read that or did I think it myself, *mon
cher compatriote?*

When I examined thus the trouble I had in
separating definitively from a woman—a trouble
which used to involve me in so many simultaneous
liaisons—I didn't blame my softheartedness. That
was not what impelled me when one of my mis-
tresses tired of waiting for the Austerlitz of our
passion and spoke of leaving me. At once I was the
one who made a step forward, who yielded, who
became eloquent. As for affection and softheartedness, I aroused them in women, experiencing merely
the appearance of them myself—simply a little excited by this refusal, alarmed also by the possible
loss of someone's affection. At times I truly thought
I was suffering, to be sure. But the rebellious female had merely to leave in fact for me to forget
her without effort, as I forgot her presence when,
on the contrary, she had decided to return. No, it
was not love or generosity that awakened me when

66

I was in danger of being forsaken, but merely the desire to be loved and to receive what in my opinion was due me. The moment I was loved and my partner again forgotten, I shone, I was at the top of my form, I became likable.

Be it said, moreover, that as soon as I had rewon that affection I became aware of its weight. In my moments of irritation I told myself that the ideal solution would have been the death of the person I was interested in. Her death would, on the one hand, have definitively fixed our relationship and, on the other, removed its compulsion. But one cannot long for the death of everyone or, in the extreme, depopulate the planet in order to enjoy a freedom that cannot be imagined otherwise. My sensibility was opposed to this, and my love of mankind.

The only deep emotion I occasionally felt in these affairs was gratitude, when all was going well and I was left, not only peace, but freedom to come and go—never kinder and gayer with one woman than when I had just left another's bed, as if I extended to all others the debt I had just contracted toward one of them. In any case, however apparently confused my feelings were, the result I achieved was clear: I kept all my affections within reach to make use of them when I wanted. On my own admission, I could live happily only on condition that all the individuals on earth, or the greatest possible number, were turned toward me, eternally in suspense, devoid of independent life and ready to answer my call at any moment, doomed in short to sterility until the day I should deign to favor them. In short, for me to live happily it was essential for the creatures I chose not to live at all. They must receive their life, sporadically, only at my bidding.

Oh, I don't feel any self-satisfaction, believe me, in telling you this. Upon thinking of that time when I used to ask for everything without paying anything myself, when I used to mobilize so many people in my service, when I used to put them in the refrigerator, so to speak, in order to have them at hand some day when it would suit me, I don't know how to name the odd feeling that comes over me. Isn't it shame, perhaps? Tell me, *mon cher compatriote*, doesn't shame sting a little? It does? Well, it's probably shame, then, or one of those silly emotions that have to do with honor. It seems to me in any case that that feeling has never left me since the adventure I found at the heart of my memory, which I cannot any longer put off relating, despite my digressions and the inventive efforts for which, I hope, you give me credit.

Look, the rain has stopped! Be kind enough to walk home with me. I am strangely tired, not from having talked so much but at the mere thought of what I still have to say. Oh, well, a few words will suffice to relate my essential discovery. What's the use of saying more, anyway? For the statue to stand bare, the fine speeches must take flight like pigeons. So here goes. That particular night in November, two or three years before the evening when I thought I heard laughter behind me, I was returning to the Left Bank and my home by way of the Pont Royal. It was an hour past midnight, a fine rain was falling, a drizzle rather, that scattered the few people on the streets. I had just left a mistress, who was surely already asleep. I was enjoying that walk, a little numbed, my body calmed and irrigated by a flow of blood gentle as the falling rain. On the bridge I passed behind a figure leaning

69

over the railing and seeming to stare at the river. On closer view, I made out a slim young woman dressed in black. The back of her neck, cool and damp between her dark hair and coat collar, stirred me. But I went on after a moment's hesitation. At the end of the bridge I followed the quays toward Saint-Michel, where I lived. I had already gone some fifty yards when I heard the sound—which, despite the distance, seemed dreadfully loud in the midnight silence—of a body striking the water. I stopped short, but without turning around. Almost at once I heard a cry, repeated several times, which was going downstream; then it suddenly ceased. The silence that followed, as the night suddenly stood still, seemed interminable. I wanted to run and yet didn't stir. I was trembling, I believe from cold and shock. I told myself that I had to be quick and I felt an irresistible weakness steal over me. I have forgotten what I thought then. "Too late, too far . . ." or something of the sort. I was still listening as I stood motionless. Then, slowly under the rain, I went away. I informed no one.

But here we are; here's my house, my shelter!

Tomorrow? Yes, if you wish. I'd like to take you to the island of Marken so you can see the Zuider Zee. Let's meet at eleven at *Mexico City*. What? That woman? Oh, I don't know. Really I don't know. The next day, and the days following, I didn't read the papers.

A DOLL's village, isn't it? No shortage of quaintness here! But I didn't bring you to this island for quaintness, *cher ami*. Anyone can show you peasant headdresses, wooden shoes, and ornamented houses with fishermen smoking choice tobacco surrounded by the smell of furniture wax. I am one of the few people, on the other hand, who can show you what really matters here.

We are reaching the dike. We'll have to follow it to get as far as possible from these too charming houses. Please, let's sit down. Well, what do you think of it? Isn't it the most beautiful negative landscape? Just see on the left that pile of ashes they call a dune here, the gray dike on the right, the livid beach at our feet, and in front of us, the sea the color of a weak lye-solution with the vast sky reflecting the colorless waters. A soggy hell, indeed! Everything horizontal, no relief; space is colorless, and life dead. Is it not universal obliteration, everlasting nothingness made visible? No human beings, above all, no human beings! You and

I alone facing the planet at last deserted! The sky is alive? You are right, *cher ami*. It thickens, becomes concave, opens up air shafts and closes cloudy doors. Those are the doves. Haven't you noticed that the sky of Holland is filled with millions of doves, invisible because of their altitude, which flap their wings, rise or fall in unison, filling the heavenly space with dense multitudes of grayish feathers carried hither and thither by the wind? The doves wait up there all year round. They wheel above the earth, look down, and would like to come down. But there is nothing but the sea and the canals, roofs covered with shop signs, and never a head on which to light.

You don't understand what I mean? I'll admit my fatigue. I lose the thread of what I am saying; I've lost that lucidity to which my friends used to enjoy paying respects. I say "my friends," moreover, as a convention. I have no more friends; I have nothing but accomplices. To make up for this, their number has increased; they are the whole human race. And within the human race, you first of all. Whoever is at hand is always the first. How do I know I have no friends? It's very easy: I dis-

covered it the day I thought of killing myself to
play a trick on them, to punish them, in a way.
But punish whom? Some would be surprised, and
no one would feel punished. I realized I had no
friends. Besides, even if I had had, I shouldn't be
any better off. If I had been able to commit suicide
and then see their reaction, why, then the game
would have been worth the candle. But the earth
is dark, *cher ami*, the coffin thick, and the shroud
opaque. The eyes of the soul—to be sure—if there
is a soul and it has eyes! But you see, we're not
sure, we can't be sure. Otherwise, there would be
a solution; at least one could get oneself taken seriously. Men are never convinced of your reasons,
of your sincerity, of the seriousness of your sufferings, except by your death. So long as you are
alive, your case is doubtful; you have a right only
to their skepticism. So if there were the least certainty that one could enjoy the show, it would be
worth proving to them what they are unwilling to
believe and thus amazing them. But you kill yourself and what does it matter whether or not they
believe you? You are not there to see their amazement and their contrition (fleeting at best), to wit-

ness, according to every man's dream, your own funeral. In order to cease being a doubtful case, one has to cease being, that's all.

Besides, isn't it better thus? We'd suffer too much from their indifference. "You'll pay for this!" a daughter said to her father who had prevented her from marrying a too well groomed suitor. And she killed herself. But the father paid for nothing. He loved fly-casting. Three Sundays later he went back to the river—to forget, as he said. He was right; he forgot. To tell the truth, the contrary would have been surprising. You think you are dying to punish your wife and actually you are freeing her. It's better not to see that. Besides the fact that you might hear the reasons they give for your action. As far as I am concerned, I can hear them now: "He killed himself because he couldn't bear . . ." Ah, *cher ami*, how poor in invention men are! They always think one commits suicide for a reason. But it's quite possible to commit suicide for two reasons. No, that never occurs to them. So what's the good of dying intentionally, of sacrificing yourself to the idea you want people to have of you? Once you are dead, they will take advantage of it to attribute idiotic or vulgar motives to your action. Martyrs, *cher ami*, must choose between being forgotten, mocked, or made use of. As for being understood—never!

Besides, let's not beat about the bush; I love life—that's my real weakness. I love it so much that I am incapable of imagining what is not life. Such avidity has something plebeian about it, don't you think? Aristocracy cannot imagine itself without a little distance surrounding itself and its life. One dies if necessary, one breaks rather than bending. But I bend, because I continue to love myself. For example, after all I have told you, what do you think I developed? An aversion for myself? Come, come, it was especially with others that I was fed up. To be sure, I knew my failings and regretted them. Yet I continued to forget them with a rather meritorious obstinacy. The prosecution of others, on the contrary, went on constantly in my heart. Of course—does that shock you? Maybe you think it's not logical? But the question is not to remain logical. The question is to slip through and, above all—yes, above all, the question is to elude judgment. I'm not saying to avoid punishment, for punishment without judgment is bearable. It has a name, besides, that guarantees our innocence: it is called misfortune. No, on the contrary, it's a matter of dodging judgment, of avoiding being forever judged without ever having a sentence pronounced.

But one can't dodge it so easily. Today we are always ready to judge as we are to fornicate. With this difference, that there are no inadequacies to fear. If you doubt this, just listen to the table conversation during August in those summer hotels where our charitable fellow citizens take the boredom cure. If you still hesitate to conclude, read the writings of our great men of the moment. Or else observe your own family and you will be edified. *Mon cher ami*, let's not give them any pretext, no matter how small, for judging us! Otherwise, we'll be left in shreds. We are forced to take the same precautions as the animal tamer. If, before going into the cage, he has the misfortune to cut himself while shaving, what a feast for the wild animals! I realized this all at once the moment I had the suspicion that maybe I wasn't so admirable. From then on, I became distrustful. Since I was bleeding slightly, there was no escape for me; they would devour me.

My relations with my contemporaries were apparently the same and yet subtly out of tune. My friends hadn't changed. On occasion, they still extolled the harmony and security they found in my company. But I was aware only of the dissonances and disorder that filled me; I felt vulnerable and open to public accusation. In my eyes my fellows ceased to be the respectful public to which I was accustomed. The circle of which I was the center broke and they lined up in a row as on the judges' bench. In short, the moment I grasped that there was something to judge in me, I realized that there was in them an irresistible vocation for judgment. Yes, they were there as before, but they were laughing. Or rather it seemed to me that every one I encountered was looking at me with a hidden smile. I even had the impression, at that time, that people were tripping me up. Two or three times, in fact, I stumbled as I entered public places. Once, even, I went sprawling on the floor. The Cartesian Frenchman in me didn't take long to catch hold of himself and attribute those accidents to the only reasonable divinity—that is, chance. Nonetheless, my distrust remained.

Once my attention was aroused, it was not hard for me to discover that I had enemies. In my profession, to begin with, and also in my social life. Some among them I had obliged. Others I should have obliged. All that, after all, was natural, and I discovered it without too much grief. It was harder and more painful, on the other hand, to admit that I had enemies among people I hardly knew or didn't know at all. I had always thought, with the ingenuousness I have already illustrated to you, that those who didn't know me couldn't resist liking me if they came to know me. Not at all! I encountered hostility especially among those who knew me only at a distance without my knowing them myself. Doubtless they suspected me of living fully, given up completely to happiness; and that cannot be forgiven. The look of success, when it is worn in a certain way, would infuriate a jackass. Then again, my life was full to bursting, and for lack of time, I used to refuse many advances. Then I would forget my refusals, for the same reason. But those advances had been made me by people whose lives were not full and who, for that very reason, would remember my refusals.

Thus it is that in the end, to take but one example, women cost me dear. The time I used to devote to them I couldn't give to men, who didn't always forgive me this. Is there any way out? Your successes and happiness are forgiven you only if you generously consent to share them. But to be happy it is essential not to be too concerned with others. Consequently, there is no escape. Happy and judged, or absolved and wretched. As for me, the injustice was even greater: I was condemned for past successes. For a long time I had lived in the illusion of a general agreement, whereas, from all sides, judgments, arrows, mockeries rained upon me, inattentive and smiling. The day I was alerted I became lucid; I received all the wounds at the same time and lost my strength all at once. The whole universe then began to laugh at me.

That is what no man (except those who are not really alive—in other words, wise men) can endure. Spitefulness is the only possible ostentation. People hasten to judge in order not to be judged themselves. What do you expect? The idea that comes most naturally to man, as if from his very nature, is the idea of his innocence. From this point of view, we are all like that little Frenchman at Buchenwald who insisted on registering a complaint with the clerk, himself a prisoner, who was recording his arrival. A complaint? The clerk and his comrades laughed: "Useless, old man. You don't lodge a complaint here." "But you see, sir," said the little Frenchman, "My case is exceptional. I am innocent!"

We are all exceptional cases. We all want to appeal against something! Each of us insists on being innocent at all cost, even if he has to accuse the whole human race and heaven itself. You won't delight a man by complimenting him on the efforts by which he has become intelligent or generous. On the other hand, he will beam if you admire his natural generosity. Inversely, if you tell a criminal that his crime is not due to his nature or his character but to unfortunate circumstances, he will be extravagantly grateful to you. During the counsel's speech, this is the moment he will choose to weep. Yet there is no credit in being honest or intelligent by birth. Just as one is surely no more responsible for being a criminal by nature than for being a criminal by circumstance. But those rascals want grace, that is irresponsibility, and they shamelessly allege the justifications of nature or the excuses of circumstances, even if they are contradictory. The essential thing is that they should be innocent, that their virtues, by grace of birth, should not be questioned and that their misdeeds, born of a momentary misfortune, should never be more than provisional. As I told you, it's a matter of dodging judgment. Since it is hard to dodge it, tricky to get one's nature simultaneously admired and excused, they all strive to be rich. Why? Did you ever ask yourself? For power, of course. But especially because wealth shields from immediate judgment, takes you out of the subway crowd to enclose you in a chromium-plated automobile, isolates you in huge protected lawns, Pullmans, first-class cabins. Wealth, *cher ami*, is not quite acquittal, but reprieve, and that's always worth taking.

Above all, don't believe your friends when they ask you to be sincere with them. They merely hope you will encourage them in the good opinion they have of themselves by providing them with the additional assurance they will find in your promise of sincerity. How could sincerity be a condition of friendship? A liking for truth at any cost is a passion that spares nothing and that nothing resists. It's a vice, at times a comfort, or a selfishness. Therefore, if you are in that situation, don't hesitate: promise to tell the truth and then lie as best you can. You will satisfy their hidden desire and doubly prove your affection.

This is so true that we rarely confide in those who are better than we. Rather, we are more inclined to flee their society. Most often, on the other hand, we confess to those who are like us and who share our weaknesses. Hence we don't want to improve ourselves or be bettered, for we should first have to be judged in default. We merely wish to be pitied and encouraged in the course we have chosen. In short, we should like, at the same time, to cease being guilty and yet not to make the effort of cleansing ourselves. Not enough cynicism and not enough virtue. We lack the energy of evil as well as the energy of good. Do you know Dante? Really? The devil you say! Then you know that Dante accepts the idea of neutral angels in the quarrel between God and Satan. And he puts them in Limbo, a sort of vestibule of his Hell. We are in the vestibule, *cher ami*.

Patience? You are probably right. It would take patience to wait for the Last Judgment. But that's it, we're in a hurry. So much in a hurry, indeed, that I was obliged to make myself a judge-penitent. However, I first had to make shift with my discoveries and put myself right with my contemporaries' laughter. From the evening when I was called—for I was really called—I had to answer or at least seek an answer. It wasn't easy; for some time I floundered. To begin with, that perpetual laugh and the laughers had to teach me to see clearly within me and to discover at last that I was not simple. Don't smile; that truth is not so basic as it seems. What we call basic truths are simply the ones we discover after all the others.

However that may be, after prolonged research on myself, I brought out the fundamental duplicity of the human being. Then I realized, as a result of delving in my memory, that modesty helped me to shine, humility to conquer, and virtue to oppress. I used to wage war by peaceful means and eventually used to achieve, through disinterested means, everything I desired. For instance, I never complained that my birthday was overlooked; people were even surprised, with a touch of admiration, by my discretion on this subject. But the reason for my disinterestedness was even more discreet: I longed to be forgotten in order to be able to complain to myself. Several days before the famous date (which I knew very well) I was on the alert, eager to let nothing slip that might arouse the attention and memory of those on whose lapse I was counting (didn't I once go so far as to contemplate falsifying a friend's calendar?). Once my solitude was thoroughly proved, I could surrender to the charms of a virile self-pity.

Thus the surface of all my virtues had a less imposing reverse side. It is true that, in another sense, my shortcomings turned to my advantage. For example, the obligation I felt to conceal the vicious part of my life gave me a cold look that was confused with the look of virtue; my indifference made me loved; my selfishness wound up in my generosities. I stop there, for too great a symmetry would upset my argument. But after all, I presented a harsh exterior and yet could never resist the offer of a glass or of a woman! I was considered active, energetic, and my kingdom was the bed. I used to advertise my loyalty and I don't believe there is a single person I loved that I didn't eventually betray. Of course, my betrayals didn't stand in the way of my fidelity; I used to knock off a considerable pile of work through successive periods of idleness; and I had never ceased aiding my neighbor, thanks to my enjoyment in doing so. But however much I repeated such facts to myself, they gave me but superficial consolations. Certain mornings, I would get up the case against myself most thoroughly, coming to the conclusion that I excelled above all in scorn. The very people I helped most often were the most scorned. Courteously, with a solidarity charged with emotion, I used to spit daily in the face of all the blind.

Tell me frankly, is there any excuse for that? There is one, but so wretched that I cannot dream of advancing it. In any case, here it is: I have never been really able to believe that human affairs were serious matters. I had no idea where the serious might lie, except that it was not in all this I saw around me—which seemed to me merely an amusing game, or tiresome. There are really efforts and convictions I have never been able to understand. I always looked with amazement, and a certain suspicion, on those strange creatures who died for money, fell into despair over the loss of a "position," or sacrificed themselves with a high and mighty manner for the prosperity of their family. I could better understand that friend who had made up his mind to stop smoking and through sheer will power had succeeded. One morning he opened the paper, read that the first H-bomb had been exploded, learned about its wonderful effects, and hastened to a tobacco shop.

To be sure, I occasionally pretended to take life seriously. But very soon the frivolity of seriousness struck me and I merely went on playing my role as well as I could. I played at being efficient, intelligent, virtuous, civic-minded, shocked, indulgent, fellow-spirited, edifying . . . In short, there's no need of going on, you have already grasped that I was like my Dutchmen who are here without being here: I was absent at the moment when I took up the most space. I have never been really sincere and enthusiastic except when I used to indulge in sports, and in the army, when I used to act in plays we put on for our own amusement. In both cases there was a rule of the game, which was not serious but which we enjoyed taking as if it were. Even now, the Sunday matches in an overflowing stadium, and the theater, which I loved with the greatest passion, are the only places in the world where I feel innocent.

But who would consider such an attitude legitimate in the face of love, death, and the wages of the poor? Yet what can be done about it? I could imagine the love of Isolde only in novels or on the stage. At times people on their deathbed seemed to me convinced of their roles. The lines spoken by my poor clients always struck me as fitting the same pattern. Whence, living among men without sharing their interests, I could not manage to believe in the commitments I made. I was courteous and indolent enough to live up to what was expected of me in my profession, my family, or my civic life, but each time with a sort of indifference that spoiled everything. I lived my whole life under a double code, and my most serious acts were often the ones in which I was the least involved. Wasn't that after all the reason that, added to my blunders, I could not forgive myself, that made me revolt most violently against the judgment I felt forming, in me and around me, and that forced me to seek an escape?

For some time, my life continued outwardly as if nothing had changed. I was on rails and speeding ahead. As if purposely, people's praises increased. And that's just where the trouble came from. You remember the remark: "Woe to you when all men speak well of you!" Ah, the one who said that spoke words of wisdom! Woe to me! Consequently, the engine began to have whims, inexplicable breakdowns.

Then it was that the thought of death burst into my daily life. I would measure the years separating me from my end. I would look for examples of men of my age who were already dead. And I was tormented by the thought that I might not have time to accomplish my task. What task? I had no idea. Frankly, was what I was doing worth continuing? But that was not quite it. A ridiculous fear pursued me, in fact: one could not die without having confessed all one's lies. Not to God or to one of his representatives; I was above that, as you well imagine. No, it was a matter of confessing to men, to a friend, to a beloved woman, for example. Otherwise, were there but one lie hidden in a life, death made it definitive. No one, ever again, would know the truth on this point, since the only one to know it was precisely the dead man sleeping on his secret. That absolute murder of a truth used to make me dizzy. Today, let me interject, it would cause me, instead, subtle joys. The idea, for instance, that I am the only one to know what everyone is looking for and that I have at home an object which kept the police of three countries on the run is a sheer delight. But let's not go into that. At the time, I had not yet found the recipe and I was fretting.

I pulled myself together, of course. What did one man's lie matter in the history of generations? And what pretension to want to drag out into the full light of truth a paltry fraud, lost in the sea of ages like a grain of sand in the ocean! I also told myself that the body's death, to judge from those I had seen, was in itself sufficient punishment that absolved all. Salvation was won (that is, the right to disappear definitively) in the sweat of the death agony. Nonetheless the discomfort grew; death was faithful at my bedside; I used to get up with it every morning, and compliments became more and more unbearable to me. It seemed to me that the falsehood increased with them so inordinately that never again could I put myself right.

A day came when I could bear it no longer. My first reaction was excessive. Since I was a liar, I would reveal this and hurl my duplicity in the face of all those imbeciles, even before they discovered it. Provoked to truth, I would accept the challenge. In order to forestall the laughter, I dreamed of hurling myself into the general derision. In short, it was still a question of dodging judgment. I wanted to put the laughers on my side, or at least to put myself on their side. I contemplated, for instance, jostling the blind on the street; and from the secret, unexpected joy this gave me I recognized how much a part of my soul loathed them; I planned to puncture the tires of invalids' vehicles, to go and shout "lousy proletarian" under the scaffoldings on which laborers were working, to slap infants in the subway. I dreamed of all that and did none of it, or if I did something of the sort, I have forgotten it. In any case, the very word "justice" gave me strange fits of rage. I continued, of necessity, to use it in my speeches to the court. But I took my revenge by publicly inveighing against the humanitarian spirit; I announced the publication of a manifesto exposing the oppression that the oppressed inflict on decent people. One day while I was eating lobster at a sidewalk restaurant and a beggar bothered me, I called the proprietor to drive him away and loudly approved the words of that administrator of justice: "You are embarrassing people," he said. "Just put yourself in the place of these ladies and gents, after all!" Finally, I used to express, to whoever would listen, my regret that it was no longer possible to act like a certain Russian landowner whose character I admired. He would have a beating administered both to his peasants who bowed to him and to those who didn't bow to him in order to punish a boldness he considered equally impudent in both cases.

However, I recall more serious excesses. I began to write an "Ode to the Police" and an "Apotheosis of the Guillotine." Above all, I used to force myself to visit regularly the special cafés where our professional humanitarian free thinkers gathered. My good past record assured me of a welcome. There, without seeming to, I would let fly a forbidden expression: "Thank God . . ." I would say, or more simply: "My God . . ." You know what shy little children our café atheists are. A moment of amazement would follow that outrageous expression, they would look at one another dumbfounded, then the tumult would burst forth. Some would flee the café, others would gabble indignantly without listening to anything, and all would writhe in convulsions like the devil in holy water.

You must look on that as childish. Yet maybe there was a more serious reason for those little jokes. I wanted to upset the game and above all to destroy that flattering reputation, the thought of which threw me into a rage. "A man like you . . ." people would say sweetly, and I would blanch. I didn't want their esteem because it wasn't general, and how could it be general since I couldn't share it? Hence it was better to cover everything, judgment and esteem, with a cloak of ridicule. I had to liberate at all cost the feeling that was stifling me.

In order to reveal to all eyes what he was made of, I wanted to break open the handsome wax-figure I presented everywhere. For instance, I recall an informal lecture I had to give to a group of young fledgling lawyers. Irritated by the fantastic praises of the President of the Bar, who had introduced me, I couldn't resist long. I had begun with the enthusiasm and emotion expected of me, which I had no trouble summoning up on order. But I suddenly began to advise alliance as a system of defense. Not, I said, that alliance perfected by modern inquisitions which judge simultaneously a thief and an honest man in order to crush the second under the crimes of the first. On the contrary, I meant to defend the thief by exposing the crimes of the honest man, the lawyer in this instance. I explained myself very clearly on this point:

"Let us suppose that I have accepted the defense of some touching citizen, a murderer through jealousy. Gentlemen of the Jury, consider, I should say, how venial it is to get angry when one sees one's natural goodness put to the test by the malignity of the fair sex. Is it not more serious, on the contrary, to be by chance on this side of the bar, on my own bench, without ever having been good or suffered from being duped? I am free, shielded from your severities, yet who am I? A Louis XIV in pride, a billy goat for lust, a Pharaoh for wrath, a king of laziness. I haven't killed anyone? Not yet, to be sure! But have I not let deserving creatures die? Maybe. And maybe I am ready to do so again. Whereas this man—just look at him—will not do so again. He is still quite amazed to have accomplished what he has." This speech rather upset my young colleagues. After a moment, they made up their minds to laugh at it. They became completely reassured when I got to my conclusion, in which I invoked the human individual and his supposed rights. That day, habit won out.

By repeating these pleasant indiscretions, I merely succeeded in disconcerting opinion somewhat. Not in disarming it, or above all in disarming myself. The amazement I generally encountered in my listeners, their rather reticent embarrassment, somewhat like what you are showing—no, don't protest—did not calm me at all. You see, it is not enough to accuse yourself in order to clear yourself; otherwise, I'd be as innocent as a lamb. One must accuse oneself in a certain way, which it took me considerable time to perfect. I did not discover it until I fell into the most utterly forlorn state. Until then, the laughter continued to drift my way, without my random efforts succeeding in divesting it of its benevolent, almost tender quality that hurt me.

But the sea is rising, it seems to me. It won't be long before our boat leaves; the day is ending. Look, the doves are gathering up there. They are crowding against one another, hardly stirring, and the light is waning. Don't you think we should be silent to enjoy this rather sinister moment? No, I interest you? You are very polite. Moreover, I now run the risk of really interesting you. Before explaining myself on the subject of judges-penitent, I must talk to you of debauchery and of the little-ease.

Y<small>OU</small> are wrong, *cher*, the boat is going at top speed. But the Zuider Zee is a dead sea, or almost. With its flat shores, lost in the fog, there's no saying where it begins or ends. So we are steaming along without any landmark; we can't gauge our speed. We are making progress and yet nothing is changing. It's not navigation but dreaming.

In the Greek archipelago I had the contrary feeling. Constantly new islands would appear on the horizon. Their treeless backbone marked the limit of the sky and their rocky shore contrasted sharply with the sea. No confusion possible; in the sharp light everything was a landmark. And from one island to another, ceaselessly on our little boat, which was nevertheless dawdling, I felt as if we were scudding along, night and day, on the crest of the short, cool waves in a race full of spray and laughter. Since then, Greece itself drifts somewhere within me, on the edge of my memory, tirelessly . . . Hold on, I, too, am drifting; I am becoming lyrical! Stop me, *cher*, I beg you.

By the way, do you know Greece? No? So much the better. What should we do there, I ask you? There one has to be pure in heart. Do you know that there male friends walk along the street in pairs holding hands? Yes, the women stay home and you often see a middle-aged, respectable man, sporting mustaches, gravely striding along the sidewalks, his fingers locked in those of his friend. In the Orient likewise, at times? All right. But tell me, would you take my hand in the streets of Paris? Oh, I'm joking. *We* have a sense of decorum; scum makes us stilted. Before appearing in the Greek islands, we should have to wash at length. There the air is chaste and sensual enjoyment as transparent as the sea. And we . . .

Let's sit down on these steamer chairs. What a fog! I interrupted myself, I believe, on the way to the little-ease. Yes, I'll tell you what I mean. After having struggled, after having used up all my insolent airs, discouraged by the uselessness of my efforts, I made up my mind to leave the society of men. No, no, I didn't look for a desert island; there *are* no more. I simply took refuge among women. As you know, they don't really condemn any weak-

ness; they would be more inclined to try to humili-
ate or disarm our strength. This is why woman is
the reward, not of the warrior, but of the criminal.
She is his harbor, his haven; it is in a woman's bed
that he is generally arrested. Is she not all that remains to us of earthly paradise? In distress, I hastened to my natural harbor. But I no longer indulged in pretty speeches. I still gambled a little,
out of habit; but invention was lacking. I hesitate
to admit it for fear of using a few more naughty
words: it seems to me that at that time I felt the
need of love. Obscene, isn't it? In any case, I experienced a secret suffering, a sort of privation that
made me emptier and allowed me, partly through
obligation and partly out of curiosity, to make a
few commitments. Inasmuch as I needed to love
and be loved, I thought I was in love. In other
words, I acted the fool.

I often caught myself asking a question which,
as a man of experience, I had always previously
avoided. I would hear myself asking: "Do you love
me?" You know that it is customary to answer in
such cases: "And you?" If I answered yes, I found
myself committed beyond my real feelings. If I

dared to say no, I ran the risk of ceasing to be loved, and I would suffer therefor. The greater the threat to the feeling in which I had hoped to find calm, the more I demanded that feeling of my partner. Hence I was led to ever more explicit promises and came to expect of my heart an ever more sweeping feeling. Thus I developed a deceptive passion for a charming fool of a woman who had so thoroughly read "true love" stories that she spoke of love with the assurance and conviction of an intellectual announcing the classless society. Such conviction, as you must know, is contagious. I tried myself out at talking likewise of love and eventually convinced myself. At least until she became my mistress and I realized that the "true love" stories, though they taught how to talk of love, did not teach how to make love. After having loved a parrot, I had to go to bed with a serpent. So I looked elsewhere for the love promised by books, which I had never encountered in life.

But I lacked practice. For more than thirty years I had been in love exclusively with myself. What hope was there of losing such a habit? I didn't lose it and remained a trifler in passion. I multiplied the promises. I contracted simultaneous loves as, at an earlier period, I had multiple liaisons. In this way I piled up more misfortunes, for others, than at the time of my fine indifference. Have I told you that in despair my parrot wanted to let herself die of hunger? Fortunately I arrived in time and submitted to holding her hand until she met, on his return from a journey to Bali, the engineer with graying temples who had already been described to her by her favorite weekly. In any case, far from finding myself transported and absolved in the whirlwind —as the saying goes—of passion, I added even more to the weight of my crimes and to my deviation from virtue. As a result, I conceived such a loathing for love that for years I could not hear *"La Vie en rose"* or the *"Liebestod"* without gritting my teeth. I tried accordingly to give up women, in a certain way, and to live in a state of chastity. After all, their friendship ought to satisfy me. But this was tantamount to giving up gambling. Without desire, women bored me beyond all expectation, and obviously I bored them too. No more gambling and no more theater—I was probably in the realm of truth. But truth, *cher ami*, is a colossal bore.

Despairing of love and of chastity, I at last bethought myself of debauchery, a substitute for love, which quiets the laughter, restores silence, and above all, confers immortality. At a certain degree of lucid intoxication, lying late at night between two prostitutes and drained of all desire, hope ceases to be a torture, you see; the mind dominates the whole past, and the pain of living is over forever. In a sense, I had always lived in debauchery, never having ceased wanting to be immortal. Wasn't this the key to my nature and also a result of the great self-love I have told you about? Yes, I was bursting with a longing to be immortal. I was too much in love with myself not to want the precious object of my love never to disappear. Since, in the waking state and with a little self-knowledge, one can see no reason why immortality should be conferred on a salacious monkey, one has to obtain substitutes for that immortality. Because I longed for eternal life, I went to bed with harlots and drank for nights on end. In the morning, to be sure, my mouth was filled with the bitter taste of the mortal state. But, for hours on end, I had soared in bliss. Dare I admit it to you? I still remember with affection certain

nights when I used to go to a sordid night club to
meet a quick-change dancer who honored me with
her favors and for whose reputation I even fought
one evening with a bearded braggart. Every night I
would strut at the bar, in the red light and dust of
that earthly paradise, lying fantastically and drinking at length. I would wait for dawn and at last
end up in the always unmade bed of my princess,
who would indulge mechanically in sex and then
sleep without transition. Day would come softly to
throw light on this disaster and I would get up and
stand motionless in a dawn of glory.

Alcohol and women provided me, I admit, the
only solace of which I was worthy. I'll reveal this
secret to you, *cher ami*, don't fear to make use of it.
Then you'll see that true debauchery is liberating
because it creates no obligations. In it you possess
only yourself; hence it remains the favorite pastime
of the great lovers of their own person. It is a jungle
without past or future, without any promise above
all, nor any immediate penalty. The places where it
is practiced are separated from the world. On entering, one leaves behind fear and hope. Conversation is not obligatory there; what one comes for

can be had without words, and often indeed without money. Ah, I beg you, let me pay honor to the unknown and forgotten women who helped me then! Even today, my recollection of them contains something resembling respect.

In any case, I freely took advantage of that liberation. I was even seen in a hotel dedicated to what is called sin, living simultaneously with a mature prostitute and an unmarried girl of the best society. I played the gallant with the first and gave the second an opportunity to learn the realities. Unfortunately the prostitute had a most middle-class nature; she since consented to write her memoirs for a confessions magazine quite open to modern ideas. The girl, for her part, got married to satisfy her unbridled instincts and make use of her remarkable gifts. I am not a little proud likewise to have been admitted as an equal, at that time, by a masculine guild too often reviled. But I'll not insist on that: you know that even very intelligent people glory in being able to empty one bottle more than the next man. I might ultimately have found peace and release in that happy dissipation. But, there too, I encountered an obstacle in myself. This time it was my liver, and a fatigue so dreadful that it hasn't yet left me. One plays at being immortal and after a few weeks one doesn't even know whether or not one can hang on till the next day.

The sole benefit of that experience, when I had given up my nocturnal exploits, was that life became less painful for me. The fatigue that was gnawing at my body had simultaneously cauterized many raw spots in me. Each excess decreases vitality, hence suffering. There is nothing frenzied about debauchery, contrary to what is thought. It is but a long sleep. You must have noticed that men who really suffer from jealousy have no more urgent desire than to go to bed with the woman they nevertheless think has betrayed them. Of course, they want to assure themselves once more that their dear treasure still belongs to them. They want to possess it, as the saying goes. But there is also the fact that immediately afterward they are less jealous. Physical jealousy is a result of the imagination at the same time that it is a self-judgment. One attributes to the rival the nasty thoughts one had oneself in the same circumstances. Fortunately excess of sensual satisfaction weakens both imagination and judgment. The suffering then lies dormant as long as virility does. For the same reasons adolescents lose their metaphysical unrest with their first mistress; and certain marriages, which are merely formalized debauches, become the monotonous hearses of daring and invention. Yes, *cher ami*, bourgeois marriage has put our country into slippers and will soon lead it to the gates of death.

I am exaggerating? No, but I am straying from the subject. I merely wanted to tell you the advantage I derived from those months of orgy. I lived in a sort of fog in which the laughter became so muffled that eventually I ceased to notice it. The indifference that already had such a hold over me now encountered no resistance and extended its sclerosis. No more emotions! An even temper, or rather no temper at all. Tubercular lungs are cured by drying up and gradually asphyxiate their happy owner. So it was with me as I peacefully died of my cure. I was still living on my work although my reputation was seriously damaged by my flights of language and the regular exercise of my profession compromised by the disorder of my life. It is noteworthy, however, that I aroused less resentment by my nocturnal excesses than by my verbal provocations. The reference, purely verbal, that I often made to God in my speeches before the court awakened mistrust in my clients. They probably feared that heaven could not represent their interests as well as a lawyer invincible when it came to the code of law. Whence it was but a step to conclude that I invoked the divinity in proportion to my ignorance. My clients took that step and became scarce. Now and then I still argued a case. At times even, forgetting that I no longer believed in what I was saying, I was a good advocate. My own voice would lead me on and I would follow it; without really soaring, as I once did, I at least got off the ground and did a little hedgehopping. Outside of my profession, I saw but few people and painfully kept alive one or two tired liaisons. It even happened that I would spend purely friendly evenings, without any element of desire, yet with the difference that, resigned to boredom, I scarcely listened to what was being said. I became a little fatter and at last was able to believe that the crisis was over. Nothing remained but to grow older.

One day, however, during a trip to which I

was treating a friend without telling her I was doing so to celebrate my cure, I was aboard an ocean liner —on the upper deck, of course. Suddenly, far off at sea, I perceived a black speck on the steel-gray ocean. I turned away at once and my heart began to beat wildly. When I forced myself to look, the black speck had disappeared. I was on the point of shouting, of stupidly calling for help, when I saw it again. It was one of those bits of refuse that ships leave behind them. Yet I had not been able to endure watching it; for I had thought at once of a drowning person. Then I realized, calmly as you resign yourself to an idea the truth of which you have long known, that that cry which had sounded over the Seine behind me years before had never ceased, carried by the river to the waters of the Channel, to travel throughout the world, across the limitless expanse of the ocean, and that it had waited for me there until the day I had encountered it. I realized likewise that it would continue to await me on seas and rivers, everywhere, in short, where lies the bitter water of my baptism. Here, too, by the way, aren't we on the water? On this flat, monotonous, interminable water whose limits are indistinguishable from those of the land? Is it credible that we shall ever reach Amsterdam? We shall never get out of this immense holy-water font. Listen. Don't you hear the cries of invisible gulls? If they are crying in our direction, to what are they calling us?

But they are the same gulls that were crying, that were already calling over the Atlantic the day I realized definitively that I was not cured, that I was still cornered and that I had to make shift with it. Ended the glorious life, but ended also the frenzy and the convulsions. I had to submit and admit my guilt. I had to live in the little-ease. To be sure, you are not familiar with that dungeon cell that was called the little-ease in the Middle Ages. In general, one was forgotten there for life. That cell was distinguished from others by ingenious dimensions. It was not high enough to stand up in nor yet wide enough to lie down in. One had to take on an awkward manner and live on the diagonal; sleep was a collapse, and waking a squatting. *Mon cher*, there was genius—and I am weighing my words— in that so simple invention. Every day through the unchanging restriction that stiffened his body, the condemned man learned that he was guilty and that innocence consists in stretching joyously. Can you imagine in that cell a frequenter of summits and upper decks? What? One could live in those cells and still be innocent? Improbable! Highly improbable! Or else my reasoning would collapse. That innocence should be reduced to living hunchbacked —I refuse to entertain for a second such a hypothesis. Moreover, we cannot assert the innocence of anyone, whereas we can state with certainty the guilt of all. Every man testifies to the crime of all the others—that is my faith and my hope.

Believe me, religions are on the wrong track the moment they moralize and fulminate commandments. God is not needed to create guilt or to punish. Our fellow men suffice, aided by ourselves. You were speaking of the Last Judgment. Allow me to laugh respectfully. I shall wait for it resolutely, for I have known what is worse, the judgment of men. For them, no extenuating circumstances; even the good intention is ascribed to crime. Have you at least heard of the spitting-cell, which a nation recently thought up to prove itself the greatest on earth? A walled-up box in which the prisoner can stand without moving. The solid door that locks him in his cement shell stops at chin level. Hence only his face is visible, and every passing jailer spits copiously on it. The prisoner, wedged into his cell, cannot wipe his face, though he is allowed, it is true, to close his eyes. Well, that, *mon cher*, is a human invention. They didn't need God for that little masterpiece.

What of it? Well, God's sole usefulness would be to guarantee innocence, and I am inclined to see religion rather as a huge laundering venture—as it was once but briefly, for exactly three years, and it wasn't called religion. Since then, soap has been lacking, our faces are dirty, and we wipe one another's noses. All dunces, all punished, let's all spit on one another and—hurry! to the little-ease! Each tries to spit first, that's all. I'll tell you a big secret, *mon cher*. Don't wait for the Last Judgment. It takes place every day.

No, it's nothing; I'm merely shivering a little in this damned humidity. We're landing anyway. Here we are. After you. But stay a little, I beg you, and walk home with me. I haven't finished; I must go on. Continuing is what is hard. Say, do you know why he was crucified—the one you are perhaps thinking of at this moment? Well, there were heaps of reasons for that. There are always reasons for murdering a man. On the contrary, it is impossible to justify his living. That's why crime always finds lawyers, and innocence only rarely. But, beside the reasons that have been very well explained to us for the past two thousand years, there was a major one for that terrible agony, and I don't know why it has been so carefully hidden. The real reason is that *he* knew he was not altogether innocent. If he did not bear the weight of the crime he was accused of, he had committed others—even though he didn't know which ones. Did he really not know them? He was at the source, after all; he must have heard of a certain Slaughter of the Innocents. The children of Judea massacred while his parents were taking him to a safe place—why did they die if not because of him? Those blood-spattered soldiers, those infants cut in two filled him with horror. But given the man he was, I am sure he could not forget them. And as for that sadness that can be felt in his every act, wasn't it the incurable melancholy of a man who heard night after night the voice of Rachel weeping for her children and refusing all comfort? The lamentation would rend the night, Rachel would call her children who had been killed for him, and he was still alive!

Knowing what he knew, familiar with everything about man—ah, who would have believed that crime consists less in making others die than in not dying oneself!—brought face to face day and night with his innocent crime, he found it too hard for him to hold on and continue. It was better to have done with it, not to defend himself, to die, in order not to be the only one to live, and to go elsewhere where perhaps he would be upheld. He was not upheld, he complained, and as a last straw, he was censored. Yes, it was the third evangelist, I believe, who first suppressed his complaint. "Why hast thou forsaken me?"—it was a seditious cry, wasn't it? Well, then, the scissors! Mind you, if Luke had suppressed nothing, the matter would hardly have been noticed; in any case, it would not have assumed such importance. Thus the censor shouts aloud what he proscribes. The world's order likewise is ambiguous.

Nonetheless, the censored one was unable to carry on. And I know, *cher*, whereof I speak. There was a time when I didn't at any minute have the slightest idea how I could reach the next one. Yes, one can wage war in this world, ape love, torture one's fellow man, or merely say evil of one's neighbor while knitting. But, in certain cases, carrying on, merely continuing, is superhuman. And he was not superhuman, you can take my word for it. He cried aloud his agony and that's why I love him, my friend who died without knowing.

The unfortunate thing is that he left us alone, to carry on, whatever happens, even when we are lodged in the little-ease, knowing in turn what he knew, but incapable of doing what he did and of dying like him. People naturally tried to get some help from his death. After all, it was a stroke of genius to tell us: "You're not a very pretty sight, that's certain! Well, we won't go into the details! We'll just liquidate it all at once, on the cross!" But too many people now climb onto the cross merely to be seen from a greater distance, even if they have to trample somewhat on the one who has been there so long. Too many people have decided to do without generosity in order to practice charity.

114

Oh, the injustice, the rank injustice that has been done him! It wrings my heart!

Good heavens, the habit has seized me again and I'm on the point of making a speech to the court. Forgive me and realize that I have my reasons. Why, a few streets from here there is a museum called "Our Lord in the Attic." At the time, they had the catacombs in the attic. After all, the cellars are flooded here. But today—set your mind at rest—their Lord is neither in the attic nor in the cellar. They have hoisted him onto a judge's bench, in the secret of their hearts, and they smite, they judge above all, they judge in his name. He spoke softly to the adulteress: "Neither do I condemn thee!" but that doesn't matter; they condemn without absolving anyone. In the name of the Lord, here is what you deserve. Lord? He, my friend, didn't expect so much. He simply wanted to be loved, nothing more. Of course, there are those who love him, even among Christians. But they are not numerous. He had foreseen that too; he had a sense of humor. Peter, you know, the coward, Peter denied him: "I know not the man . . . I know not

what thou sayest . . . etc." Really, he went too
far! And my friend makes a play on words: "Thou
art Peter, and upon this rock I will build my
church." Irony could go no further, don't you
think? But no, they still triumph! "You see, he had
said it!" He had said it indeed; he knew the question
thoroughly. And then he left forever, leaving them
to judge and condemn, with pardon on their lips
and the sentence in their hearts.

For it cannot be said there is no more pity;
no, good Lord, we never stop talking of it. Simply,
no one is ever acquitted any more. On dead innocence the judges swarm, the judges of all species,
those of Christ and those of the Antichrist, who
are the same anyway, reconciled in the little-ease.
For one mustn't blame everything exclusively on
the Christians. The others are involved too. Do you
know what has become of one of the houses in this
city that sheltered Descartes? A lunatic asylum.
Yes, general delirium and persecution. We, too,
naturally, are obliged to come to it. You have had a
chance to observe that I spare nothing, and as for
you, I know that you agree in thought. Wherefor,
since we are all judges, we are all guilty before one

116

another, all Christs in our mean manner, one by one crucified, always without knowing. We should be at least if I, Clamence, had not found a way out, the only solution, truth at last . . .

No, I am stopping, *cher ami*, fear nothing! Besides, I'm going to leave you, for we are at my door. In solitude and when fatigued, one is after all inclined to take oneself for a prophet. When all is said and done, that's really what I am, having taken refuge in a desert of stones, fogs, and stagnant waters—an empty prophet for shabby times, Elijah without a messiah, choked with fever and alcohol, my back up against this moldy door, my finger raised toward a threatening sky, showering imprecations on lawless men who cannot endure any judgment. For they can't endure it, *très cher*, and that's the whole question. He who clings to a law does not fear the judgment that reinstates him in an order he believes in. But the keenest of human torments is to be judged without a law. Yet we are in that torment. Deprived of their natural curb, the judges, loosed at random, are racing through their job. Hence we have to try to go faster than they, don't we? And it's a real madhouse. Prophets and quacks multiply; they hasten to get there with a good law or a flawless organization before the world is deserted. Fortunately, *I* arrived! I am the end and the beginning; I announce the law. In short, I am a judge-penitent.

Yes, yes, I'll tell you tomorrow what this noble profession consists of. You are leaving the day after tomorrow, so we are in a hurry. Come to my place, will you? Just ring three times. You are going back to Paris? Paris is far; Paris is beautiful; I haven't forgotten it. I remember its twilights at about this same season. Evening falls, dry and rustling, over the roofs blue with smoke, the city rumbles, the river seems to flow backward. Then I used to wander in the streets. They wander now too, I know! They wander, pretending to hasten toward the tired wife, the forbidding home . . . Ah, *mon ami*, do you know what the solitary creature is like as he wanders in big cities? . . .

I'M EMBARRASSED to be in bed when you arrive. It's nothing, just a little fever that I'm treating with gin. I'm accustomed to these attacks. Malaria, I think, that I caught at the time I was pope. No, I'm only half joking. I know what you're thinking: it's very hard to disentangle the true from the false in what I'm saying. I admit you are right. I myself . . . You see, a person I knew used to divide human beings into three categories: those who prefer having nothing to hide rather than being obliged to lie, those who prefer lying to having nothing to hide, and finally those who like both lying and the hidden. I'll let you choose the pigeonhole that suits me.

But what do I care? Don't lies eventually lead to the truth? And don't all my stories, true or false, tend toward the same conclusion? Don't they all have the same meaning? So what does it matter whether they are true or false if, in both cases, they are significant of what I have been and of what I am? Sometimes it is easier to see clearly into the liar than into the man who tells the truth. Truth, like light, blinds. Falsehood, on the contrary, is a beautiful twilight that enhances every object. Well, make of it what you will, but I was named pope in a prison camp. Sit down, please. You are examining this room. Bare, to be sure, but clean. A Vermeer, without furniture or copper pots. Without books either, for I gave up reading some time ago. At one time, my house was full of half-read books. That's just as disgusting as those people who cut a piece off a *foie gras* and have the rest thrown out. Anyway, I have ceased to like anything but confessions, and authors of confessions write especially to avoid confessing, to tell nothing of what they know. When they claim to get to the painful admissions, you have to watch out, for they are about to dress the corpse. Believe me, I know what I'm talking about. So I put a stop to it. No more books, no more useless objects either; the bare necessities, clean and polished like a coffin. Besides, these Dutch beds, so hard and with their immaculate sheets—one dies in them as if already wrapped in a shroud, embalmed in purity.

You are curious to know my pontifical adventures? Nothing out of the ordinary, you know. Shall I have the strength to tell you of them? Yes, the fever is going down. It was all so long ago. It was in Africa where, thanks to a certain Rommel, war was raging. I wasn't involved in it—no, don't worry. I had already dodged the one in Europe. Mobilized of course, but I never saw action. In a way, I regret it. Maybe that would have changed many things? The French army didn't need me on the front; it merely asked me to take part in the retreat. A little later I got back to Paris, and the Germans. I was tempted by the Resistance, about which people were beginning to talk just about the time I discovered that I was patriotic. You are smiling? You are wrong. I made my discovery on a subway platform, at the Châtelet station. A dog had strayed into the labyrinth of passageways. Big, wiry-haired, one ear cocked, eyes laughing, he was cavorting and sniffing the passing legs. I have a very old and very faithful attachment for dogs. I like them because they always forgive. I called this one, who hesitated, obviously won over, wagging his tail enthusiastically a few yards ahead of me. Just then, a young German soldier, who was walking

121

briskly, passed me. Having reached the dog, he caressed the shaggy head. Without hesitating, the animal fell in step with the same enthusiasm and disappeared with him. From the resentment and the sort of rage I felt against the German soldier, it was clear to me that my reaction was patriotic. If the dog had followed a French civilian, I'd not even have thought of it. But, on the contrary, I imagined that friendly dog as the mascot of a German regiment and that made me fly into a rage. Hence the test was convincing.

I reached the Southern Zone with the intention of finding out about the Resistance. But once there and having found out, I hesitated. The undertaking struck me as a little mad and, in a word, romantic. I think especially that underground action suited neither my temperament nor my preference for exposed heights. It seemed to me that I was being asked to do some weaving in a cellar, for days and nights on end, until some brutes should come to haul me from hiding, undo my weaving, and then drag me to another cellar to beat me to death. I admired those who indulged in such heroism of the depths, but couldn't imitate them.

So I crossed over to North Africa with the vague intention of getting to London. But in Africa the situation was not clear; the opposing parties seemed to be equally right and I stood aloof. I can see from your manner that I am skipping rather fast, in your opinion, over these details which have a certain significance. Well, let's say that, having judged you at your true value, I am skipping over them so that you will notice them the better. In any case, I eventually reached Tunisia, where a fond friend gave me work. That friend was a very intelligent woman who was involved in the movies. I followed her to Tunis and didn't discover her real business until the days following the Allied landing in Algeria. She was arrested that day by the Germans and I, too, but without having intended it. I don't know what became of her. As for me, no harm was done me and I realized, after considerable anguish, that it was chiefly as a security measure. I was interned near Tripoli in a camp where we suffered from thirst and destitution more than from brutality. I'll not describe it to you. We children of the mid-century don't need a diagram to imagine such places. A hundred and fifty years ago, people became sentimental about lakes and forests. Today we have the lyricism of the prison cell. Hence, I'll leave it to you. You need add but a few details: the heat, the vertical sun, the flies, the sand, the lack of water.

There was a young Frenchman with me who had faith. Yes, it's decidedly a fairy tale! The Du Guesclin type, if you will. He had crossed over from France into Spain to go and fight. The Catholic general had interned him, and having seen that in the Franco camps the chick-peas were, if I may say so, blessed by Rome, he had developed a profound melancholy. Neither the sky of Africa, where he had next landed, nor the leisures of the camp had distracted him from that melancholy. But his reflections, and the sun, too, had somewhat unhinged him. One day when, under a tent that seemed to drip molten lead, the ten or so of us were panting among the flies, he repeated his diatribes against the Roman, as he called him. He looked at us with a wild stare, his face unshaven for days. Bare to the waist and covered with sweat, he drummed with his hands on the visible keyboard of his ribs.

124

He declared to us the need for a new pope who should live among the wretched instead of praying on a throne, and the sooner the better. He stared with wild eyes as he shook his head. "Yes," he repeated, "as soon as possible!" Then he calmed down suddenly and in a dull voice said that we must choose him among us, pick a complete man with his vices and virtues and swear allegiance to him, on the sole condition that he should agree to keep alive, in himself and in others, the community of our sufferings. "Who among us," he asked, "has the most failings?" As a joke, I raised my hand and was the only one to do so. "O.K., Jean-Baptiste will do." No, he didn't say just that because I had another name then. He declared at least that nominating oneself as I had done presupposed also the greatest virtue and proposed electing me. The others agreed, in fun, but with a trace of seriousness all the same. The truth is that Du Guesclin had impressed us. It seems to me that even I was not altogether laughing. To begin with, I considered that my little prophet was right; and then with the sun, the exhausting labor, the struggle for water, we were not up to snuff. In any case, I exercised my pontificate for several weeks, with increasing seriousness.

Of what did it consist? Well, I was something like a group leader or the secretary of a cell. The others, in any case, and even those who lacked faith, got into the habit of obeying me. Du Guesclin was suffering; I administered his suffering. I discovered then that it was not so easy as I thought to be a pope, and I remembered this just yesterday after having given you such a scornful speech on judges, our brothers. The big problem in the camp was the water allotment. Other groups, political or sectarian, had formed, and each prisoner favored his comrades. I was consequently led to favor mine, and this was a little concession to begin with. Even among us, I could not maintain complete equality. According to my comrades' condition, or the work they had to do, I gave an advantage to this or that one. Such distinctions are far-reaching, you can take my word for it. But decidedly I am tired and no longer want to think of that period. Let's just say that I closed the circle the day I drank the water of a dying comrade. No, no, it wasn't Du Guesclin; he was already dead, I believe, for he stinted himself too much. Besides, had he been there, out of love for him I'd have resisted longer, for I loved him—yes, I loved him, or so it seems to me. But I drank the water, that's certain, while convincing myself that the others needed me more than this fellow who was going to die anyway and that I had a duty to keep myself alive for them. Thus, *cher*, empires and churches are born under the sun of death. And in order to correct somewhat what I said yesterday, I am going to tell you the great idea that has come to me while telling all this, which—I'm not sure now—I may have lived or only dreamed. My great idea is that one must forgive the pope. To begin with, he needs it more than anyone else. Secondly, that's the only way to set oneself above him . . .

Did you close the door thoroughly? Yes? Make sure, please. Forgive me, I have the bolt complex. On the point of going to sleep, I can never remember whether or not I pushed the bolt. And every night I must get up to verify. One can be sure of nothing, as I've told you. Don't think that this worry about the bolt is the reaction of a frightened possessor. Formerly I didn't lock my apartment or my car. I didn't lock up my money; I didn't cling to what I owned. To tell the truth, I was a little ashamed to own anything. Didn't I occasionally, in my social remarks, exclaim with conviction: "Property, gentlemen, is murder!" Not being sufficiently big-hearted to share my wealth with a deserving poor man, I left it at the disposal of possible thieves, hoping thus to correct injustice by chance. Today, moreover, I possess nothing. Hence I am not worried about my safety, but about myself and my presence of mind. I am also eager to block the door of the closed little universe of which I am the king, the pope, and the judge.

By the way, will you please open that cupboard? Yes, look at that painting. Don't you recognize it? It is "The Just Judges." That doesn't make you jump? Can it be that your culture has gaps? Yet if you read the papers, you would recall the theft in 1934 in the St. Bavon Cathedral of Ghent, of one of the panels of the famous van Eyck altarpiece, "The Adoration of the Lamb." That panel was called "The Just Judges." It represented judges on horseback coming to adore the sacred animal. It was replaced by an excellent copy, for the original was never found. Well, here it is. No, I had nothing to do with it. A frequenter of *Mexico City* —you had a glimpse of him the other evening— sold it to the ape for a bottle, one drunken evening. I first advised our friend to hang it in a place of honor, and for a long time, while they were being looked for throughout the world, our devout judges sat enthroned at *Mexico City* above the drunks and pimps. Then the ape, at my request, put it in custody here. He balked a little at doing so, but he got a fright when I explained the matter to him. Since then, these estimable magistrates form my sole company. At *Mexico City*, above the bar, you saw what a void they left.

Why I did not return the panel? Ah! Ah! You have a policeman's reflex, you do! Well, I'll answer you as I would the state's attorney, if it could ever occur to anyone that this painting had wound up in my room. First, because it belongs not to me but to the proprietor of *Mexico City*, who deserves it as much as the Archbishop of Ghent. Secondly, because among all those who file by "The Adoration of the Lamb" no one could distinguish the copy from the original and hence no one is wronged by my misconduct. Thirdly, because in this way I dominate. False judges are held up to the world's admiration and I alone know the true ones. Fourth, because I thus have a chance of being sent to prison—an attractive idea in a way. Fifth, because those judges are on their way to meet the Lamb, because there is no more lamb or innocence, and because the clever rascal who stole the panel was an instrument of the unknown justice that one ought not to thwart. Finally, because this way everything is in harmony. Justice being definitively separated from innocence—the latter on the cross and the former in the cupboard—I have the way clear to work according to my convictions. With a clear conscience I can practice the difficult profession of judge-penitent, in which I have set myself up after so many blighted hopes and contradictions; and now it is time, since you are leaving, for me to tell you what it is.

Allow me first to sit up so I can breathe more easily. Oh, how weak I am! Lock up my judges, please. As for the profession of judge-penitent, I am practicing it at present. Ordinarily, my offices are at *Mexico City*. But real vocations are carried beyond the place of work. Even in bed, even with a fever, I am functioning. Besides, one doesn't practice this profession, one breathes it constantly. Don't get the idea that I have talked to you at such length for five days just for the fun of it. No, I used to talk through my hat quite enough in the past. Now my words have a purpose. They have the purpose, obviously, of silencing the laughter, of avoiding judgment personally, though there is apparently no escape. Is not the great thing that stands in the way of our escaping it the fact that we are the first to condemn ourselves? Therefore it is essential to begin by extending the condemnation to all, without distinction, in order to thin it out at the start.

No excuses ever, for anyone; that's my principle at the outset. I deny the good intention, the respectable mistake, the indiscretion, the extenuating circumstance. With me there is no giving of absolution or blessing. Everything is simply totted up, and then: "It comes to so much. You are an evildoer, a satyr, a congenital liar, a homosexual, an artist, etc." Just like that. Just as flatly. In philosophy as in politics, I am for any theory that re-

131

fuses to grant man innocence and for any practice that treats him as guilty. You see in me, *très cher*, an enlightened advocate of slavery.

Without slavery, as a matter of fact, there is no definitive solution. I very soon realized that. Once upon a time, I was always talking of freedom. At breakfast I used to spread it on my toast, I used to chew it all day long, and in company my breath was delightfully redolent of freedom. With that key word I would bludgeon whoever contradicted me; I made it serve my desires and my power. I used to whisper it in bed in the ear of my sleeping mates and it helped me to drop them. I would slip it . . . Tchk! Tchk! I am getting excited and losing all sense of proportion. After all, I did on occasion make a more disinterested use of freedom and even—just imagine my naïveté—defended it two or three times without of course going so far as to die for it, but nevertheless taking a few risks. I must be forgiven such rash acts; I didn't know what I was doing. I didn't know that freedom is not a reward or a decoration that is celebrated with champagne. Nor yet a gift, a box of dainties designed to make you lick your chops. Oh, no! It's a chore, on the contrary, and a long-distance race, quite solitary and very exhausting. No champagne, no friends raising their glasses as they look at you affectionately. Alone in a forbidding room, alone in the prisoner's box before the judges, and alone to decide in face of oneself or in the face of others' judgment. At the end of all freedom is a court sentence; that's why freedom is too heavy to bear, especially when you're down with a fever, or are distressed, or love nobody.

Ah, *mon cher*, for anyone who is alone, without God and without a master, the weight of days is dreadful. Hence one must choose a master, God being out of style. Besides, that word has lost its meaning; it's not worth the risk of shocking anyone. Take our moral philosophers, for instance, so serious, loving their neighbor and all the rest— nothing distinguishes them from Christians, except that they don't preach in churches. What, in your opinion, keeps them from becoming converted? Respect perhaps, respect for men; yes, human respect. They don't want to start a scandal, so they keep their feelings to themselves. For example, I knew an atheistic novelist who used to pray every night. That didn't stop anything: how he gave it to God in his books! What a dusting off, as some-one or other would say. A militant freethinker to whom I spoke of this raised his hands—with no evil intention, I assure you—to heaven: "You're telling me nothing new," that apostle sighed, "they are all like that." According to him, eighty per cent of our writers, if only they could avoid signing, would write and hail the name of God. But they sign, according to him, because they love themselves, and they hail nothing at all because they loathe themselves. Since, nevertheless, they cannot keep themselves from judging, they make up for it by moralizing. In short, their satanism is virtuous. An odd epoch, indeed! It's not at all surprising that minds are confused and that one of my friends, an atheist when he was a model husband, got con-verted when he became an adulterer!

Ah, the little sneaks, play actors, hypocrites —and yet so touching! Believe me, they all are, even when they set fire to heaven. Whether they are atheists or churchgoers, Muscovites or Bosto-nians, all Christians from father to son. But it so hap-pens that there is no more father, no more rule!

134

They are free and hence have to shift for themselves; and since they don't want freedom or its judgments, they ask to be rapped on the knuckles, they invent dreadful rules, they rush out to build piles of faggots to replace churches. Savonarolas, I tell you. But they believe solely in sin, never in grace. They think of it, to be sure. Grace is what they want—acceptance, surrender, happiness, and maybe, for they are sentimental too, betrothal, the virginal bride, the upright man, the organ music. Take me, for example, and I am not sentimental— do you know what I used to dream of? A total love of the whole heart and body, day and night, in an uninterrupted embrace, sensual enjoyment and mental excitement—all lasting five years and ending in death. Alas!

So, after all, for want of betrothal or uninterrupted love, it will be marriage, brutal marriage, with power and the whip. The essential is that everything should become simple, as for the child, that every act should be ordered, that good and evil should be arbitrarily, hence obviously, pointed out. And I agree, however Sicilian and Javanese I may be and not at all Christian, though I feel friendship for the first Christian of all. But on the bridges of Paris I, too, learned that I was afraid of freedom. So hurray for the master, whoever he may be, to take the place of heaven's law. "Our Father who art provisionally here . . . Our guides, our delightfully severe masters, O cruel and beloved leaders . . ." In short, you see, the essential is to cease being free and to obey, in repentance, a greater rogue than oneself. When we are all guilty, that will be democracy. Without counting, *cher ami*, that we must take revenge for having to die alone. Death is solitary, whereas slavery is collective. The others get theirs, too, and at the same time as we—that's what counts. All together at last, but on our knees and heads bowed.

Isn't it good likewise to live like the rest of the world, and for that doesn't the rest of the world have to be like me? Threat, dishonor, police are the sacraments of that resemblance. Scorned, hunted down, compelled, I can then show what I am worth, enjoy what I am, be natural at last. This is why, *très cher*, after having solemnly paid my respects to freedom, I decided on the sly that it had to be handed over without delay to anyone who comes along. And every time I can, I preach in my church of *Mexico City*, I invite the good people to submit to authority and humbly to solicit the comforts of slavery, even if I have to present it as true freedom.

But I'm not being crazy; I'm well aware that slavery is not immediately realizable. It will be one of the blessings of the future, that's all. In the meantime, I must get along with the present and seek at least a provisional solution. Hence I had to find another means of extending judgment to everybody in order to make it weigh less heavily on my own shoulders. I found the means. Open the window a little, please; it's frightfully hot. Not too much, for I am cold also. My idea is both simple and fertile. How to get everyone involved in order to have the right to sit calmly on the outside myself? Should I climb up to the pulpit, like many of my illustrious contemporaries, and curse humanity? Very dangerous, that is! One day, or one night, laughter bursts out without a warning. The judgment you are passing on others eventually snaps back in your face, causing some damage. And so what? you ask. Well, here's the stroke of genius,

I discovered that while waiting for the masters with their rods, we should, like Copernicus, reverse the reasoning to win out. Inasmuch as one couldn't condemn others without immediately judging oneself, one had to overwhelm oneself to have the right to judge others. Inasmuch as every judge some day ends up as a penitent, one had to travel the road in the opposite direction and practice the profession of penitent to be able to end up as a judge. You follow me? Good. But to make myself even clearer, I'll tell you how I operate.

First I closed my law office, left Paris, traveled. I aimed to set up under another name in some place where I shouldn't lack for a practice. There are many in the world, but chance, convenience, irony, and also the necessity for a certain mortification made me choose a capital of waters and fogs, girdled by canals, particularly crowded, and visited by men from all corners of the earth. I set up my office in a bar in the sailors' quarter. The clientele of a port-town is varied. The poor don't go into the luxury districts, whereas eventually the gentlefolk always wind up at least once, as you have seen, in the disreputable places. I lie in wait particularly for the bourgeois, and the straying bourgeois at that; it's with him that I get my best results. Like a virtuoso with a rare violin, I draw my subtlest sounds from him.

So I have been practicing my useful profession at *Mexico City* for some time. It consists to begin with, as you know from experience, in indulging in public confession as often as possible. I accuse myself up and down. It's not hard, for I now have acquired a memory. But let me point out that I don't accuse myself crudely, beating my breast. No, I navigate skillfully, multiplying distinctions and digressions, too—in short I adapt my words to my listener and lead him to go me one better. I mingle what concerns me and what concerns others. I choose the features we have in common, the experiences we have endured together, the failings we share—good form, in other words, the man of the hour as he is rife in me and in others. With all that I construct a portrait which is the image of all and of no one. A mask, in short, rather like those carnival masks which are both lifelike and stylized, so that they make people say: "Why, surely I've met him!" When the portrait is finished, as it is this evening, I show it with great sorrow: "This, alas, is what I am!" The prosecutor's charge is finished. But at the same time the portrait I hold out to my contemporaries becomes a mirror.

Covered with ashes, tearing my hair, my face scored by clawing, but with piercing eyes, I stand before all humanity recapitulating my shames without losing sight of the effect I am producing, and saying: "I was the lowest of the low." Then imperceptibly I pass from the "I" to the "we." When I get to "This is what we are," the trick has been played and I can tell them off. I am like them, to be sure; we are in the soup together. However, I have a superiority in that I know it and this gives me the right to speak. You see the advantage, I am sure. The more I accuse myself, the more I have a right to judge you. Even better, I provoke you into judging yourself, and this relieves me of that much of the burden. Ah, *mon cher*, we are odd, wretched creatures, and if we merely look back over our lives, there's no lack of occasions to amaze and horrify ourselves. Just try. I shall listen, you may be sure, to your own confession with a great feeling of fraternity.

Don't laugh! Yes, you are a difficult client; I saw that at once. But you'll come to it inevitably. Most of the others are more sentimental than intelligent; they are disconcerted at once. With the intelligent ones it takes time. It is enough to explain the method fully to them. They don't forget it; they reflect. Sooner or later, half as a game and half out of emotional upset, they give up and tell all. *You* are not only intelligent, you look polished by use. Admit, however, that today you feel less pleased with yourself than you felt five days ago? Now I shall wait for you to write me or come back. For you will come back, I am sure! You'll find me unchanged. And why should I change, since I have found the happiness that suits me? I have accepted duplicity instead of being upset about it. On the contrary, I have settled into it and found there the comfort I was looking for throughout life. I was wrong, after all, to tell you that the essential was to avoid judgment. The essential is being able to permit oneself everything, even if, from time to time, one has to profess vociferously one's own infamy. I permit myself everything again, and without the laughter this

141

time. I haven't changed my way of life; I continue
to love myself and to make use of others. Only, the
confession of my crimes allows me to begin again
lighter in heart and to taste a double enjoyment,
first of my nature and secondly of a charming repentance.

Since finding my solution, I yield to everything, to women, to pride, to boredom, to resentment, and even to the fever that I feel delightfully
rising at this moment. I dominate at last, but forever. Once more I have found a height to which
I am the only one to climb and from which I can
judge everybody. At long intervals, on a really
beautiful night I occasionally hear a distant laugh
and again I doubt. But quickly I crush everything,
people and things, under the weight of my own infirmity, and at once I perk up.

So I shall await your respects at *Mexico City*
as long as necessary. But remove this blanket; I
want to breathe. You will come, won't you? I'll
show you the details of my technique, for I feel a
sort of affection for you. You will see me teaching
them night after night that they are vile. This very
evening, moreover, I shall resume. I can't do with-

out it or deny myself those moments when one of them collapses, with the help of alcohol, and beats his breast. Then I grow taller, *très cher*, I grow taller, I breathe freely, I am on the mountain, the plain stretches before my eyes. How intoxicating to feel like God the Father and to hand out definitive testimonials of bad character and habits. I sit enthroned among my bad angels at the summit of the Dutch heaven and I watch ascending toward me, as they issue from the fogs and the water, the multitude of the Last Judgment. They rise slowly; I already see the first of them arriving. On his bewildered face, half hidden by his hand, I read the melancholy of the common condition and the despair of not being able to escape it. And as for me, I pity without absolving, I understand without forgiving, and above all, I feel at last that I am being adored!

Yes, I am moving about. How could I remain in bed like a good patient? I must be higher than you, and my thoughts lift me up. Such nights, or such mornings rather (for the fall occurs at dawn), I go out and walk briskly along the canals. In the livid sky the layers of feathers become thinner, the

143

doves move a little higher, and above the roofs a rosy light announces a new day of my creation. On the Damrak the first streetcar sounds its bell in the damp air and marks the awakening of life at the extremity of this Europe where, at the same moment, hundreds of millions of men, my subjects, painfully slip out of bed, a bitter taste in their mouths, to go to a joyless work. Then, soaring over this whole continent which is under my sway without knowing it, drinking in the absinthe-colored light of breaking day, intoxicated with evil words, I am happy—I am happy, I tell you, I won't let you think I'm not happy, I am happy unto death! Oh, sun, beaches, and the islands in the path of the trade winds, youth whose memory drives one to despair!

I'm going back to bed; forgive me. I fear I got worked up; yet I'm not weeping. At times one wanders, doubting the facts, even when one has discovered the secrets of the good life. To be sure, my solution is not the ideal. But when you don't like your own life, when you know that you must change lives, you don't have any choice, do you? What can one do to become another? Impossible.

One would have to cease being anyone, forget one-self for someone else, at least once. But how? Don't bear down too hard on me. I'm like that old beggar who wouldn't let go of my hand one day on a café terrace: "Oh, sir," he said, "it's not just that I'm no good, but you lose track of the light." Yes, we have lost track of the light, the mornings, the holy innocence of those who forgive themselves.

Look, it's snowing! Oh, I must go out! Amsterdam asleep in the white night, the dark jade canals under the little snow-covered bridges, the empty streets, my muffled steps—there will be purity, even if fleeting, before tomorrow's mud. See the huge flakes drifting against the windowpanes. It must be the doves, surely. They finally make up their minds to come down, the little dears; they are covering the waters and the roofs with a thick layer of feathers; they are fluttering at every window. What an invasion! Let's hope they are bringing good news. Everyone will be saved, eh?—and not only the elect. Possessions and hardships will be shared and you, for example, from today on you will sleep every night on the ground for me. The whole shooting match, eh! Come now, admit that

145

you would be flabbergasted if a chariot came down from heaven to carry me off, or if the snow suddenly caught fire. You don't believe it? Nor do I. But still I must go out.

All right, all right, I'll be quiet; don't get upset! Don't take my emotional outbursts or my ravings too seriously. They are controlled. Say, now that you are going to talk to me about yourself, I shall find out whether or not one of the objectives of my absorbing confession is achieved. I always hope, in fact, that my interlocutor will be a policeman and that he will arrest me for the theft of "The Just Judges." For the rest—am I right?—no one can arrest me. But as for that theft, it falls within the provisions of the law and I have arranged everything so as to make myself an accomplice: I am harboring that painting and showing it to whoever wants to see it. You would arrest me then; that would be a good beginning. Perhaps the rest would be taken care of subsequently; I would be decapitated, for instance, and I'd have no more fear of death; I'd be saved. Above the gathered crowd, you would hold up my still warm head, so that they could recognize themselves in it and I could again dominate—an exemplar. All would be consummated; I should have brought to a close, unseen and unknown, my career as a false prophet crying in the wilderness and refusing to come forth.

But of course you are not a policeman; that would be too easy. What? Ah, I suspected as much, you see. That strange affection I felt for you had sense to it then. In Paris you practice the noble profession of lawyer! I sensed that we were of the same species. Are we not all alike, constantly talking and to no one, forever up against the same questions although we know the answers in advance? Then please tell me what happened to you one night on the quays of the Seine and how you managed never to risk your life. You yourself utter the words that for years have never ceased echoing through my nights and that I shall at last say through your mouth: "O young woman, throw yourself into the water again so that I may a second time have the chance of saving both of us!" A second time, eh, what a risky suggestion! Just suppose, *cher maître*, that we should be taken literally? We'd have to go through with it. Brr . . .! The water's so cold! But let's not worry! It's too late now. It will always be too late. Fortunately!

147

EXILE AND
THE KINGDOM

FOR FRANCINE

CONTENTS

THE
ADULTEROUS
WOMAN

A HOUSEFLY had been circling for the
last few minutes in the bus, though the windows
were closed. An odd sight here, it had been silently
flying back and forth on tired wings. Janine lost
track of it, then saw it light on her husband's
motionless hand. The weather was cold. The fly
shuddered with each gust of sandy wind that
scratched against the windows. In the meager light
of the winter morning, with a great fracas of sheet
metal and axles, the vehicle was rolling, pitching,
and making hardly any progress. Janine looked at

her husband. With wisps of graying hair growing low on a narrow forehead, a broad nose, a flabby mouth, Marcel looked like a pouting faun. At each hollow in the pavement she felt him jostle against her. Then his heavy torso would slump back on his widespread legs and he would become inert again and absent, with vacant stare. Nothing about him seemed active but his thick hairless hands, made even shorter by the flannel underwear extending below his cuffs and covering his wrists. His hands were holding so tight to a little canvas suitcase set between his knees that they appeared not to feel the fly's halting progress.

Suddenly the wind was distinctly heard to howl and the gritty fog surrounding the bus became even thicker. The sand now struck the windows in packets as if hurled by invisible hands. The fly shook a chilled wing, flexed its legs, and took flight. The bus slowed and seemed on the point of stopping. But the wind apparently died down, the fog lifted slightly, and the vehicle resumed speed. Gaps of light opened up in the dust-drowned landscape. Two or three frail, whitened palm trees which seemed cut out of metal flashed into sight in the window only to disappear the next moment.

"What a country!" Marcel said.

The bus was full of Arabs pretending to sleep, shrouded in their burnooses. Some had folded their legs on the seat and swayed more than the others in the car's motion. Their silence and impassivity began to weigh upon Janine; it seemed to her as if she had been traveling for days with that mute escort. Yet the bus had left only at dawn from the end of the rail line and for two hours in the cold morning it had been advancing on a stony, desolate plateau which, in the beginning at least, extended its straight lines all the way to reddish horizons. But the wind had risen and gradually swallowed up the vast expanse. From that moment on, the passengers had seen nothing more; one after another, they had ceased talking and were silently progressing in a sort of sleepless night, occasionally wiping their lips and eyes irritated by the sand that filtered into the car.

"Janine!" She gave a start at her husband's call. Once again she thought how ridiculous that name was for someone tall and sturdy like her. Marcel wanted to know where his sample case was. With her foot she explored the empty space under the seat and encountered an object which she decided must be it. She could not stoop over without gasping somewhat. Yet in school she had won the first prize in gymnastics and hadn't known what it was to be winded. Was that so long ago? Twenty-five years. Twenty-five years were nothing, for it seemed to her only yesterday when she was hesitating between an independent life and marriage, just yesterday when she was thinking anxiously of the time she might be growing old alone. She was not alone and that law-student who always wanted to be with her was now at her side. She had eventually accepted him although he was a little shorter than she and she didn't much like his eager, sharp laugh or his black protruding eyes. But she liked his courage in facing up to life, which he shared with all the French of this country. She also liked his crestfallen look when events or men failed to live up to his expectations. Above all, she liked being loved, and he had showered her with attentions. By so often making her aware that she existed for him he made her exist in reality. No, she was not alone. . . .

The bus, with many loud honks, was plowing its way through invisible obstacles. Inside the car, however, no one stirred. Janine suddenly felt someone staring at her and turned toward the seat across the aisle. He was not an Arab, and she was surprised not to have noticed him from the beginning.

154

He was wearing the uniform of the French regiments of the Sahara and an unbleached linen cap above his tanned face, long and pointed like a jackal's. His gray eyes were examining her with a sort of glum disapproval, in a fixed stare. She suddenly blushed and turned back to her husband, who was still looking straight ahead in the fog and wind. She snuggled down in her coat. But she could still see the French soldier, long and thin, so thin in his fitted tunic that he seemed constructed of a dry, friable material, a mixture of sand and bone. Then it was that she saw the thin hands and burned faces of the Arabs in front of her and noticed that they seemed to have plenty of room, despite their ample garments, on the seat where she and her husband felt wedged in. She pulled her coat around her knees. Yet she wasn't so fat—tall and well rounded rather, plump and still desirable, as she was well aware when men looked at her, with her rather childish face, her bright, naïve eyes contrasting with this big body she knew to be warm and inviting.

No, nothing had happened as she had expected. When Marcel had wanted to take her along on his trip she had protested. For some time he had been thinking of this trip—since the end of the war, to be precise, when business had returned to normal. Before the war the small dry-goods business he had taken over from his parents on giving up his study of law had provided a fairly good living. On the coast the years of youth can be happy ones. But he didn't much like physical effort and very soon had given up taking her to the beaches. The little car took them out of town solely for the Sunday afternoon ride. The rest of the time he preferred his shop full of multicolored piece-goods shaded by the arcades of this half-native, half-European quarter. Above the shop they lived in three rooms furnished with Arab hangings and furniture from the Galerie Barbès. They had not had children. The years had passed in the semi-darkness behind the half-closed shutters. Summer, the beaches, excursions, the mere sight of the sky were things of the past. Nothing seemed to interest Marcel but business. She felt she had discovered his true passion to be money, and, without really knowing why, she didn't like that. After all, it was to her advantage. Far from being miserly, he was generous, especially where she was concerned. "If something happened to me," he used to say, "you'd be provided for." And, in fact, it is essential to provide for one's needs. But for all the rest, for what is not the most elementary need, how to provide? This is what she felt vaguely, at infrequent intervals. Meanwhile she helped Marcel keep his books and occasionally substituted for him in the shop. Summer was always the hardest, when the heat stifled even the sweet sensation of boredom.

Suddenly, in summer as it happened, the war, Marcel called up then rejected on grounds of health, the scarcity of piece-goods, business at a standstill, the streets empty and hot. If something happened now, she would no longer be provided for. This is why, as soon as piece-goods came back on the market, Marcel had thought of covering the villages of the Upper Plateaus and of the South himself in order to do without a middleman and sell directly to the Arab merchants. He had wanted to take her along. She knew that travel was difficult, she had trouble breathing, and she would have preferred staying at home. But he was obstinate and she had accepted because it would have taken too much energy to refuse. Here they were and, truly, nothing was like what she had imagined. She had feared the heat, the swarms of flies, the filthy hotels reeking of aniseed. She had not thought of the cold, of the biting wind, of these semi-polar plateaus cluttered with moraines. She had dreamed too of palm trees and soft sand. Now she saw that the desert was not that at all, but merely stone, stone everywhere, in the sky full of nothing but stone-dust, rasping and cold, as on the ground, where nothing grew among the stones except dry grasses.

The bus stopped abruptly. The driver shouted a few words in that language she had heard all her life without ever understanding it. "What's the matter?" Marcel asked. The driver, in French this time, said that the sand must have clogged the carburetor, and again Marcel cursed this country. The driver laughed hilariously and asserted that it was nothing, that he would clean the carburetor and they'd be off again. He opened the door and the cold wind blew into the bus, lashing their faces with a myriad grains of sand. All the Arabs silently plunged their noses into their burnooses and huddled up. "Shut the door," Marcel shouted. The driver laughed as he came back to the door. Without hurrying, he took some tools from under the dashboard, then, tiny in the fog, again disappeared ahead without closing the door. Marcel sighed. "You may be sure he's never seen a motor in his life." "Oh, be quiet!" said Janine. Suddenly she gave a start. On the shoulder of the road close to the bus, draped forms were standing still. Under the burnoose's hood and behind a rampart of veils, only their eyes were visible. Mute, come from nowhere, they were staring at the travelers. "Shepherds," Marcel said.

Inside the car there was total silence. All the passengers, heads lowered, seemed to be listening to the voice of the wind loosed across these endless plateaus. Janine was all of a sudden struck by the almost complete absence of luggage. At the end of the railroad line the driver had hoisted their trunk and a few bundles onto the roof. In the racks inside the bus could be seen nothing but gnarled sticks and shopping-baskets. All these people of the South apparently were traveling empty-handed.

But the driver was coming back, still brisk. His eyes alone were laughing above the veils with which he too had masked his face. He announced that they would soon be under way. He closed the door, the wind became silent, and the rain of sand on the windows could be heard better. The motor coughed and died. After having been urged at great length by the starter, it finally sparked and the driver raced it by pressing on the gas. With a big hiccough the bus started off. From the ragged clump of shepherds, still motionless, a hand rose and then faded into the fog behind them. Almost at once the vehicle began to bounce on the road, which had become worse. Shaken up, the Arabs constantly swayed. Nonetheless, Janine was feeling overcome with sleep when there suddenly appeared in front of her a little yellow box filled with lozenges. The jackal-soldier was smiling at her. She hesitated, took one, and thanked him. The jackal pocketed the box and simultaneously swallowed his smile. Now he was staring at the road, straight in front of him. Janine turned toward Marcel and saw only the solid back of his neck. Through the window he was watching the denser fog rising from the crumbly embankment.

They had been traveling for hours and fatigue had extinguished all life in the car when shouts burst forth outside. Children wearing burnooses, whirling like tops, leaping, clapping their hands, were running around the bus. It was now going down a long street lined with low houses; they were entering the oasis. The wind was still blowing, but the walls intercepted the grains of sand which had previously cut off the light. Yet the sky was still cloudy. Amidst shouts, in a great screeching of brakes, the bus stopped in front of the adobe arcades of a hotel with dirty windows. Janine got out and, once on the pavement, staggered. Above

160

the houses she could see a slim yellow minaret. On her left rose the first palm trees of the oasis, and she would have liked to go toward them. But although it was close to noon, the cold was bitter; the wind made her shiver. She turned toward Marcel and saw the soldier coming toward her. She was expecting him to smile or salute. He passed without looking at her and disappeared. Marcel was busy getting down the trunk of piece-goods, a black foot-locker perched on the bus's roof. It would not be easy. The driver was the only one to take care of the luggage and he had already stopped, standing on the roof, to hold forth to the circle of burnooses gathered around the bus. Janine, surrounded with faces that seemed cut out of bone and leather, besieged by guttural shouts, suddenly became aware of her fatigue. "I'm going in," she said to Marcel, who was shouting impatiently at the driver.

She entered the hotel. The manager, a thin, laconic Frenchman, came to meet her. He led her to a second-floor balcony overlooking the street and into a room which seemed to have but an iron bed, a white-enameled chair, an uncurtained wardrobe, and, behind a rush screen, a washbasin covered with fine sand-dust. When the manager had closed the door, Janine felt the cold coming from the bare, whitewashed walls. She didn't know where to put her bag, where to put herself. She had either to lie down or to remain standing, and to shiver in either case. She remained standing, holding her bag and staring at a sort of window-slit that opened onto the sky near the ceiling. She was waiting, but she didn't know for what. She was aware only of her solitude, and of the penetrating cold, and of a greater weight in the region of her heart. She was in fact dreaming, almost deaf to the sounds rising from the street along with Marcel's vocal outbursts, more aware on the other hand of that sound of a river coming from the window-slit and caused by the wind in the palm trees, so close now, it seemed to her. Then the wind seemed to increase and the gentle ripple of waters became a hissing of waves. She imagined, beyond the walls, a sea of erect, flexible palm trees unfurling in the storm. Nothing was like what she had expected, but those invisible waves refreshed her tired eyes. She was standing, heavy, with dangling arms, slightly stooped, as the cold climbed her thick legs. She was dreaming of the erect and flexible palm trees and of the girl she had once been.

. . .

After having washed, they went down to the dining-room. On the bare walls had been painted camels and palm trees drowned in a sticky background of pink and lavender. The arcaded windows let in a meager light. Marcel questioned the hotel manager about the merchants. Then an elderly Arab wearing a military decoration on his tunic served them. Marcel, preoccupied, tore his bread into little pieces. He kept his wife from drinking water. "It hasn't been boiled. Take wine." She didn't like that, for wine made her sleepy. Besides, there was pork on the menu. "They don't eat it because of the Koran. But the Koran didn't know that well-done pork doesn't cause illness. We French know how to cook. What are you thinking about?" Janine was not thinking of anything, or perhaps of that victory of the cooks over the prophets. But she had to hurry. They were to leave the next morning for still farther south; that afternoon they had to see all the important merchants. Marcel urged the elderly Arab to hurry the coffee. He nodded without smiling and pattered out. "Slowly in the morning, not too fast in the afternoon," Marcel said, laughing. Yet eventually the coffee came. They barely took time to swallow it and went out into the dusty, cold street.

163

Marcel called a young Arab to help him carry the trunk, but as a matter of principle quibbled about the payment. His opinion, which he once more expressed to Janine, was in fact based on the vague principle that they always asked for twice as much in the hope of settling for a quarter of the amount. Janine, ill at ease, followed the two trunk-bearers. She had put on a wool dress under her heavy coat and would have liked to take up less space. The pork, although well done, and the small quantity of wine she had drunk also bothered her somewhat.

They walked along a diminutive public garden planted with dusty trees. They encountered Arabs who stepped out of their way without seeming to see them, wrapping themselves in their burnooses. Even when they were wearing rags, she felt they had a look of dignity unknown to the Arabs of her town. Janine followed the trunk, which made a way for her through the crowd. They went through the gate in an earthen rampart and emerged on a little square planted with the same mineral trees and bordered on the far side, where it was widest, with arcades and shops. But they stopped on the square itself in front of a small construction shaped like an artillery shell and painted chalky blue. Inside, in the single room lighted solely by the entrance, an old Arab with white mustaches stood behind a shiny plank. He was serving tea, raising and lowering the teapot over three tiny multicolored glasses. Before they could make out anything else in the darkness, the cool scent of mint tea greeted Marcel and Janine at the door. Marcel had barely crossed the threshold and dodged the garlands of pewter teapots, cups and trays, and the postcard displays when he was up against the counter. Janine stayed at the door. She stepped a little aside so as not to cut off the light. At that moment she perceived in the darkness behind the old merchant two Arabs smiling at them, seated on the bulging sacks that filled the back of the shop. Red-and-black rugs and embroidered scarves hung on the walls; the floor was cluttered with sacks and little boxes filled with aromatic seeds. On the counter, beside a sparkling pair of brass scales and an old yardstick with figures effaced, stood a row of loaves of sugar. One of them had been unwrapped from its coarse blue paper and cut into on top. The smell of wool and spices in the room became apparent behind the scent of tea when the old merchant set down the teapot and said good-day.

Marcel talked rapidly in the low voice he assumed when talking business. Then he opened the trunk, exhibited the wools and silks, pushed back the scale and yardstick to spread out his merchandise in front of the old merchant. He got excited, raised his voice, laughed nervously, like a woman who wants to make an impression and is not sure of herself. Now, with hands spread wide, he was going through the gestures of selling and buying. The old man shook his head, passed the tea tray to the two Arabs behind him, and said just a few words that seemed to discourage Marcel. He picked up his goods, piled them back into the trunk, then wiped an imaginary sweat from his forehead. He called the little porter and they started off toward the arcades. In the first shop, although the merchant began by exhibiting the same Olympian manner, they were a little luckier. "They think they're God almighty," Marcel said, "but they're in business too! Life is hard for everyone."

Janine followed without answering. The wind had almost ceased. The sky was clearing in spots. A cold, harsh light came from the deep holes that opened up in the thickness of the clouds. They had now left the square. They were walking in narrow streets along earthen walls over which hung rotted December roses or, from time to time, a pomegranate, dried and wormy. An odor of dust and coffee, the smoke of a wood fire, the smell of stone and of sheep permeated this quarter. The shops, hollowed out of the walls, were far from one another; Janine felt her feet getting heavier. But her husband was gradually becoming more cheerful. He was beginning to sell and was feeling more kindly; he called Janine "Baby"; the trip would not be wasted. "Of course," Janine said mechanically, "it's better to deal directly with them."

They came back by another street, toward the center. It was late in the afternoon; the sky was now almost completely clear. They stopped in the square. Marcel rubbed his hands and looked affectionately at the trunk in front of them. "Look," said Janine. From the other end of the square was coming a tall Arab, thin, vigorous, wearing a sky-blue burnoose, soft brown boots and gloves, and bearing his bronzed aquiline face loftily. Nothing but the *chèche* that he was wearing swathed as a turban distinguished him from those French officers in charge of native affairs whom Janine had occasionally admired. He was advancing steadily toward them, but seemed to be looking beyond their group as he slowly removed the glove from one hand. "Well," said Marcel as he shrugged his shoulders, "there's one who thinks he's a general." Yes, all of them here had that look of pride; but this one, really, was going too far. Although they were surrounded by the empty space of the square, he was walking straight toward the trunk without seeing it, without seeing them. Then the distance separating them decreased rapidly and the Arab was upon them when Marcel suddenly seized the handle of the foot-locker and pulled it out of the way. The Arab passed without seeming to notice anything and headed with the same regular step toward the ramparts. Janine looked at her husband; he had his crestfallen look. "They think they can get away with anything now," he said. Janine did not reply. She loathed that Arab's stupid arrogance and suddenly felt unhappy. She wanted to leave and thought of her little apartment. The idea of going back to the hotel, to that icy room, discouraged her. It suddenly occurred to her that the manager had advised her to climb up to the terrace around the fort to see the desert. She said this to Marcel and that he could leave the trunk at the hotel. But he was tired and wanted to sleep a little before dinner. "Please," said Janine. He looked at her, suddenly attentive. "Of course, my dear," he said.

She waited for him in the street in front of the hotel. The white-robed crowd was becoming larger and larger. Not a single woman could be seen, and it seemed to Janine that she had never seen so many men. Yet none of them looked at her. Some of them, without appearing to see her, slowly turned toward her that thin, tanned face that made them all look alike to her, the face of the French soldier in the bus and that of the gloved Arab, a face both shrewd and proud. They turned that face toward the foreign woman, they didn't see her, and then, light and silent, they walked around her as she stood there with swelling ankles. And her discomfort, her need of getting away increased. "Why did I come?" But already Marcel was coming back.

When they climbed the stairs to the fort, it was five o'clock. The wind had died down altogether. The sky, completely clear, was now periwinkle blue. The cold, now drier, made their cheeks smart. Halfway up the stairs an old Arab, stretched out against the wall, asked them if they wanted a guide, but didn't budge, as if he had been sure of their refusal in advance. The stairs were long and steep despite several landings of packed earth. As they climbed, the space widened and they rose into an ever broader light, cold and dry, in which every sound from the oasis reached them pure and distinct. The bright air seemed to vibrate around them with a vibration increasing in length as they advanced, as if their progress struck from the crystal of light a sound wave that kept spreading out. And as soon as they reached the terrace and their gaze was lost in the vast horizon beyond the palm grove, it seemed to Janine that the whole sky rang with a single short and piercing note, whose echoes gradually filled the space above her, then suddenly died and left her silently facing the limitless expanse.

From east to west, in fact, her gaze swept slowly, without encountering a single obstacle, along a perfect curve. Beneath her, the blue-and-white terraces of the Arab town overlapped one another, splattered with the dark-red spots of peppers drying in the sun. Not a soul could be seen, but from the inner courts, together with the aroma of roasting coffee, there rose laughing voices or incomprehensible stamping of feet. Farther off, the palm grove, divided into uneven squares by clay walls, rustled its upper foliage in a wind that could not be felt up on the terrace. Still farther off and all the way to the horizon extended the ocher-and-gray realm of stones, in which no life was visible. At some distance from the oasis, however, near the wadi that bordered the palm grove on the west could be seen broad black tents. All around them a flock of motionless dromedaries, tiny at that distance, formed against the gray ground the black signs of a strange handwriting, the meaning of which had to be deciphered. Above the desert, the silence was as vast as the space.

Janine, leaning her whole body against the parapet, was speechless, unable to tear herself away from the void opening before her. Beside her, Marcel was getting restless. He was cold; he wanted to go back down. What was there to see here, after all? But she could not take her gaze from the horizon. Over yonder, still farther south, at that point where sky and earth met in a pure line —over yonder it suddenly seemed there was awaiting her something of which, though it had always been lacking, she had never been aware until now. In the advancing afternoon the light relaxed and softened; it was passing from the crystalline to the liquid. Simultaneously, in the heart of a woman brought there by pure chance a knot tightened by the years, habit, and boredom was slowly loosening. She was looking at the nomads' encampment. She had not even seen the men living in it; nothing was stirring among the black tents, and yet she could think only of them whose existence she had barely known until this day. Homeless, cut off from the world, they were a handful wandering over the vast territory she could see, which however was but a paltry part of an even greater expanse whose dizzying course stopped only thousands of miles farther south, where the first river finally waters the forest. Since the beginning of time, on the dry earth of this limitless land scraped to the bone, a few men had been ceaselessly trudging, possessing nothing but serving no one, poverty-stricken but free lords of a strange kingdom. Janine did not know why this thought filled her with such a sweet, vast melancholy that it closed her eyes. She knew that this kingdom had been eternally promised her and yet that it would never be hers, never again, except in this fleeting moment perhaps when she opened her eyes again on the suddenly motionless sky and on its waves of steady light, while the voices rising from the Arab town suddenly fell silent. It seemed to her that the world's course had just stopped and that, from that moment on, no one would ever age any more or die. Everywhere, henceforth, life was suspended—except in her heart, where, at the same moment, someone was weeping with affliction and wonder.

But the light began to move; the sun, clear and devoid of warmth, went down toward the west, which became slightly pink, while a gray wave took shape in the east ready to roll slowly over the vast expanse. A first dog barked and its distant bark rose in the now even colder air. Janine noticed that her teeth were chattering. "We are catching our death of cold," Marcel said. "You're a fool. Let's go back." But he took her hand awkwardly. Docile now, she turned away from the parapet and followed him. Without moving, the old Arab on the stairs watched them go down toward the town. She walked along without seeing anyone, bent under a tremendous and sudden fatigue, dragging her body, whose weight now seemed to her unbearable. Her exaltation had left her. Now she felt too tall, too thick, too white too for this world she had just entered. A child, the girl, the dry man, the furtive jackal were the only creatures who could silently walk that earth. What would she do there henceforth except to drag herself toward sleep, toward death?

She dragged herself, in fact, toward the restaurant with a husband suddenly taciturn unless he was telling how tired he was, while she was struggling weakly against a cold, aware of a fever rising within her. Then she dragged herself toward her bed, where Marcel came to join her and put the light out at once without asking anything of her. The room was frigid. Janine felt the cold creeping up while the fever was increasing. She breathed with difficulty, her blood pumped without warming her; a sort of fear grew within her. She turned over and the old iron bedstead groaned under her weight. No, she didn't want to fall ill. Her husband was already asleep; she too had to sleep; it was essential. The muffled sounds of the town reached her through the window-slit. With a nasal twang old phonographs in the Moorish cafés ground out tunes she recognized vaguely; they reached her borne on the sound of a slow-moving crowd. She must sleep. But she was counting black tents; behind her eyelids motionless camels were grazing; immense solitudes were whirling within her. Yes, why had she come? She fell asleep on that question.

She awoke a little later. The silence around her was absolute. But, on the edges of town, hoarse dogs were howling in the soundless night. Janine shivered. She turned over, felt her husband's hard shoulder against hers, and suddenly, half asleep, huddled against him. She was drifting on the surface of sleep without sinking in and she clung to that shoulder with unconscious eagerness as her safest haven. She was talking, but no sound issued from her mouth. She was talking, but she herself hardly heard what she was saying. She could feel only Marcel's warmth. For more than twenty years every night thus, in his warmth, just the two of them, even when ill, even when traveling, as at present . . . Besides, what would she have done alone at home? No child! Wasn't that what she lacked? She didn't know. She simply followed Marcel, pleased to know that someone needed her. The only joy he gave her was the knowledge that she was necessary. Probably he didn't love her. Love, even when filled with hate, doesn't have that sullen face. But what is his face like? They made love in the dark by feel, without seeing each other.

Is there another love than that of darkness, a love that would cry aloud in daylight? She didn't know, but she did know that Marcel needed her and that she needed that need, that she lived on it night and day, at night especially—every night, when he didn't want to be alone, or to age or die, with that set expression he assumed which she occasionally recognized on other men's faces, the only common expression of those madmen hiding under an appearance of wisdom until the madness seizes them and hurls them desperately toward a woman's body to bury in it, without desire, everything terrifying that solitude and night reveals to them.

Marcel stirred as if to move away from her. No, he didn't love her; he was merely afraid of what was not she, and she and he should long ago have separated and slept alone until the end. But who can always sleep alone? Some men do, cut off from others by a vocation or misfortune, who go to bed every night in the same bed as death. Marcel never could do so—he above all, a weak and disarmed child always frightened by suffering, her own child indeed who needed her and who, just at that moment, let out a sort of whimper. She cuddled a little closer and put her hand on his chest. And to herself she called him with the little love-name she had once given him, which they still used from time to time without even thinking of what they were saying.

She called him with all her heart. After all, she too needed him, his strength, his little eccentricities, and she too was afraid of death. "If I could overcome that fear, I'd be happy. . . ." Immediately, a nameless anguish seized her. She drew back from Marcel. No, she was overcoming nothing, she was not happy, she was going to die, in truth, without having been liberated. Her heart pained her; she was stifling under a huge weight that she suddenly discovered she had been dragging around for twenty years. Now she was struggling under it with all her strength. She wanted to be liberated even if Marcel, even if the others, never were! Fully awake, she sat up in bed and listened to a call that seemed very close. But from the edges of night the exhausted and yet indefatigable voices of the dogs of the oasis were all that reached her ears. A slight wind had risen and she heard its light waters flow in the palm grove. It came from the south, where desert and night mingled now under the again unchanging sky, where life stopped, where no one would ever age or die any more. Then the waters of the wind dried up and she was not even

sure of having heard anything except a mute call
that she could, after all, silence or notice. But never
again would she know its meaning unless she re-
sponded to it at once. At once—yes, that much
was certain at least!

She got up gently and stood motionless beside
the bed, listening to her husband's breathing. Marcel was asleep. The next moment, the bed's warmth
left her and the cold gripped her. She dressed
slowly, feeling for her clothes in the faint light
coming through the blinds from the street-lamps.
Her shoes in her hand, she reached the door. She
waited a moment more in the darkness, then gently
opened the door. The knob squeaked and she
stood still. Her heart was beating madly. She listened with her body tense and, reassured by the silence, turned her hand a little more. The knob's
turning seemed to her interminable. At last she
opened the door, slipped outside, and closed the
door with the same stealth. Then, with her cheek
against the wood, she waited. After a moment she
made out, in the distance, Marcel's breathing. She
faced about, felt the icy night air against her cheek,
and ran the length of the balcony. The outer
door was closed. While she was slipping the bolt,
the night watchman appeared at the top of the

stairs, his face blurred with sleep, and spoke to her in Arabic. "I'll be back," said Janine as she stepped out into the night.

Garlands of stars hung down from the black sky over the palm trees and houses. She ran along the short avenue, now empty, that led to the fort. The cold, no longer having to struggle against the sun, had invaded the night; the icy air burned her lungs. But she ran, half blind, in the darkness. At the top of the avenue, however, lights appeared, then descended toward her zigzagging. She stopped, caught the whir of turning sprockets and, behind the enlarging lights, soon saw vast burnooses surmounting fragile bicycle wheels. The burnooses flapped against her; then three red lights sprang out of the black behind her and disappeared at once. She continued running toward the fort. Halfway up the stairs, the air burned her lungs with such cutting effect that she wanted to stop. A final burst of energy hurled her despite herself onto the terrace, against the parapet, which was now pressing her belly. She was panting and everything was hazy before her eyes. Her running had not warmed her and she was still trembling all over. But the cold air she was gulping down soon flowed evenly inside her and a spark of warmth began to glow amidst her shivers. Her eyes opened at last on the expanse of night.

Not a breath, not a sound—except at intervals the muffled crackling of stones that the cold was reducing to sand—disturbed the solitude and silence surrounding Janine. After a moment, however, it seemed to her that the sky above her was moving in a sort of slow gyration. In the vast reaches of the dry, cold night, thousands of stars were constantly appearing, and their sparkling icicles, loosened at once, began to slip gradually toward the horizon. Janine could not tear herself away from contemplating those drifting flares. She was turning with them, and the apparently stationary progress little by little identified her with the core of her being, where cold and desire were now vying with each other. Before her the stars were falling one by one and being snuffed out among the stones of the desert, and each time Janine opened a little more to the night. Breathing deeply, she forgot the cold, the dead weight of others, the craziness or stuffiness of life, the long anguish of living and dying. After so many years of mad, aimless fleeing from fear, she had come to a stop at last. At the same time, she seemed to recover her roots and the sap again rose in her body, which had ceased trembling. Her whole belly pressed against the parapet as she strained toward the moving sky; she was merely waiting for her fluttering heart to calm down and establish silence within her. The last stars of the constellations dropped their clusters a little lower on the desert horizon and became still. Then, with unbearable gentleness, the water of night began to fill Janine, drowned the cold, rose gradually from the hidden core of her being and overflowed in wave after wave, rising up even to her mouth full of moans. The next moment, the whole sky stretched out over her, fallen on her back on the cold earth.

When Janine returned to the room, with the same precautions, Marcel was not awake. But he whimpered as she got back in bed and a few seconds later sat up suddenly. He spoke and she didn't understand what he was saying. He got up, turned on the light, which blinded her. He staggered toward the washbasin and drank a long draught from the bottle of mineral water. He was about to slip between the sheets when, one knee on the bed, he looked at her without understanding. She was weeping copiously, unable to restrain herself. "It's nothing, dear," she said, "it's nothing."

THE
RENEGADE

What a jumble! What a jumble! I must tidy up my mind. Since they cut out my tongue, another tongue, it seems, has been constantly wagging somewhere in my skull, something has been talking, or someone, that suddenly falls silent and then it all begins again—oh, I hear too many things I never utter, what a jumble, and if I open my mouth it's like pebbles rattling together. Order and method, the tongue says, and then goes on talking of other matters simultaneously—yes, I always longed for order. At least one thing is certain, I am waiting for the missionary who is to come and take my place. Here I am on the trail, an hour away from Taghâsa, hidden in a pile of rocks,

182

sitting on my old rifle. Day is breaking over the desert, it's still very cold, soon it will be too hot, this country drives men mad and I've been here I don't know how many years. . . . No, just a little longer. The missionary is to come this morning, or this evening. I've heard he'll come with a guide, perhaps they'll have but one camel between them. I'll wait, I am waiting, it's only the cold making me shiver. Just be patient a little longer, lousy slave!

But I have been patient for so long. When I was home on that high plateau of the Massif Central, my coarse father, my boorish mother, the wine, the pork soup every day, the wine above all, sour and cold, and the long winter, the frigid wind, the snowdrifts, the revolting bracken—oh, I wanted to get away, leave them all at once and begin to live at last, in the sunlight, with fresh water. I believed the priest, he spoke to me of the seminary, he tutored me daily, he had plenty of time in that Protestant region, where he used to hug the walls as he crossed the village. He told me of the future and of the sun, Catholicism is the sun, he used to say, and he would get me to read, he beat Latin into my hard head ('The kid's bright but he's pig-headed'), my head was so hard that, despite all my falls, it has never once bled in my life: 'Bull-headed,' my pig of a father used to say. At the seminary they were proud as punch, a recruit from the Protestant region was a victory, they greeted me like the sun at Austerlitz. The sun was pale and feeble, to be sure, because of the alcohol, they have drunk sour wine and the children's teeth are set on edge, *gra gra*, one really ought to kill one's father, but after all there's no danger that *he*'ll hurl himself into missionary work since he's now long dead, the tart wine eventually cut through his stomach, so there's nothing left but to kill the missionary.

I have something to settle with him and with his teachers, with my teachers who deceived me, with the whole of lousy Europe, everybody deceived me. Missionary work, that's all they could say, go out to the savages and tell them: 'Here is my Lord, just look at him, he never strikes or kills, he issues his orders in a low voice, he turns the other cheek, he's the greatest of masters, choose him, just see how much better he's made me, offend me and you will see.' Yes, I believed, *gra gra*, and I felt better, I had put on weight, I was almost handsome, I wanted to be offended. When we would walk out in tight black rows, in summer, under Grenoble's hot sun and would meet girls in cotton dresses, *I* didn't look away, I despised them, I waited for them to offend me, and sometimes they would laugh. At such times I would think: 'Let them strike me and spit in my face,' but their laughter, to tell the truth, came to the same thing, bristling with teeth and quips that tore me to shreds, the offense and the suffering were sweet to me! My confessor couldn't understand when I used to heap accusations on myself: 'No, no, there's good in you!' Good! There was nothing but sour wine in me, and that was all for the best, how can a man become better if he's not bad, I had grasped that in everything they taught me. That's the only thing I did grasp, a single idea, and, pig-headed bright boy, I carried it to its logical conclusion, I went out of my way for punishments, I groused at the normal, in short I too wanted to be an example in order to be noticed and so that after noticing me people would give credit to what had made me better, through me praise my Lord.

Fierce sun! It's rising, the desert is changing, it has lost its mountain-cyclamen color, O my mountain, and the snow, the soft enveloping snow, no, it's a rather grayish yellow, the ugly moment before the great resplendence. Nothing, still nothing from here to the horizon over yonder where the plateau disappears in a circle of still soft colors. Behind me, the trail climbs to the dune hiding Taghâsa, whose iron name has been beating in my head for so many years. The first to mention it to me was the half-blind old priest who had retired to our monastery, but why do I say the first, he was the only one, and it wasn't the city of salt, the white walls under the blinding sun, that struck me in his account but the cruelty of the savage inhabitants and the town closed to all outsiders, only one of those who had tried to get in, one alone, to his knowledge, had lived to relate what he had seen. They had whipped him and driven him out into the desert after having put salt on his wounds and in his mouth, he had met nomads who for once were compassionate, a stroke of luck, and since then I had been dreaming about his tale, about the fire of the salt and the sky, about the House of the Fetish and his slaves, could anything more barbarous, more exciting be imagined, yes, that was my mission and I had to go and reveal to them my Lord.

They all expatiated on the subject at the seminary to discourage me, pointing out the necessity of waiting, that it was not missionary country, that I wasn't ready yet, I had to prepare myself specially, know who I was, and even then I had to go through tests, then they would see! But go on waiting, ah, no!—yes, if they insisted, for the special preparation and the tryouts because they took place at Algiers and brought me closer, but for all the rest I shook my pig-head and repeated the same thing, to get among the most barbarous and live as they did, to show them at home, and even in the House of the Fetish, through example, that my Lord's truth would prevail. They would offend me, of course, but I was not afraid of offenses, they were essential to the demonstration, and as a result of the way I endured them I'd get the upper hand of those savages like a strong sun. Strong, yes, that was the word I constantly had on the tip of my tongue, I dreamed of absolute power, the kind that makes people kneel down, that forces the adversary to capitulate, converts him in short, and the blinder, the crueler he is, the more he's sure of himself, mired in his own conviction, the more his consent establishes the royalty of whoever brought about his collapse. Converting good folk who had strayed somewhat was the shabby ideal of our priests, I despised them for daring so little when they could do so much, they lacked faith and I had it, I wanted to be acknowledged by the torturers themselves, to fling them on their knees and make them say: 'O Lord, here is thy victory,' to rule in short by the sheer force of words over an army of the wicked. Oh, I was sure of reasoning logically on that subject, never quite sure of myself otherwise, but once I get an idea I don't let go of it, that's my strong point, yes the strong point of the fellow they all pitied!

The sun has risen higher, my forehead is beginning to burn. Around me the stones are beginning to crack open with a dull sound, the only cool thing is the rifle's barrel, cool as the fields, as the evening rain long ago when the soup was simmering, they would wait for me, my father and mother who would occasionally smile at me, perhaps I loved them. But that's all in the past, a film of heat is beginning to rise from the trail, come on, missionary, I'm waiting for you, now I know how to answer the message, my new masters taught me, and I know they are right, you have to settle accounts with that question of love. When I fled the seminary in Algiers I had a different idea of the savages and only one detail of my imaginings was true, they are cruel. I had robbed the treasurer's office, cast off my habit, crossed the Atlas, the upper plateaus and the desert, the bus-driver of the

Trans-Sahara line made fun of me: 'Don't go there,' he too, what had got into them all, and the gusts of sand for hundreds of wind-blown kilometers, progressing and backing in the face of the wind, then the mountains again made up of black peaks and ridges sharp as steel, and after them it took a guide to go out on the endless sea of brown pebbles, screaming with heat, burning with the fires of a thousand mirrors, to the spot on the confines of the white country and the land of the blacks where stands the city of salt. And the money the guide stole from me, ever naïve I had shown it to him, but he left me on the trail—just about here, it so happens—after having struck me: 'Dog, there's the way, the honor's all mine, go ahead, go on, they'll show you,' and they did show me, oh yes, they're like the sun that never stops, except at night, beating sharply and proudly, that is beating me hard at this moment, too hard, with a multitude of lances burst from the ground, oh shelter, yes shelter, under the big rock, before everything gets muddled.

The shade here is good. How can anyone live in the city of salt, in the hollow of that basin full of dazzling heat? On each of the sharp right-angle walls cut out with a pickax and coarsely planed, the gashes left by the pickax bristle with blinding scales, pale scattered sand yellows them somewhat except when the wind dusts the upright walls and terraces, then everything shines with dazzling whiteness under a sky likewise dusted even to its blue rind. I was going blind during those days when the stationary fire would crackle for hours on the surface of the white terraces that all seemed to meet as if, in the remote past, they had all together tackled a mountain of salt, flattened it first, and then had hollowed out streets, the insides of houses and windows directly in the mass, or as if —yes, this is more like it, they had cut out their white, burning hell with a powerful jet of boiling water just to show that they could live where no one ever could, thirty days' travel from any living thing, in this hollow in the middle of the desert where the heat of day prevents any contact among creatures, separates them by a portcullis of invisible flames and of searing crystals, where without transition the cold of night congeals them individually in their rock-salt shells, nocturnal dwellers in a dried-up icefloe, black Eskimos suddenly shivering in their cubical igloos. Black because they wear long black garments, and the salt that collects even under their nails, that they continue tasting bitterly and swallowing during the sleep of those polar nights, the salt they drink in the water from the only spring in the hollow of a dazzling groove, often spots their dark garments with something like the trail of snails after a rain.

Rain, O Lord, just one real rain, long and hard, rain from your heaven! Then at last the hideous city, gradually eaten away, would slowly and irresistibly cave in and, utterly melted in a slimy torrent, would carry off its savage inhabitants toward the sands. Just one rain, Lord! But what do I mean, what Lord, they are the lords and masters! They rule over their sterile homes, over their black slaves that they work to death in the mines and each slab of salt that is cut out is worth a man in the region to the south, they pass by, silent, wearing their mourning veils in the mineral whiteness of the streets, and at night, when the whole town looks like a milky phantom, they stoop down and enter the shade of their homes, where the salt walls shine dimly. They sleep with a weightless sleep and, as soon as they wake, they give orders, they strike, they say they are a united people, that their god is the true god, and that one must obey. They are my masters, they are ignorant of pity and, like masters, they want to be alone, to progress alone, to rule alone, because they alone had the daring to build in the salt and the sands a cold torrid city. And I . . .

What a jumble when the heat rises, I'm sweating, they never do, now the shade itself is heating up, I feel the sun on the stone above me, it's striking, striking like a hammer on all the stones and it's the music, the vast music of noon, air and stones vibrating over hundreds of kilometers, *gra*, I hear the silence as I did once before. Yes, it was the same silence, years ago, that greeted me when the guards led me to them, in the sunlight, in the center of the square, whence the concentric terraces rose gradually toward the lid of hard blue sky sitting on the edge of the basin. There I was, thrown on my knees in the hollow of that white shield, my eyes corroded by the swords of salt and fire issuing from all the walls, pale with fatigue, my ear bleeding from the blow given by my guide, and they, tall and black, looked at me without saying a word. The day was at its midcourse. Under the blows of the iron sun the sky resounded at length, a sheet of white-hot tin, it was the same silence, and they stared at me, time passed, they kept on staring at me, and I couldn't face their stares, I panted more and more violently, eventually I wept, and suddenly they turned their backs on me in silence and all together went off in the same direction. On my knees, all I could see, in the red-and-black sandals, was their feet sparkling with salt as they raised the long black gowns, the tip rising somewhat, the heel striking the ground lightly, and when the square was empty I was dragged to the House of the Fetish.

Squatting, as I am today in the shelter of the rock and the fire above my head pierces the rock's thickness, I spent several days within the dark of the House of the Fetish, somewhat higher than the others, surrounded by a wall of salt, but without windows, full of a sparkling night. Several days, and I was given a basin of brackish water and some grain that was thrown before me the way chickens are fed, I picked it up. By day the door remained closed and yet the darkness became less oppressive, as if the irresistible sun managed to flow through the masses of salt. No lamp, but by feeling my way along the walls I touched garlands of dried palms decorating the walls and, at the end, a small door, coarsely fitted, of which I could make out the bolt with my fingertips. Several days, long after—I couldn't count the days or the hours, but my handful of grain had been thrown me some ten times and I had dug out a hole for my excrements that I covered up in vain, the stench of an animal den hung on anyway—long after, yes, the door opened wide and they came in.

One of them came toward me where I was squatting in a corner. I felt the burning salt against my cheek, I smelled the dusty scent of the palms, I watched him approach. He stopped a yard away from me, he stared at me in silence, a signal, and I stood up, he stared at me with his metallic eyes that shone without expression in his brown horse-face, then he raised his hand. Still impassive, he seized me by the lower lip, which he twisted slowly until he tore my flesh and, without letting go, made me turn around and back up to the center of the room, he pulled on my lip to make me fall on my knees there, mad with pain and my mouth bleeding, then he turned away to join the others standing against the walls. They watched me moaning in the unbearable heat of the unbroken daylight that came in the wide-open door, and in that light suddenly appeared the Sorcerer with his raffia hair, his chest covered with a breastplate of pearls, his legs bare under a straw skirt, wearing a mask of reeds and wire with two square openings for the eyes. He was followed by musicians and women wearing heavy motley gowns that revealed nothing of their bodies. They danced in front of the door at the end, but a coarse, scarcely rhythmical dance, they just barely moved, and finally the Sorcerer opened the little door behind me, the masters did not stir, they were watching me, I turned around and saw the Fetish, his double ax-head, his iron nose twisted like a snake.

I was carried before him, to the foot of the pedestal, I was made to drink a black, bitter, bitter water, and at once my head began to burn, I was laughing, that's the offense, I have been offended. They undressed me, shaved my head and body, washed me in oil, beat my face with cords dipped in water and salt, and I laughed and turned my head away, but each time two women would take me by the ears and offer my face to the Sorcerer's blows while I could see only his square eyes, I was still laughing, covered with blood. They stopped, no one spoke but me, the jumble was beginning in my head, then they lifted me up and forced me to raise my eyes toward the Fetish, I had ceased laughing. I knew that I was now consecrated to him to serve him, adore him, no, I was not laughing any more, fear and pain stifled me. And there, in that white house, between those walls that the sun was assiduously burning on the outside, my face taut, my memory exhausted, yes, I tried to pray to the Fetish, he was all there was and even his horrible face was less horrible than the rest of the world. Then it was that my ankles were tied with a cord that permitted just one step, they danced again, but this time in front of the Fetish, the masters went out one by one.

The door once closed behind them, the music again, and the Sorcerer lighted a bark fire around which he pranced, his long silhouette broke on the angles of the white walls, fluttered on the flat surfaces, filled the room with dancing shadows. He traced a rectangle in a corner to which the women dragged me, I felt their dry and gentle hands, they set before me a bowl of water and a little pile of grain and pointed to the Fetish, I grasped that I was to keep my eyes fixed on him. Then the Sorcerer called them one after the other over to the fire, he beat some of them who moaned and who then went and prostrated themselves before the Fetish my god, while the Sorcerer kept on dancing and he made them all leave the room until only one was left, quite young, squatting near the musicians and not yet beaten. He held her by a shock of hair which he kept twisting around his wrist, she dropped backward with eyes popping until she finally fell on her back. Dropping her, the Sorcerer screamed, the musicians turned to the wall, while behind the square-eyed mask the scream rose to an impossible pitch, and the woman rolled on the ground in a sort of fit and, at last on all fours, her head hidden in her locked arms, she too screamed, but with a hollow, muffled sound, and in this position, without ceasing to scream and to look at the Fetish, the Sorcerer took her nimbly and nastily, without the woman's face being visible, for it was covered with the heavy folds of her garment. And, wild as a result of the solitude, *I* screamed too, yes, howled with fright toward the Fetish until a kick hurled me against the wall, biting the salt as I am biting this rock today with my tongueless mouth, while waiting for the man I must kill.

Now the sun has gone a little beyond the middle of the sky. Through the breaks in the rock I can see the hole it makes in the white-hot metal of the sky, a mouth voluble as mine, constantly vomiting rivers of flame over the colorless desert. On the trail in front of me, nothing, no cloud of dust on the horizon, behind me they must be looking for me, no, not yet, it's only in the late afternoon that they opened the door and I could go out a little, after having spent the day cleaning the House of the Fetish, set out fresh offerings, and in the evening the ceremony would begin, in which I was sometimes beaten, at others not, but always I served the Fetish, the Fetish whose image is engraved in iron in my memory and now in my hope also. Never had a god so possessed or enslaved me, my whole life day and night was devoted to him, and pain and the absence of pain, wasn't that joy, were due him and even, yes, desire, as a result of being present, almost every day, at that impersonal and nasty act which I heard without seeing it inasmuch as I now had to face the wall or else be beaten. But, my face up against the salt, obsessed by the bestial shadows moving on the wall, I listened to the long scream, my throat was dry, a burning sexless desire squeezed my temples and my belly as in a vise. Thus the days followed one another, I barely distinguished them as if they had liquefied in the torrid heat and the treacherous reverberation from the walls of salt, time had become merely a vague lapping of waves in which there would burst out, at regular intervals, screams of pain or possession, a long ageless day in which the Fetish ruled as this fierce sun does over my house of rocks, and now, as I did then, I weep with unhappiness and longing, a wicked hope consumes me, I want to betray, I lick the barrel of my gun and its soul inside, its soul, only guns have souls —oh, yes! the day they cut out my tongue, I learned to adore the immortal soul of hatred!

What a jumble, what a rage, *gra gra*, drunk with heat and wrath, lying prostrate on my gun. Who's panting here? I can't endure this endless heat, this waiting, I must kill him. Not a bird, not a blade of grass, stone, an arid desire, their screams, this tongue within me talking, and, since they mutilated me, the long, flat, deserted suffering deprived even of the water of night, the night of which I would dream, when locked in with the god, in my den of salt. Night alone with its cool stars and dark fountains could save me, carry me off at last from the wicked gods of mankind, but ever locked up I could not contemplate it. If the newcomer tarries more, I shall see it at least rise from the desert and sweep over the sky, a cold golden vine that will hang from the dark zenith and from which I can drink at length, moisten this black dried hole that no muscle of live flexible flesh revives now, forget at last that day when madness took away my tongue.

How hot it was, really hot, the salt was melting

or so it seemed to me, the air was corroding my
eyes, and the Sorcerer came in without his mask.
Almost naked under grayish tatters, a new woman
followed him and her face, covered with a tattoo
reproducing the mask of the Fetish, expressed only
an idol's ugly stupor. The only thing alive about
her was her thin flat body that flopped at the foot
of the god when the Sorcerer opened the door of
the niche. Then he went out without looking at
me, the heat rose, I didn't stir, the Fetish looked
at me over that motionless body whose muscles
stirred gently and the woman's idol-face didn't
change when I approached. Only her eyes enlarged as she stared at me, my feet touched hers,
the heat then began to shriek, and the idol, without
a word, still staring at me with her dilated eyes,
gradually slipped onto her back, slowly drew her
legs up and raised them as she gently spread her
knees. But, immediately afterward, *gra*, the Sorcerer was lying in wait for me, they all entered and
tore me from the woman, beat me dreadfully on
the sinful place, what sin, I'm laughing, where is it
and where is virtue, they clapped me against a wall,
a hand of steel gripped my jaws, another opened
my mouth, pulled on my tongue until it bled, was
it I screaming with that bestial scream, a cool cut-

ting caress, yes cool at last, went over my tongue. When I came to, I was alone in the night, glued to the wall, covered with hardened blood, a gag of strange-smelling dry grasses filled my mouth, it had stopped bleeding, but it was vacant and in that absence the only living thing was a tormenting pain. I wanted to rise, I fell back, happy, desperately happy to die at last, death too is cool and its shadow hides no god.

I did not die, a new feeling of hatred stood up one day, at the same time I did, walked toward the door of the niche, opened it, closed it behind me, I hated my people, the Fetish was there and from the depths of the hole in which I was I did more than pray to him, I believed in him and denied all I had believed up to then. Hail! he was strength and power, he could be destroyed but not converted, he stared over my head with his empty, rusty eyes. Hail! he was the master, the only lord, whose indisputable attribute was malice, there are no good masters. For the first time, as a result of offenses, my whole body crying out a single pain, I surrendered to him and approved his maleficent order, I adored in him the evil principle of the world. A prisoner of his kingdom—the sterile city carved out of a mountain of salt, divorced from

nature, deprived of those rare and fleeting flower-
ings of the desert, preserved from those strokes of
chance or marks of affection such as an unexpected
cloud or a brief violent downpour that are familiar
even to the sun or the sands, the city of order in
short, right angles, square rooms, rigid men—I
freely became its tortured, hate-filled citizen, I re-
pudiated the long history that had been taught me.
I had been misled, solely the reign of malice was
devoid of defects, I had been misled, truth is square,
heavy, thick, it does not admit distinctions, good is
an idle dream, an intention constantly postponed
and pursued with exhausting effort, a limit never
reached, its reign is impossible. Only evil can reach
its limits and reign absolutely, it must be served to
establish its visible kingdom, then we shall see, but
what does 'then' mean, only evil is present, down
with Europe, reason, honor, and the cross. Yes, I
was to be converted to the religion of my masters,
yes indeed, I was a slave, but if I too become vicious I cease to be a slave, despite my shackled feet
and my mute mouth. Oh, this heat is driving me
crazy, the desert cries out everywhere under the
unbearable light, and he, the Lord of kindness,
whose very name revolts me, I disown him, for I
know him now. He dreamed and wanted to lie, his

tongue was cut out so that his word would no longer be able to deceive the world, he was pierced with nails even in his head, his poor head, like mine now, what a jumble, how weak I am, and the earth didn't tremble, I am sure, it was not a righteous man they had killed, I refuse to believe it, there are no righteous men but only evil masters who bring about the reign of relentless truth. Yes, the Fetish alone has power, he is the sole god of this world, hatred is his commandment, the source of all life, the cool water, cool like mint that chills the mouth and burns the stomach.

Then it was that I changed, they realized it, I would kiss their hands when I met them, I was on their side, never wearying of admiring them, I trusted them, I hoped they would mutilate my people as they had mutilated me. And when I learned that the missionary was to come, I knew what I was to do. That day like all the others, the same blinding daylight that had been going on so long! Late in the afternoon a guard was suddenly seen running along the edge of the basin, and, a few minutes later, I was dragged to the House of the Fetish and the door closed. One of them held me on the ground in the dark, under threat of his cross-shaped sword, and the silence lasted for a long time until a strange sound filled the ordinarily peaceful town, voices that it took me some time to recognize because they were speaking my language, but as soon as they rang out the point of the sword was lowered toward my eyes, my guard stared at me in silence. Then two voices came closer and I can still hear them, one asking why that house was guarded and whether they should break in the door, Lieutenant, the other said: 'No' sharply, then added, after a moment, that an agreement had been reached, that the town accepted a garrison of twenty men on condition that they would camp outside the walls and respect the customs. The private laughed, 'They're knuckling under,' but the officer didn't know, for the first time in any case they were willing to receive someone to take care of the children and that would be the chaplain, later on they would see about the territory. The other said they would cut off the chaplain's you know what if the soldiers were not there. 'Oh, no!' the officer answered. 'In fact, Father Beffort will come before the garrison; he'll be here in two days.' That was all I heard, motionless, lying under the sword, I was in pain, a wheel of needles and knives was whirling in me. They were crazy, they were crazy, they were allowing a hand to be laid on the city, on their invincible power, on the true god, and the fellow who was to come would not have his tongue cut out, he would show off his insolent goodness without paying for it, without enduring any offense. The reign of evil would be postponed, there would be doubt again, again time would be wasted dreaming of the impossible good, wearing oneself out in fruitless efforts instead of hastening the realization of the only possible kingdom and I looked at the sword threatening me, O sole power to rule over the world! O power, and the city gradually emptied of its sounds, the door finally opened, I remained alone, burned and bitter, with the Fetish, and I swore to him to save my new faith, my true masters, my despotic God, to betray well, whatever it might cost me.

Gra, the heat is abating a little, the stone has ceased to vibrate, I can go out of my hole, watch the desert gradually take on yellow and ocher tints that will soon be mauve. Last night I waited until they were asleep, I had blocked the lock on the door, I went out with the same step as usual, measured by the cord, I knew the streets, I knew where to get the old rifle, what gate wasn't guarded, and I reached here just as the night was beginning to fade around a handful of stars while the desert was getting a little darker. And now it seems days and days that I have been crouching in these rocks. Soon, soon, I hope he comes soon! In a moment they'll begin to look for me, they'll speed over the trails in all directions, they won't know that I left for them and to serve them better, my legs are weak, drunk with hunger and hate. Oh! over there, *gra*, at the end of the trail, two camels are growing bigger, ambling along, already multiplied by short shadows, they are running with that lively and dreamy gait they always have. Here they are, here at last!

Quick, the rifle, and I load it quickly. O Fetish, my god over yonder, may your power be preserved, may the offense be multiplied, may hate rule pitilessly over a world of the damned, may the wicked forever be masters, may the kingdom come, where in a single city of salt and iron black tyrants will enslave and possess without pity! And now, *gra gra*, fire on pity, fire on impotence and its charity, fire on all that postpones the coming of evil, fire twice, and there they are toppling over, falling, and the camels flee toward the horizon, where a geyser of black birds has just risen in the unchanged sky. I laugh, I laugh, the fellow is writh-

ing in his detested habit, he is raising his head a little, he sees me—me his all-powerful shackled master, why does he smile at me, I'll crush that smile!
How pleasant is the sound of a rifle butt on the
face of goodness, today, today at last, all is consummated and everywhere in the desert, even
hours away from here, jackals sniff the nonexistent
wind, then set out in a patient trot toward the
feast of carrion awaiting them. Victory! I raise
my arms to a heaven moved to pity, a lavender
shadow is just barely suggested on the opposite
side, O nights of Europe, home, childhood, why
must I weep in the moment of triumph?

He stirred, no the sound comes from somewhere
else, and from the other direction here they come
rushing like a flight of dark birds, my masters, who
fall upon me, seize me, ah yes! strike, they fear
their city sacked and howling, they fear the aveng-
ing soldiers I called forth, and this is only right,
upon the sacred city. Defend yourselves now,
strike! strike me first, you possess the truth! O my
masters, they will then conquer the soldiers, they'll
conquer the word and love, they'll spread over the
deserts, cross the seas, fill the light of Europe with
their black veils—strike the belly, yes, strike the
eyes—sow their salt on the continent, all vegeta-

tion, all youth will die out, and dumb crowds with shackled feet will plod beside me in the world-wide desert under the cruel sun of the true faith, I'll not be alone. Ah! the pain, the pain they cause me, their rage is good and on this cross-shaped war-saddle where they are now quartering me, pity! I'm laughing, I love the blow that nails me down crucified.

* * *

How silent the desert is! Already night and I am alone, I'm thirsty. Still waiting, where is the city, those sounds in the distance, and the soldiers perhaps the victors, no, it can't be, even if the soldiers are victorious, they're not wicked enough, they won't be able to rule, they'll still say one must become better, and still millions of men between evil and good, torn, bewildered, O Fetish, why hast thou forsaken me? All is over, I'm thirsty, my body is burning, a darker night fills my eyes.

This long, this long dream, I'm awaking, no, I'm going to die, dawn is breaking, the first light, daylight for the living, and for me the inexorable sun, the flies. Who is speaking, no one, the sky is not opening up, no, no, God doesn't speak in the desert, yet whence comes that voice saying: 'If you consent to die for hate and power, who will forgive us?' Is it another tongue in me or still that other fellow refusing to die, at my feet, and repeating: 'Courage! courage! courage!'? Ah! supposing I were wrong again! Once fraternal men, sole recourse, O solitude, forsake me not! Here, here who are you, torn, with bleeding mouth, is it you, Sorcerer, the soldiers defeated you, the salt is burning over there, it's you my beloved master! Cast off that hate-ridden face, be good now, we were mistaken, we'll begin all over again, we'll rebuild the city of mercy, I want to go back home. Yes, help me, that's right, give me your hand. . . ."

A handful of salt fills the mouth of the garrulous slave.

THE
SILENT
MEN

Iт was тне dead of winter and yet a radiant sun was rising over the already active city. At the end of the jetty, sea and sky fused in a single dazzling light. But Yvars did not see them. He was cycling slowly along the boulevards above the harbor. On the fixed pedal of his cycle his crippled leg rested stiffly while the other labored to cope with the slippery pavement still wet with the night's moisture. Without raising his head, a slight figure astride the saddle, he avoided the rails of the former car-line, suddenly turned the handlebars to let autos pass him, and occasionally elbowed back into place the musette bag in which Fernande had put his lunch. At such moments he would think bitterly of the bag's contents. Between the two slices of coarse bread, instead of the Spanish omelet he liked or the beefsteak fried in oil, there was nothing but cheese.

The ride to the shop had never seemed to him so long. To be sure, he was aging. At forty, though he had remained as slim as a vine shoot, a man's muscles don't warm up so quickly. At times, reading sports commentaries in which a thirty-year-old athlete was referred to as a veteran, he would shrug his shoulders. "If he's a veteran," he would say to Fernande, "then I'm practically in a wheelchair." Yet he knew that the reporter wasn't altogether wrong. At thirty a man is already beginning to lose his wind without noticing it. At forty he's not yet in a wheelchair, but he's definitely heading in that direction. Wasn't that just why he now avoided looking toward the sea during the ride to the other end of town where the cooper's shop was? When he was twenty he never got tired of watching it, for it used to hold in store a happy weekend on the beach. Despite or because of his lameness, he had always liked swimming. Then the years had passed, there had been Fernande, the birth of the boy, and, to make ends meet, the overtime, at the shop on Saturdays and on various odd jobs for others on Sundays. Little by little he had lost the habit of those violent days that used to satiate him. The deep, clear water, the hot sun, the girls, the physical life—there was no other form of happiness in this country. And that happiness disappeared with youth. Yvars continued to love the sea, but only at the end of the day when the water in the bay became a little darker. The moment was pleasant on the terrace beside his house where he would sit down after work, grateful for his clean shirt that Fernande ironed so well and for the glass of anisette all frosted over. Evening would fall, the sky would become all soft and mellow, the neighbors talking with Yvars would suddenly lower their voices. At those times he didn't know whether he was happy or felt like crying. At least he felt in harmony at such moments, he had nothing to do but wait quietly, without quite knowing for what.

In the morning when he went back to work, on the other hand, he didn't like to look at the sea. Though it was always there to greet him, he refused to see it until evening. This morning he was

pedaling along with head down, feeling even
heavier than usual; his heart too was heavy. When
he had come back from the meeting, the night before, and had announced that they were going
back to work, Fernande had gaily said: "Then the
boss is giving you all a raise?" The boss was not
giving any raise; the strike had failed. They hadn't
managed things right, it had to be admitted. An
impetuous walkout, and the union had been right
to back it up only halfheartedly. After all, some
fifteen workers hardly counted; the union had to
consider the other cooper's shops that hadn't gone
along. You couldn't really blame the union. Cooperage, threatened by the building of tankers and
tank trucks, was not thriving. Fewer and fewer
barrels and large casks were being made; work
consisted chiefly in repairing the huge tuns already
in existence. Employers saw their business compromised, to be sure, but even so they wanted to
maintain a margin of profit and the easiest way
still seemed to them to block wages despite the rise
in living costs. What can coopers do when cooperage disappears? You don't change trades when
you've gone to the trouble of learning one; this
one was hard and called for a long apprenticeship.
The good cooper, the one who fits his curved staves

and tightens them in the fire with an iron hoop, almost hermetically, without calking with raffia or oakum, was rare. Yvars knew this and was proud of it. Changing trades is nothing, but to give up what you know, your master craftsmanship, is not easy. A fine craft without employment and you're stuck, you have to resign yourself. But resignation isn't easy either. It was hard to have one's mouth shut, not to be able to discuss really, and to take the same road every morning with an accumulating fatigue, in order to receive at the end of every week merely what they are willing to give you, which is less and less adequate.

So they had got angry. Two or three of them had hesitated, but the anger had spread to them too after the first discussions with the boss. He had told them flatly, in fact, that they could take it or leave it. A man doesn't talk that way. "What's he expect of us?" Esposito had said. "That we'll stoop over and wait to be kicked in the ass?" The boss wasn't a bad sort, however. He had inherited from his father, had grown up in the shop, and had known almost all the workers for years. Occasionally he invited them to have a snack in the shop; they would cook sardines or sausage meat over fires of shavings and, thanks partly to the wine, he was really very nice. At New Year's he always gave five bottles of vintage wine to each of the men, and often, when one of them was ill or celebrated an event like marriage or first communion, he would make a gift of money. At the birth of his daughter, there had been sugar-coated almonds for everyone. Two or three times he had invited Yvars to hunt on his coastal property. He liked his workmen, no doubt, and often recalled the fact that his father had begun as an apprentice. But he had never gone to their homes; he wasn't aware. He thought only of himself because he knew nothing but himself, and now you could take it or leave it. In other words, he had become obstinate likewise. But, in his position, he could allow himself to be.

He had forced the union's hand, and the shop had closed its doors. "Don't go to the trouble of picketing," the boss had said; "when the shop's not working, I save money." That wasn't true, but it didn't help matters since he was telling them to their faces that he gave them work out of charity. Esposito was wild with fury and had told him he wasn't a man. The boss was hot-blooded and they had to be separated. But, at the same time, it had made an impression on the workers. Twenty days on strike, the wives sad at home, two or three of them discouraged, and, in the end, the union had advised them to give in on the promise of arbitration and recovery of the lost days through overtime. They had decided to go back to work. Swaggering, of course, and saying that it wasn't all settled, that it would have to be reconsidered. But this morning, with a fatigue that resembled defeat, cheese instead of meat, the illusion was no longer possible. No matter how the sun shone, the sea held forth no more promises. Yvars pressed on his single pedal and with each turn of the wheel it seemed to him he was aging a little. He couldn't think of the shop, of the fellow workers and the boss he would soon be seeing again without feeling his heart become a trifle heavier. Fernande had been worried: "What will you men say to him?" "Nothing." Yvars had straddled his bicycle, and had shaken his head. He had clenched his teeth; his small, dark, and wrinkled face with its delicate features had become hard. "We're going back to work. That's enough." Now he was cycling along, his teeth still clenched, with a sad, dry anger that darkened even the sky itself.

He left the boulevard, and the sea, to attack the moist streets of the old Spanish quarter. They led to an area occupied solely by sheds, junkyards, and garages, where the shop was—a sort of low shed that was faced with stone up to a halfway point and then glassed in up to the corrugated metal roof. This shop opened onto the former cooperage, a courtyard surrounded by a covered shed that had been abandoned when the business had enlarged and now served only as a storehouse for worn-out machines and old casks. Beyond the courtyard, separated from it by a sort of path covered with old tiles, the boss's garden began, at the end of which his house stood. Big and ugly, it was nevertheless prepossessing because of the Virginia creeper and the straggling honeysuckle surrounding the outside steps.

Yvars saw at once that the doors of the shop were closed. A group of workmen stood silently in front of them. This was the first time since he had been working here that he had found the doors closed when he arrived. The boss had wanted to emphasize that he had the upper hand. Yvars turned toward the left, parked his bicycle under the lean-to that prolonged the shed on that side, and walked toward the door. From a distance he recognized Esposito, a tall dark, hairy fellow who worked beside him, Marcou, the union delegate, with his tenor's profile, Saïd, the only Arab in the shop, then all the others who silently watched him approach. But before he had joined them, they all suddenly looked in the direction of the shop doors, which had just begun to open. Ballester, the foreman, appeared in the opening. He opened one of the heavy doors and, turning his back to the workmen, pushed it slowly on its iron rail.

Ballester, who was the oldest of all, disapproved of the strike but had kept silent as soon as Esposito had told him that he was serving the boss's interests. Now he stood near the door, broad and short in his navy-blue jersey, already barefoot (he was the only one besides Saïd who worked barefoot), and he watched them go in one by one with his eyes that were so pale they seemed colorless in his old tanned face, his mouth downcast under his thick, drooping mustache. They were silent, humiliated by this return of the defeated, furious at their own silence, but the more it was prolonged the less capable they were of breaking it. They went in without looking at Ballester, for they knew he was carrying out an order in making them go in like that, and his bitter and downcast look told them what he was thinking. Yvars, for one, looked at him. Ballester, who liked him, nodded his head without saying a word.

Now they were all in the little locker-room on the right of the entrance: open stalls separated by unpainted boards to which had been attached, on either side, little locked cupboards; the farthest stall from the entrance, up against the walls of the shed, had been transformed into a shower above a gutter hollowed out of the earthen floor. In the center of the shop could be seen work in various stages, already finished large casks, loose-hooped, waiting for the forcing in the fire, thick benches with a long slot hollowed out in them (and in some of them had been slipped circular wooden bottoms waiting to be planed to a sharp edge), and finally cold fires. Along the wall, on the left of the entrance, the workbenches extended in a row. In front of them stood piles of staves to be planed. Against the right wall, not far from the dressing-room, two large power saws, thoroughly oiled, strong and silent, gleamed.

Some time ago, the workshop had become too big for the handful of men who worked there. This was an advantage in the hot season, a disadvantage in winter. But today, in this vast space, the work dropped half finished, the casks abandoned in every corner with a single hoop holding the base of the staves spreading at the top like coarse wooden

flowers, the sawdust covering the benches, the tool-
boxes and machines—everything gave the shop a
look of neglect. They looked at it, dressed now in
their old jumpers and their faded and patched pants,
and they hesitated. Ballester was watching them.
"So," he said, "we pitch in?" One by one, they
went to their posts without saying a word. Ballester
went from one to another, briefly reminding them
of the work to be begun or finished. No one answered. Soon the first hammer resounded against
the iron-tipped wedge sinking a hoop over the
convex part of a barrel, a plane groaned as it hit a
knot, and one of the saws, started up by Eposito,
got under way with a great whirring of blade.
Saïd would bring staves on request or light fires
of shavings on which the casks were placed to make
them swell in their corset of iron hoops. When no
one called for him, he stood at a workbench riv-
eting the big rusty hoops with heavy hammer
blows. The scent of burning shavings began to fill
the shop. Yvars, who was planing and fitting the
staves cut out by Esposito, recognized the old scent
and his heart relaxed somewhat. All were working
in silence, but a warmth, a life was gradually beginning to reawaken in the shop. Through the broad
windows a clean, fresh light began to fill the shed.

The smoke rose bluish in the golden sunlight; Yvars even heard an insect buzz close to him.

At that moment the door into the former shop opened in the end wall and M. Lassalle, the boss, stopped on the threshold. Thin and dark, he was scarcely more than thirty. His white coverall hanging open over a tan gabardine suit, he looked at ease in his body. Despite his very bony face cut like a hatchet, he generally aroused liking, as do most people who exude vitality. Yet he seemed somewhat embarrassed as he came through the door. His greeting was less sonorous than usual; in any case, no one answered it. The sound of the hammers hesitated, lost the beat, and resumed even louder. M. Lassalle took a few hesitant steps, then he headed toward little Valery, who had been working with them for only a year. Near the power saw, a few feet away from Yvars, he was putting a bottom on a big hogshead and the boss watched him. Valery went on working without saying anything. "Well, my boy," said M. Lassalle, "how are things?" The young man suddenly became more awkward in his movements. He glanced at Esposito, who was close to him, picking up a pile of staves in his huge arms to take them to Yvars. Esposito looked at him too while going on with his work, and Valery peered back into his hogshead without answering the boss. Lassalle, rather nonplused, remained a moment planted in front of the young man, then he shrugged his shoulders and turned toward Marcou. The latter, astride his bench, was giving the finishing touches, with slow, careful strokes, to sharpening the edge of a bottom. "Hello, Marcou," Lassalle said in a flatter voice. Marcou did not answer, entirely occupied with taking very thin shavings off his wood. "What's got into you?" Lassalle asked in a loud voice as he turned toward the other workmen. "We didn't agree, to be sure. But that doesn't keep us from having to work together. So what's the use of this?" Marcou got up, raised his bottom piece, verified the circular sharp edge with the palm of his hand, squinted his languorous eyes with a look of satisfaction, and, still silent, went toward another workman who was putting together a hogshead. Throughout the whole shop could be heard nothing but the sound of hammers and of the power saw. "O.K.," Lassalle said. "When you get over this, let me know through Ballester." Calmly, he walked out of the shop.

Almost immediately afterward, above the din of the shop, a bell rang out twice. Ballester, who had just sat down to roll a cigarette, got up slowly and went to the door at the end. After he had left, the hammers resounded with less noise; one of the workmen had even stopped when Ballester came back. From the door he said merely: "The boss wants you, Marcou and Yvars." Yvars's first impulse was to go and wash his hands, but Marcou grasped him by the arm as he went by and Yvars limped out behind him.

Outside in the courtyard, the light was so clear, so liquid, that Yvars felt it on his face and bare arms. They went up the outside stairs, under the honeysuckle on which a few blossoms were already visible. When they entered the corridor, whose walls were covered with diplomas, they heard a child crying and M. Lassalle's voice saying: "Put her to bed after lunch. We'll call the doctor if she doesn't get over it." Then the boss appeared suddenly in the corridor and showed them into the little office they already knew, furnished with imitation-rustic furniture and its walls decorated with sports trophies. "Sit down," Lassalle said as he took his place behind the desk. They remained standing. "I called you in because you, Marcou, are the delegate and you, Yvars, my oldest employee after Ballester. I don't want to get back to the discussions, which are now over. I cannot, absolutely not, give you what you ask. The matter has been settled, and we reached the conclusion that work had to be resumed. I see that you are angry with me, and that hurts me, I'm telling you just as I feel it. I merely want to add this: what I can't do today I may perhaps be able to do when business picks up. And if I can do it, I'll do it even before you ask me. Meanwhile, let's try to work together." He stopped talking, seemed to reflect, then looked up at them. "Well?" he said. Marcou was looking out the window. Yvars, his teeth clenched, wanted to speak but couldn't. "Listen," said Lassalle, "you have all closed your minds. You'll get over it. But when you become reasonable again, don't forget what I've just said to you." He rose, went toward Marcou, and held out his hand. "Chao!" he said. Marcou suddenly turned pale, his popular tenor's face hardened and, for a second only, became mean-looking. Then he abruptly turned on his heel and went out. Lassalle, likewise pale, looked at Yvars without holding out his hand. "Go to hell!" he shouted.

When they went back into the shop, the men were lunching. Ballester had gone out. Marcou simply said: "Just wind," and returned to his bench.

Esposito stopped biting into his bread to ask what they had answered; Yvars said they hadn't answered anything. Then he went to get his musette bag and came back and sat down on his workbench. He was beginning to eat when, not far from him, he noticed Saïd lying on his back in a pile of shavings, his eyes looking vaguely at the windows made blue by a sky that had become less luminous. He asked him if he had already finished. Saïd said he had eaten his figs. Yvars stopped eating. The uneasy feeling that hadn't left him since the interview with Lassalle suddenly disappeared to make room for a pleasant warmth. He broke his bread in two as he got up and, faced with Saïd's refusal, said that everything would be better next week. "Then it'll be your turn to treat," he said. Saïd smiled. Now he bit into the piece of Yvars's sandwich, but in a gingerly way like a man who isn't hungry.

Esposito took an old pot and lighted a little fire of shavings and chips. He heated some coffee that he had brought in a bottle. He said it was a gift to the shop that his grocer had made when he learned of the strike's failure. A mustard jar passed from hand to hand. Each time Esposito poured out the already sugared coffee. Saïd swallowed it with more pleasure than he had taken in eating. Esposito drank the rest of the coffee right from the burning pot, smacking his lips and swearing. At that moment Ballester came in to give the back-to-work signal.

While they were rising and gathering papers and utensils into their musette bags, Ballester came and stood in their midst and said suddenly that it was hard for all, and for him too, but that this was no reason to act like children and that there was no use in sulking. Esposito, the pot in his hand, turned toward him; his long, coarse face had suddenly become flushed. Yvars knew what he was about to say—and what everyone was thinking at the same time—that they were not sulking, that their mouths had been closed, they had to take it or leave it, and that anger and helplessness sometimes hurt so much that you can't even cry out. They were men, after all, and they weren't going to begin smiling and simpering. But Esposito said none of this, his face finally relaxed, and he slapped Ballester's shoulder gently while the others went back to their work. Again the hammers rang out, the big shed filled with the familiar din, with the smell of shavings and of old clothes damp with sweat. The big saw whined and bit into the fresh wood of the stave that Esposito was slowly pushing in front of him.

Where the saw bit, a damp sawdust spurted out and covered with something like bread-crumbs the big hairy hands firmly gripping the wood on each side of the moaning blade. Once the stave was ripped, you could hear only the sound of the motor.

At present Yvars felt only the strain in his back as he leaned over the plane. Generally the fatigue didn't come until later on. He had got out of training during these weeks of inactivity, it was clear. But he thought also of age, which makes manual labor harder when it's not mere precision work. That strain also foreshadowed old age. Wherever the muscles are involved, work eventually becomes hateful, it precedes death, and on evenings following great physical effort sleep itself is like death. The boy wanted to become a schoolteacher, he was right; those who indulge in clichés about manual work don't know what they're talking about.

When Yvars straightened up to catch his breath and also to drive away these evil thoughts, the bell rang out again. It was insistent, but in such a strange way, with stops and imperious starts, that the men interrupted their work. Ballester listened, surprised, then made up his mind and went slowly to the door. He had disappeared for several seconds when the

ringing finally ceased. They resumed work. Again
the door was flung open and Ballester ran toward
the locker-room. He came out wearing canvas
shoes and, slipping on his jacket, said to Yvars as
he went by: "The kid has had an attack. I'm off to
get Germain," and he ran toward the main door.
Dr. Germain took care of the shop's health; he
lived in this outlying quarter. Yvars repeated the
news without commentary. They gathered around
him and looked at one another, embarrassed. Nothing could be heard but the motor of the power saw
running freely. "It's perhaps nothing," one of them
said. They went back to their places, the shop filled
again with their noises, but they were working
slowly, as if waiting for something.

A quarter of an hour later, Ballester came in
again, hung up his jacket, and, without saying a
word, went out through the little door. On the
windows the light was getting dimmer. A little
later, in the intervals when the saw was not ripping
into the wood, the dull bell of an ambulance could
be heard, at first in the distance, then nearer,
finally just outside. Then silence. After a moment
Ballester came back and everyone went up to him.
Esposito had turned off the motor. Ballester said
that while undressing in her room the child had sud-

denly keeled over as if mowed down. "Did you ever hear anything like it!" Marcou said. Ballester shook his head and gestured vaguely toward the shop; but he looked as if he had had quite a turn. Again the ambulance bell was heard. They were all there, in the silent shop, under the yellow light coming through the glass panels, with their rough, useless hands hanging down along their old saw-dust-covered pants.

The rest of the afternoon dragged. Yvars now felt only his fatigue and his still heavy heart. He would have liked to talk. But he had nothing to say, nor did the others. On their uncommunicative faces could be read merely sorrow and a sort of ob-stinacy. Sometimes the word "calamity" took shape in him, but just barely, for it disappeared immedi-ately—as a bubble forms and bursts simultaneously. He wanted to get home, to be with Fernande again, and the boy, on the terrace. As it happened, Balles-ter announced closing-time. The machines stopped. Without hurrying, they began to put out the fires and to put everything in order on their benches, then they went one by one to the locker-room. Saïd remained behind; he was to clean up the shop and water down the dusty soil. When Yvars reached the locker-room, Esposito, huge and hairy, was already under the shower. His back was turned to them as he soaped himself noisily. Generally, they kidded him about his modesty; the big bear, indeed, obstinately hid his pudenda. But no one seemed to notice on this occasion. Esposito backed out of the shower and wrapped a towel around him like a loincloth. The others took their turns, and Marcou was vigorously slapping his bare sides when they heard the big door roll slowly open on its cast-iron wheel. Lassalle came in.

He was dressed as at the time of his first visit, but his hair was rather disheveled. He stopped on the threshold, looked at the vast deserted shop, took a few steps, stopped again, and looked toward the locker-room. Esposito, still covered with his loin-cloth, turned toward him. Naked, embarrassed, he teetered from one foot to the other. Yvars thought that it was up to Marcou to say something. But Marcou remained invisible behind the sheet of water that surrounded him. Esposito grabbed a shirt and was nimbly slipping it on when Lassalle said: "Good night," in a rather toneless voice and began to walk toward the little door. When it occurred to Yvars that someone ought to call him, the door had already closed.

Yvars dressed without washing, said good-night likewise, but with his whole heart, and they answered with the same warmth. He went out rapidly, got his bicycle, and, when he straddled it, he felt the strain in his back again. He was cycling along now in the late afternoon through the trafficky city. He was going fast because he was eager to get back to the old house and the terrace. He would wash in the wash-house before sitting down to look at the sea, which was already accompanying him, darker than in the morning, above the parapet of the boulevard. But the little girl accompanied him too and he couldn't stop thinking of her.

At home, his boy was back from school and reading the pictorials. Fernande asked Yvars whether everything had gone all right. He said nothing, cleaned up in the wash-house, then sat down on the bench against the low wall of the terrace. Mended washing hung above his head and the sky was becoming transparent; over the wall the soft evening sea was visible. Fernande brought the anisette, two glasses, and the jug of cool water. She sat down beside her husband. He told her everything, holding her hand as in the early days of their marriage. When he had finished, he didn't stir, looking toward the sea where already, from one end of the horizon to the other, the twilight was swiftly falling. "Ah! it's his own fault!" he said. If only he were young again, and Fernande too, they would have gone away, across the sea.

THE
GUEST

THE SCHOOLMASTER was watching the two men climb toward him. One was on horseback, the other on foot. They had not yet tackled the abrupt rise leading to the schoolhouse built on the hillside. They were toiling onward, making slow progress in the snow, among the stones, on the vast expanse of the high, deserted plateau. From time to time the horse stumbled. Without hearing anything yet, he could see the breath issuing from the horse's nostrils. One of the men, at least, knew the region. They were following the trail although it had disappeared days ago under a layer of dirty white snow. The schoolmaster calculated that it would take them half an hour to get onto the hill.

It was cold; he went back into the school to get a sweater.

He crossed the empty, frigid classroom. On the blackboard the four rivers of France, drawn with four different colored chalks, had been flowing toward their estuaries for the past three days. Snow had suddenly fallen in mid-October after eight months of drought without the transition of rain, and the twenty pupils, more or less, who lived in the villages scattered over the plateau had stopped coming. With fair weather they would return. Daru now heated only the single room that was his lodging, adjoining the classroom and giving also onto the plateau to the east. Like the class windows, his window looked to the south too. On that side the school was a few kilometers from the point where the plateau began to slope toward the south. In clear weather could be seen the purple mass of the mountain range where the gap opened onto the desert.

Somewhat warmed, Daru returned to the window from which he had first seen the two men. They were no longer visible. Hence they must have tackled the rise. The sky was not so dark, for the snow had stopped falling during the night. The morning had opened with a dirty light which had scarcely become brighter as the ceiling of clouds lifted. At two in the afternoon it seemed as if the day were merely beginning. But still this was better than those three days when the thick snow was falling amidst unbroken darkness with little gusts of wind that rattled the double door of the classroom. Then Daru had spent long hours in his room, leaving it only to go to the shed and feed the chickens or get some coal. Fortunately the delivery truck from Tadjid, the nearest village to the north, had brought his supplies two days before the blizzard. It would return in forty-eight hours.

Besides, he had enough to resist a siege, for the little room was cluttered with bags of wheat that the administration left as a stock to distribute to those of his pupils whose families had suffered from the drought. Actually they had all been victims because they were all poor. Every day Daru would distribute a ration to the children. They had missed it, he knew, during these bad days. Possibly one of the fathers or big brothers would come this afternoon and he could supply them with grain. It was just a matter of carrying them over to the next harvest. Now shiploads of wheat were arriving from France and the worst was over. But it would be hard to forget that poverty, that army of ragged ghosts wandering in the sunlight, the plateaus burned to a cinder month after month, the earth shriveled up little by little, literally scorched, every stone bursting into dust under one's foot. The sheep had died then by thousands and even a few men, here and there, sometimes without anyone's knowing.

In contrast with such poverty, he who lived almost like a monk in his remote schoolhouse, nonetheless satisfied with the little he had and with the rough life, had felt like a lord with his whitewashed walls, his narrow couch, his unpainted shelves, his well, and his weekly provision of water and food. And suddenly this snow, without warning, without the foretaste of rain. This is the way the region was, cruel to live in, even without men —who didn't help matters either. But Daru had been born here. Everywhere else, he felt exiled.

He stepped out onto the terrace in front of the schoolhouse. The two men were now halfway up the slope. He recognized the horseman as Balducci, the old gendarme he had known for a long time. Balducci was holding on the end of a rope an Arab who was walking behind him with hands bound and head lowered. The gendarme waved a greeting to which Daru did not reply, lost as he was in contemplation of the Arab dressed in a faded blue jellaba, his feet in sandals but covered with socks of heavy raw wool, his head surmounted by a narrow, short *chèche*. They were approaching. Balducci was holding back his horse in order not to hurt the Arab, and the group was advancing slowly.

Within earshot, Balducci shouted: "One hour to do the three kilometers from El Ameur!" Daru did not answer. Short and square in his thick sweater, he watched them climb. Not once had the Arab raised his head. "Hello," said Daru when they got up onto the terrace. "Come in and warm up." Balducci painfully got down from his horse without letting go the rope. From under his bristling mustache he smiled at the schoolmaster. His little dark eyes, deep-set under a tanned forehead, and his mouth surrounded with wrinkles made him look attentive and studious. Daru took the bridle, led the horse to the shed, and came back to the two men, who were now waiting for him in the school. He led them into his room. "I am going to heat up the classroom," he said. "We'll be more comfortable there." When he entered the room again, Balducci was on the couch. He had undone the rope tying him to the Arab, who had squatted near the stove.

His hands still bound, the *chèche* pushed back on his head, he was looking toward the window. At first Daru noticed only his huge lips, fat, smooth, almost Negroid; yet his nose was straight, his eyes were dark and full of fever. The *chèche* revealed an obstinate forehead and, under the weathered skin now rather discolored by the cold, the whole face had a restless and rebellious look that struck Daru when the Arab, turning his face toward him, looked him straight in the eyes. "Go into the other room," said the schoolmaster, "and I'll make you some mint tea." "Thanks," Balducci said. "What a chore! How I long for retirement." And addressing his prisoner in Arabic: "Come on, you." The Arab got up and, slowly, holding his bound wrists in front of him, went into the classroom.

With the tea, Daru brought a chair. But Balducci was already enthroned on the nearest pupil's desk and the Arab had squatted against the teacher's platform facing the stove, which stood between the desk and the window. When he held out the glass of tea to the prisoner, Daru hesitated at the sight of his bound hands. "He might perhaps be untied." "Sure," said Balducci. "That was for the trip." He started to get to his feet. But Daru, setting the glass on the floor, had knelt beside the Arab.

Without saying anything, the Arab watched him with his feverish eyes. Once his hands were free, he rubbed his swollen wrists against each other, took the glass of tea, and sucked up the burning liquid in swift little sips.

"Good," said Daru. "And where are you headed?"

Balducci withdrew his mustache from the tea. "Here, son."

"Odd pupils! And you're spending the night?"

"No. I'm going back to El Ameur. And you will deliver this fellow to Tinguit. He is expected at police headquarters."

Balducci was looking at Daru with a friendly little smile.

"What's this story?" asked the schoolmaster. "Are you pulling my leg?"

"No, son. Those are the orders."

"The orders? I'm not . . ." Daru hesitated, not wanting to hurt the old Corsican. "I mean, that's not my job."

"What! What's the meaning of that? In wartime people do all kinds of jobs."

"Then I'll wait for the declaration of war!"

Balducci nodded.

"O.K. But the orders exist and they concern you

too. Things are brewing, it appears. There is talk
of a forthcoming revolt. We are mobilized, in a
way."

Daru still had his obstinate look.

"Listen, son," Balducci said. "I like you and you
must understand. There's only a dozen of us at El
Ameur to patrol throughout the whole territory of
a small department and I must get back in a hurry.
I was told to hand this guy over to you and return
without delay. He couldn't be kept there. His village was beginning to stir; they wanted to take him
back. You must take him to Tinguit tomorrow before the day is over. Twenty kilometers shouldn't
faze a husky fellow like you. After that, all will be
over. You'll come back to your pupils and your
comfortable life."

Behind the wall the horse could be heard snorting
and pawing the earth. Daru was looking out the
window. Decidedly, the weather was clearing and
the light was increasing over the snowy plateau.
When all the snow was melted, the sun would take
over again and once more would burn the fields of
stone. For days, still, the unchanging sky would
shed its dry light on the solitary expanse where
nothing had any connection with man.

"After all," he said, turning around toward Balducci, "what did he do?" And, before the gendarme had opened his mouth, he asked: "Does he speak French?"

"No, not a word. We had been looking for him for a month, but they were hiding him. He killed his cousin."

"Is he against us?"

"I don't think so. But you can never be sure."

"Why did he kill?"

"A family squabble, I think. One owed the other grain, it seems. It's not at all clear. In short, he killed his cousin with a billhook. You know, like a sheep, *kreezk!*"

Balducci made the gesture of drawing a blade across his throat and the Arab, his attention attracted, watched him with a sort of anxiety. Daru felt a sudden wrath against the man, against all men with their rotten spite, their tireless hates, their blood lust.

But the kettle was singing on the stove. He served Balducci more tea, hesitated, then served the Arab again, who, a second time, drank avidly. His raised arms made the jellaba fall open and the schoolmaster saw his thin, muscular chest.

"Thanks, kid," Balducci said. "And now, I'm off."

He got up and went toward the Arab, taking a small rope from his pocket.

"What are you doing?" Daru asked dryly.

Balducci, disconcerted, showed him the rope.

"Don't bother."

The old gendarme hesitated. "It's up to you. Of course, you are armed?"

"I have my shotgun."

"Where?"

"In the trunk."

"You ought to have it near your bed."

"Why? I have nothing to fear."

"You're crazy, son. If there's an uprising, no one is safe, we're all in the same boat."

"I'll defend myself. I'll have time to see them coming."

Balducci began to laugh, then suddenly the mustache covered the white teeth.

"You'll have time? O.K. That's just what I was saying. You have always been a little cracked. That's why I like you, my son was like that."

At the same time he took out his revolver and put it on the desk.

"Keep it; I don't need two weapons from here to El Ameur."

The revolver shone against the black paint of

the table. When the gendarme turned toward him, the schoolmaster caught the smell of leather and horseflesh.

"Listen, Balducci," Daru said suddenly, "every bit of this disgusts me, and first of all your fellow here. But I won't hand him over. Fight, yes, if I have to. But not that."

The old gendarme stood in front of him and looked at him severely.

"You're being a fool," he said slowly. "I don't like it either. You don't get used to putting a rope on a man even after years of it, and you're even ashamed—yes, ashamed. But you can't let them have their way."

"I won't hand him over," Daru said again.

"It's an order, son, and I repeat it."

"That's right. Repeat to them what I've said to you: I won't hand him over."

Balducci made a visible effort to reflect. He looked at the Arab and at Daru. At last he decided.

"No, I won't tell them anything. If you want to drop us, go ahead; I'll not denounce you. I have an order to deliver the prisoner and I'm doing so. And now you'll just sign this paper for me."

"There's no need. I'll not deny that you left him with me."

"Don't be mean with me. I know you'll tell the truth. You're from hereabouts and you are a man. But you must sign, that's the rule."

Daru opened his drawer, took out a little square bottle of purple ink, the red wooden penholder with the "sergeant-major" pen he used for making models of penmanship, and signed. The gendarme carefully folded the paper and put it into his wallet. Then he moved toward the door.

"I'll see you off," Daru said.

"No," said Balducci. "There's no use being polite. You insulted me."

He looked at the Arab, motionless in the same spot, sniffed peevishly, and turned away toward the door. "Good-by, son," he said. The door shut behind him. Balducci appeared suddenly outside the window and then disappeared. His footsteps were muffled by the snow. The horse stirred on the other side of the wall and several chickens fluttered in fright. A moment later Balducci reappeared outside the window leading the horse by the bridle. He walked toward the little rise without turning around and disappeared from sight with the horse following him. A big stone could be heard bouncing down. Daru walked back toward the prisoner, who, without stirring, never took his eyes off him.

"Wait," the schoolmaster said in Arabic and went toward the bedroom. As he was going through the door, he had a second thought, went to the desk, took the revolver, and stuck it in his pocket. Then, without looking back, he went into his room.

For some time he lay on his couch watching the sky gradually close over, listening to the silence. It was this silence that had seemed painful to him during the first days here, after the war. He had requested a post in the little town at the base of the foothills separating the upper plateaus from the desert. There, rocky walls, green and black to the north, pink and lavender to the south, marked the frontier of eternal summer. He had been named to a post farther north, on the plateau itself. In the beginning, the solitude and the silence had been hard for him on these wastelands peopled only by stones. Occasionally, furrows suggested cultivation, but they had been dug to uncover a certain kind of stone good for building. The only plowing here was to harvest rocks. Elsewhere a thin layer of soil accumulated in the hollows would be scraped out to enrich paltry village gardens. This is the way it was: bare rock covered three quarters of the region. Towns sprang up, flourished, then disappeared; men came by, loved one another or fought bitterly, then died. No one in this desert, neither he nor his guest, mattered. And yet, outside this desert neither of them, Daru knew, could have really lived.

When he got up, no noise came from the classroom. He was amazed at the unmixed joy he derived from the mere thought that the Arab might have fled and that he would be alone with no decision to make. But the prisoner was there. He had merely stretched out between the stove and the desk. With eyes open, he was staring at the ceiling. In that position, his thick lips were particularly noticeable, giving him a pouting look. "Come," said Daru. The Arab got up and followed him. In the bedroom, the schoolmaster pointed to a chair near the table under the window. The Arab sat down without taking his eyes off Daru.

"Are you hungry?"

"Yes," the prisoner said.

Daru set the table for two. He took flour and oil, shaped a cake in a frying-pan, and lighted the little stove that functioned on bottled gas. While the cake was cooking, he went out to the shed to get cheese, eggs, dates, and condensed milk. When the cake was done he set it on the window sill to cool, heated some condensed milk diluted with water, and beat up the eggs into an omelette. In one of his motions he knocked against the revolver stuck in his right pocket. He set the bowl down, went into the classroom, and put the revolver in his desk drawer. When he came back to the room, night was falling. He put on the light and served the Arab. "Eat," he said. The Arab took a piece of the cake, lifted it eagerly to his mouth, and stopped short.

"And you?" he asked.

"After you. I'll eat too."

The thick lips opened slightly. The Arab hesitated, then bit into the cake determinedly.

The meal over, the Arab looked at the schoolmaster. "Are you the judge?"

"No, I'm simply keeping you until tomorrow."

"Why do you eat with me?"

"I'm hungry."

The Arab fell silent. Daru got up and went out. He brought back a folding bed from the shed, set it up between the table and the stove, perpendicular to his own bed. From a large suitcase which, upright in a corner, served as a shelf for papers, he took two blankets and arranged them on the camp bed. Then he stopped, felt useless, and sat down on his bed. There was nothing more to do or to get ready. He had to look at this man. He looked at him, therefore, trying to imagine his face bursting with rage. He couldn't do so. He could see nothing but the dark yet shining eyes and the animal mouth.

"Why did you kill him?" he asked in a voice whose hostile tone surprised him.

The Arab looked away.

"He ran away. I ran after him."

He raised his eyes to Daru again and they were full of a sort of woeful interrogation. "Now what will they do to me?"

"Are you afraid?"

He stiffened, turning his eyes away.

"Are you sorry?"

The Arab stared at him openmouthed. Obviously he did not understand. Daru's annoyance was growing. At the same time he felt awkward and self-conscious with his big body wedged between the two beds.

"Lie down there," he said impatiently. "That's your bed."

The Arab didn't move. He called to Daru:

"Tell me!"

The schoolmaster looked at him.

"Is the gendarme coming back tomorrow?"

"I don't know."

248

"Are you coming with us?"

"I don't know. Why?"

The prisoner got up and stretched out on top of the blankets, his feet toward the window. The light from the electric bulb shone straight into his eyes and he closed them at once.

"Why?" Daru repeated, standing beside the bed.

The Arab opened his eyes under the blinding light and looked at him, trying not to blink.

"Come with us," he said.

In the middle of the night, Daru was still not asleep. He had gone to bed after undressing completely; he generally slept naked. But when he suddenly realized that he had nothing on, he hesitated. He felt vulnerable and the temptation came to him to put his clothes back on. Then he shrugged his shoulders; after all, he wasn't a child and, if need be, he could break his adversary in two. From his bed he could observe him, lying on his back, still motionless with his eyes closed under the harsh light. When Daru turned out the light, the darkness seemed to coagulate all of a sudden. Little by little, the night came back to life in the window where the starless sky was stirring gently. The schoolmaster soon made out the body lying at his feet. The Arab still did not move, but his eyes seemed open. A faint wind was prowling around the schoolhouse. Perhaps it would drive away the clouds and the sun would reappear.

During the night the wind increased. The hens fluttered a little and then were silent. The Arab turned over on his side with his back to Daru, who thought he heard him moan. Then he listened for his guest's breathing, become heavier and more regular. He listened to that breath so close to him and mused without being able to go to sleep. In this room where he had been sleeping alone for a year, this presence bothered him. But it bothered him also by imposing on him a sort of brotherhood he knew well but refused to accept in the present circumstances. Men who share the same rooms, soldiers or prisoners, develop a strange alliance as if, having cast off their armor with their clothing, they fraternized every evening, over and above their differences, in the ancient community of dream and fatigue. But Daru shook himself; he didn't like such musings, and it was essential to sleep.

A little later, however, when the Arab stirred slightly, the schoolmaster was still not asleep. When the prisoner made a second move, he stiffened, on the alert. The Arab was lifting himself slowly on his arms with almost the motion of a sleepwalker. Seated upright in bed, he waited motionless without turning his head toward Daru, as if he were listening attentively. Daru did not stir; it had just occurred to him that the revolver was still in the drawer of his desk. It was better to act at once. Yet he continued to observe the prisoner, who, with the same slithery motion, put his feet on the ground, waited again, then began to stand up slowly. Daru was about to call out to him when the Arab began to walk, in a quite natural but extraordinarily silent way. He was heading toward the door at the end of the room that opened into the shed. He lifted the latch with precaution and went out, pushing the door behind him but without shutting it. Daru had not stirred. "He is running away," he merely thought. "Good riddance!" Yet he listened attentively. The hens were not fluttering; the guest must be on the plateau. A faint sound of water reached him, and he didn't know what it was until the Arab again stood framed in the doorway, closed the door carefully, and came back to bed without a sound. Then Daru turned his back on him and fell asleep. Still later he seemed, from the depths of his sleep, to hear furtive steps around the schoolhouse. "I'm dreaming! I'm dreaming!" he repeated to himself. And he went on sleeping.

When he awoke, the sky was clear; the loose window let in a cold, pure air. The Arab was asleep, hunched up under the blankets now, his mouth open, utterly relaxed. But when Daru shook him, he started dreadfully, staring at Daru with wild eyes as if he had never seen him and such a frightened expression that the schoolmaster stepped back. "Don't be afraid. It's me. You must eat." The Arab nodded his head and said yes. Calm had returned to his face, but his expression was vacant and listless.

The coffee was ready. They drank it seated together on the folding bed as they munched their pieces of the cake. Then Daru led the Arab under the shed and showed him the faucet where he washed. He went back into the room, folded the blankets and the bed, made his own bed and put the room in order. Then he went through the classroom and out onto the terrace. The sun was already rising in the blue sky; a soft, bright light was bathing the deserted plateau. On the ridge the snow was melting in spots. The stones were about to reappear. Crouched on the edge of the plateau, the schoolmaster looked at the deserted expanse.

He thought of Balducci. He had hurt him, for he had sent him off in a way as if he didn't want to be associated with him. He could still hear the gendarme's farewell and, without knowing why, he felt strangely empty and vulnerable. At that moment, from the other side of the schoolhouse, the prisoner coughed. Daru listened to him almost despite himself and then, furious, threw a pebble that whistled through the air before sinking into the snow. That man's stupid crime revolted him, but to hand him over was contrary to honor. Merely thinking of it made him smart with humiliation. And he cursed at one and the same time his own people who had sent him this Arab and the Arab too who had dared to kill and not managed to get away. Daru got up, walked in a circle on the terrace, waited motionless, and then went back into the schoolhouse.

The Arab, leaning over the cement floor of the shed, was washing his teeth with two fingers. Daru looked at him and said: "Come." He went back into the room ahead of the prisoner. He slipped a hunting-jacket on over his sweater and put on walking-shoes. Standing, he waited until the Arab had put on his *chèche* and sandals. They went into the classroom and the schoolmaster pointed to the exit,

253

saying: "Go ahead." The fellow didn't budge. "I'm coming," said Daru. The Arab went out. Daru went back into the room and made a package of pieces of rusk, dates, and sugar. In the classroom, before going out, he hesitated a second in front of his desk, then crossed the threshold and locked the door. "That's the way," he said. He started toward the east, followed by the prisoner. But, a short distance from the schoolhouse, he thought he heard a slight sound behind them. He retraced his steps and examined the surroundings of the house; there was no one there. The Arab watched him without seeming to understand. "Come on," said Daru.

They walked for an hour and rested beside a sharp peak of limestone. The snow was melting faster and faster and the sun was drinking up the puddles at once, rapidly cleaning the plateau, which gradually dried and vibrated like the air itself. When they resumed walking, the ground rang under their feet. From time to time a bird rent the space in front of them with a joyful cry. Daru breathed in deeply the fresh morning light. He felt a sort of rapture before the vast familiar expanse, now almost entirely yellow under its dome of blue sky. They walked an hour more, descending toward the south. They reached a level height made up of crumbly rocks. From there on, the plateau sloped down, eastward, toward a low plain where there were a few spindly trees and, to the south, toward outcroppings of rock that gave the landscape a chaotic look.

Daru surveyed the two directions. There was nothing but the sky on the horizon. Not a man could be seen. He turned toward the Arab, who was looking at him blankly. Daru held out the package to him. "Take it," he said. "There are dates, bread, and sugar. You can hold out for two days. Here are a thousand francs too." The Arab took the package and the money but kept his full hands at chest level as if he didn't know what to do with what was being given him. "Now look," the schoolmaster said as he pointed in the direction of the east, "there's the way to Tinguit. You have a two-hour walk. At Tinguit you'll find the administration and the police. They are expecting you." The Arab looked toward the east, still holding the package and the money against his chest. Daru took his elbow and turned him rather roughly toward the south. At the foot of the height on which they stood could be seen a faint path. "That's the trail across the plateau. In a day's walk from here you'll find pasturelands and the first nomads.

They'll take you in and shelter you according to their law." The Arab had now turned toward Daru and a sort of panic was visible in his expression. "Listen," he said. Daru shook his head: "No, be quiet. Now I'm leaving you." He turned his back on him, took two long steps in the direction of the school, looked hesitantly at the motionless Arab, and started off again. For a few minutes he heard nothing but his own step resounding on the cold ground and did not turn his head. A moment later, however, he turned around. The Arab was still there on the edge of the hill, his arms hanging now, and he was looking at the schoolmaster. Daru felt something rise in his throat. But he swore with impatience, waved vaguely, and started off again. He had already gone some distance when he again stopped and looked. There was no longer anyone on the hill.

Daru hesitated. The sun was now rather high in the sky and was beginning to beat down on his head. The schoolmaster retraced his steps, at first somewhat uncertainly, then with decision. When he reached the little hill, he was bathed in sweat. He climbed it as fast as he could and stopped, out of breath, at the top. The rock-fields to the south stood out sharply against the blue sky, but on the plain to the east a steamy heat was already rising. And in that slight haze, Daru, with heavy heart, made out the Arab walking slowly on the road to prison.

A little later, standing before the window of the classroom, the schoolmaster was watching the clear light bathing the whole surface of the plateau, but he hardly saw it. Behind him on the blackboard, among the winding French rivers, sprawled the clumsily chalked-up words he had just read: "You handed over our brother. You will pay for this." Daru looked at the sky, the plateau, and, beyond, the invisible lands stretching all the way to the sea. In this vast landscape he had loved so much, he was alone.

THE
ARTIST
AT
WORK

*Take me up and cast me forth
into the sea . . . for I know
that for my sake this great
tempest is upon you.*

JONAH i, 12

GILBERT JONAS, the painter, believed in his star. Indeed, he believed solely in it, although he felt respect, and even a sort of admiration, for other people's religion. His own faith, however, was not

258

lacking in virtues since it consisted in acknowledging obscurely that he would be granted much without ever deserving anything. Consequently when, around his thirty-fifth year, a dozen critics suddenly disputed as to which had discovered his talent, he showed no surprise. But his serenity, attributed by some to smugness, resulted, on the contrary, from a trusting modesty. Jonas credited everything to his star rather than to his own merits.

He was somewhat more astonished when a picture dealer offered him a monthly remittance that freed him from all care. The architect Rateau, who had loved Jonas and his star since their school days, vainly pointed out to him that the remittance would provide only a bare living and that the dealer was taking no risk. "All the same . . ." Jonas said. Rateau—who succeeded, but by dint of hard work, in everything he did—chided his friend. "What do you mean by 'all the same'? You must bargain." But nothing availed. In his heart Jonas thanked his star. "Just as you say," he told the dealer. And he gave up his job in the paternal publishing-house to devote himself altogether to painting. "What luck!" he said.

In reality he thought: "It's the same old luck." As far back as he could remember, he found the same luck at work. He felt, for instance, an affectionate gratitude toward his parents, first because they had brought him up carelessly and this had given free rein to his daydreaming, secondly because they had separated, on grounds of adultery. At least that was the pretext given by his father, who forgot to specify that it was a rather peculiar adultery: he could not endure the good works indulged in by his wife, who, a veritable lay saint, had, without seeing any wrong in it, given herself body and soul to suffering humanity. But the husband intended to be the master of his wife's virtues. "I'm sick and tired," that Othello used to say, "of sharing her with the poor."

This misunderstanding was profitable to Jonas. His parents, having read or heard about the many cases of sadistic murderers who were children of divorced parents, vied with each other in pampering him with a view to stamping out the spark of such an unfortunate evolution. The less obvious were the effects of the trauma experienced, according to them, by the child's psyche, the more worried they were, for invisible havoc must be deepest. Jonas had merely to announce that he was pleased with himself or his day for his parents' ordinary anxiety to become panic. Their attentions multiplied and the child wanted for nothing.

His alleged misfortune finally won Jonas a devoted brother in the person of his friend Rateau. Rateau's parents often entertained his little schoolmate because they pitied his hapless state. Their commiserating remarks inspired their strong and athletic son with the desire to take under his protection the child whose nonchalant successes he already admired. Admiration and condescension mixed well to form a friendship that Jonas received, like everything else, with encouraging simplicity.

When without any special effort Jonas had finished his formal studies, he again had the luck to get into his father's publishing-house, to find a job there and, indirectly, his vocation as a painter. As the leading publisher in France, Jonas's father was of the opinion that books, because of the very slump in culture, represented the future. "History shows," he would say, "that the less people read, the more books they buy." Consequently, he but rarely read the manuscripts submitted to him and decided to publish them solely on the basis of the author's personality or the subject's topical interest (from this point of view, sex being the only subject always topical, the publisher had eventually gone in for specialization) and spent his time looking for novel formats and free publicity. Hence at the same time he took over the manuscript-reading department, Jonas also took over considerable leisure time that had to be filled up. Thus it was that he made the acquaintance of painting.

For the first time he discovered in himself an unsuspected and tireless enthusiasm, soon devoted his days to painting, and, still without effort, excelled in that exercise. Nothing else seemed to interest him, and he was barely able to get married at the suitable age, since painting consumed him wholly. For human beings and the ordinary circumstances of life he merely reserved a kindly smile, which dispensed him from paying attention to them. It took a motorcycle accident when Rateau was riding too exuberantly with his friend on the rear seat to interest Jonas—bored and with his right hand inert and bandaged—in love. Once again, he was inclined to see in that serious accident the good effects of his star, for without it he wouldn't have taken the time to look at Louise Poulin as she deserved.

According to Rateau, it must be added, Louise did not deserve to be looked at. Short and strapping himself, he liked nothing but tall women. "I don't know what you find in that insect," he would say. Louise was in fact small and dark in skin, hair, and eye, but well built and pretty in the face. Jonas, tall and rugged, was touched at the sight of the insect, especially as she was industrious. Louise's vocation was activity. Such a vocation fitted well with Jonas's preference for inertia and its advantages. Louise dedicated herself first to literature, so long at least as she thought that publishing interested Jonas. She read everything, without order, and in a few weeks became capable of talking about everything. Jonas admired her and considered himself definitely dispensed from reading, since Louise informed him sufficiently and made it possible for him to know the essence of contemporary discoveries. "You mustn't say," Louise asserted, "that so-and-so is wicked or ugly, but that he poses as wicked or ugly." The distinction was important and might even lead, as Rateau pointed out, to the condemnation of the human race. But Louise settled the question once and for all by showing that since this truth was supported simultaneously by the sentimental press and the philosophical reviews, it was universal and not open to discussion. "Just as you say," said Jonas, who immediately forgot that cruel discovery to dream of his star.

Louise deserted literature as soon as she realized that Jonas was interested only in painting. She dedicated herself at once to the visual arts, visited museums and exhibitions, dragged Jonas to them though he didn't quite understand what his contemporaries were painting and felt bothered in his artistic simplicity. Yet he rejoiced to be so well informed about everything that concerned his art. To be sure, the next day he forgot even the name of the painter whose works he had just seen. But Louise was right when she peremptorily reminded him of one of the certainties she had kept from her literary period, namely that in reality one never forgets anything. His star decidedly protected Jonas, who could thus, without suffering in his conscience, combine the certainties of remembering and the comforts of forgetting.

But the treasures of self-sacrifice that Louise showered upon him shone most brilliantly in Jonas's daily life. That angel spared him the purchases of shoes, suits, and shirts that, for the normal man, shorten the days of an already too short life. She resolutely took upon herself the thousand inventions of the machine for killing time, from the hermetic brochures of social security to the constantly changing moods of the internal-revenue office.

"O.K.," said Rateau, "but she can't go to the dentist in your place." She may not have gone, but she telephoned and made the appointments, at the most convenient hours; she took care of changing the oil in the tiny car, of booking rooms in vacation hotels, of the coal for his stove; she herself bought the gifts Jonas wanted to give, chose and sent his flowers, and even found time, certain evenings, to go by his house in his absence and open his bed to spare him the trouble when he came home.

With the same enthusiasm, of course, she entered that bed, then took care of the appointment with the mayor, led Jonas to the town hall two years before his talent was at last recognized, and arranged the wedding trip so that they didn't miss a museum. Not without having first found, in the midst of the housing shortage, a three-room apartment into which they settled on their return. Then she produced, in rapid succession, two children, a boy and a girl. Her intention of going up to three was realized soon after Jonas had left the publishing-house to devote himself to painting.

As soon as she had become a mother, it must be added, Louise devoted herself solely to her child, and later to her children. She still tried to help her husband, but didn't have the time. To be sure, she regretted her neglect of Jonas, but her resolute character kept her from wasting time in such regrets. "It can't be helped," she would say, "each of us has his workbench." Jonas was, in any case, delighted with this expression, for, like all the artists of his epoch, he wanted to be looked upon as an artisan. Hence the artisan was somewhat neglected and had to buy his shoes himself. However, besides the fact that this was in the nature of things, Jonas was again tempted to rejoice. Of course, he had to make an effort to visit the shops, but that effort was rewarded by one of those hours of solitude that give such value to marital bliss.

The problem of living-space was, however, by far the greatest of their problems, for time and space shrank simultaneously around them. The birth of the children, Jonas's new occupation, their restricted quarters, the modesty of the monthly remittance which prevented them from getting a larger apartment did not leave much room for the double activity of Louise and Jonas. The apartment was on the second floor of what had been a private house in the eighteenth century, in the old section of the capital. Many artists lived in that quarter, faithful to the principle that in art the pursuit of the new can take place only in an old setting. Jonas, who shared that conviction, was delighted to live in that quarter.

There could be no question as to the apartment's being old. But a few very modern arrangements had given it an original appearance resulting chiefly from the fact that it provided a great volume of air while occupying but a limited surface. The rooms, particularly high and graced with magnificent tall windows, had certainly been intended, to judge from their majestic proportions, for receptions and ceremonies. But the necessities of urban congestion and of income from real estate had forced the successive owners to cut up those over-large rooms with partitions and thus to multiply the stalls they rented at exorbitant prices to their flock of tenants. They nonetheless talked up what they called "the considerable cubic space." No one could deny the advantage. It simply had to be attributed to the impossibility of partitioning the rooms horizontally as well. Otherwise the landlords would certainly not have hesitated to make the necessary sacrifices in order to provide a few more shelters for the rising generation, particularly inclined at that moment to marry and reproduce. Besides, the cubic air-space was not all to the good. It had the inconvenience of making the rooms hard to heat in winter, and this unfortunately forced the landlords to increase the rent supplement for heat. In summer, because of the great window surface, the apartment was literally flooded with light, for there were no blinds. The landlords had neglected to put them in, doubtless discouraged by the height of the windows and the cost of carpentry. After all, thick draperies could perform the same service and presented no problem as to the cost, since they were the tenants' responsibility. Furthermore, the landlords were not unwilling to help them by furnishing curtains from their own stores at cost prices. Real-estate philanthropy, in fact, was merely their avocation. In their regular daily life those new princes sold percale and velvet.

Jonas had gone into raptures over the apartment's advantages and had accepted its drawbacks without difficulties. "Just as you say," he said to the landlord about the supplement for heat. As for the curtains, he agreed with Louise that it was enough to provide them just for the bedroom and to leave the other windows bare. "We have nothing to hide," that pure heart said. Jonas had been particularly entranced by the largest room, the ceiling of which was so high that there could be no question of installing a lighting system. The entrance door opened directly into that room, which was joined by a narrow hall to the two others, much smaller and strung in a row. At the end of the hall were the kitchen, the water-closet, and a nook graced with the name of shower-room. Indeed, it might have been a shower if only the fixture had been installed, vertically of course, and one were willing to stand utterly motionless under the spray.

The really extraordinary height of the ceilings and the narrowness of the rooms made of the apartment an odd assortment of parallelepipeds almost entirely glassed in, all doors and windows, with no wall space for the furniture, and with th human beings floating about like bottle imps in a vertical aquarium. Furthermore, all the windows opened onto a court—in other words, onto other windows in the same style just across the way, behind which one could discern the lofty outline of other windows opening onto a second court. "It's the hall of mirrors," Jonas said in delight. On Rateau's advice, it was decided to locate the master bedroom in one of the small rooms, the other to be for the already expected baby. The big room served as a studio for Jonas during the day, as a living-room in the evening and at mealtimes. They could also in a pinch eat in the kitchen, provided that Jonas or

Louise was willing to remain standing. For his part, Rateau had outdone himself in ingenious inventions. By means of sliding doors, retractable shelves, and folding tables, he had managed to make up for the paucity of furniture while emphasizing the jack-in-the-box appearance of that unusual apartment.

But when the rooms were full of paintings and children, they had to think up a new arrangement. Before the birth of the third child, in fact, Jonas worked in the big room, Louise knitted in the bedroom, while the two children occupied the last room, raised a great rumpus there, and also tumbled at will throughout the rest of the apartment. They agreed to put the newborn in a corner of the studio, which Jonas walled off by propping up his canvases like a screen; this offered the advantage of having the baby within earshot and being able to answer his calls. Besides, Jonas never needed to bestir himself, for Louise forestalled him. She wouldn't wait until the baby cried before entering the studio, though with every possible precaution and always on tiptoe. Jonas, touched by such discretion, one day assured Louise that he was not so sensitive and could easily go on working despite the noise of her steps. Louise replied that she was also aiming not to waken the baby. Jonas, full of admiration for the workings of the maternal instinct, laughed heartily at his misunderstanding. As a result, he didn't dare confess that Louise's cautious entries bothered him more than an out-and-out invasion. First, because they lasted longer, and secondly because they followed a pantomime in which Louise —her arms outstretched, her shoulders thrown back, and her leg raised high—could not go unnoticed. This method even went against her avowed intentions, since Louise constantly ran the risk of bumping into one of the canvases with which the studio was cluttered. At such moments the noise would waken the baby, who would manifest his displeasure according to his capacities, which were considerable. The father, delighted by his son's pulmonary prowess, would rush to cuddle him and soon be relieved in this by his wife. Then Jonas would pick up his canvases and, brushes in hand, would listen ecstatically to his son's insistent and sovereign voice.

This was just about the time that Jonas's success brought him many friends. Those friends turned up on the telephone or in impromptu visits. The telephone, which, after due deliberation, had been put in the studio, rang often and always to the detriment of the baby's sleep, who would then mingle his cries with the urgent ringing of the phone. If it so happened that Louise was busy caring for the other children, she strove to get to the telephone with them, but most of the time she would find Jonas holding the baby in one arm and in his other hand his brushes and the receiver, which was extending a friendly invitation to lunch. Jonas was always amazed that anyone was willing to lunch with him, for his conversation was dull, but he preferred going out in the evening in order to keep his workday unbroken. Most of the time, unfortunately, the friend would be free only for lunch, and just for this particular lunch; he would insist upon holding it for his dear Jonas. His dear Jonas would accept: "Just as you say!" and after hanging up would add: "Isn't he thoughtful!" while handing the baby to Louise. Then he would go back to work, soon interrupted by lunch or dinner. He had to move the canvases out of the way, unfold the special table, and sit down with the children. During the meal Jonas would keep an eye on the painting he was working on and occasionally, in the beginning at least, he would find his children rather slow in chewing and swallowing, so that each meal was excessively long. But he read in his newspaper that it was essential to eat slowly in order to assimilate, and thenceforth each meal provided reasons for rejoicing at length.

On other occasions his new friends would drop in. Rateau, for one, never came until after dinner. He was at his office during the day and, besides, he knew that painters work during the daylight hours. But Jonas's new friends almost all belonged to the species of artists and critics. Some had painted, others were about to paint, and the remainder were concerned with what had been, or would be, painted. All, to be sure, held the labors of art in high esteem and complained of the organization of the modern world that makes so difficult the pursuit of those labors, as well as the exercise of meditation, indispensable to the artist. They complained of this for whole afternoons, begging Jonas to go on working, to behave as if they weren't there, to treat them cavalierly, for they weren't philistines and knew the value of an artist's time. Jonas, pleased to have friends capable of allowing one to go on working in their presence, would go back to his picture without ceasing to answer the questions asked him or to laugh at the anecdotes told him.

Such simplicity put his friends more and more at ease. Their good spirits were so genuine that they forgot the meal hour. But the children had a better memory. They would rush in, mingle with the guests, howl, be cuddled by the visitors, and pass from lap to lap. At last the light would dwindle in the square of sky outlined by the court, and Jonas would lay down his brushes. There was nothing to do but to invite the friends to share pot-luck and to go on talking, late into the night, about art of course, but especially about the untalented painters, plagiarists or self-advertisers, who weren't there. Jonas liked to get up early to take advantage of the first hours of daylight. He knew that this would be difficult, that breakfast wouldn't be ready on time and that he himself would be tired. But on the other hand he rejoiced to learn in an evening so many things that could not fail to be helpful to him, though in an invisible way, in his art. "In art, as in nature, nothing is ever wasted," he used to say. "This is a result of the star."

To the friends were sometimes added the disciples, for Jonas now had a following. At first he had been surprised, not seeing what anyone could learn from him who still had everything to discover. The artist in him was groping in the darkness; how could he have pointed out the right paths? But he readily realized that a disciple is not necessarily someone who longs to learn something. Most often,

on the contrary, one became a disciple for the disinterested pleasure of teaching one's master.
Thenceforth he could humbly accept such a surfeit
of honors. Jonas's disciples explained to him at
length what he had painted, and why. In this way
Jonas discovered in his work many intentions that
rather surprised him, and a host of things he hadn't
put there. He had thought himself poor and, thanks
to his pupils, suddenly found himself rich. At times,
faced with such hitherto unsuspected wealth, Jonas
would feel a tingle of pride. "Nonetheless it's true,"
he would say. "That face in the background stands
out. I don't quite understand what they mean by
indirect humanization. Yet, with that effect I've
really gone somewhere." But very soon he would
transfer that uncomfortable mastery to his star.
"It's the star," he would say, "that's gone somewhere. I'm staying home with Louise and the children."

In addition, the disciples had another advantage:
they forced Jonas to be more severe with himself.
They ranked him so high in their conversations,
and especially in regard to his conscientiousness
and energy, that henceforth no weakness was permitted him. Thus he lost his old habit of nibbling a
piece of sugar or chocolate when he had finished a

difficult passage and before he went back to work. If he were alone, he would nevertheless have given in clandestinely to that weakness. But he was helped in his moral progress by the almost constant presence of his disciples and friends in whose sight he would have been embarrassed to nibble chocolate and whose interesting conversation he couldn't interrupt anyway for such a petty idiosyncrasy.

Furthermore, his disciples insisted on his remaining faithful to his esthetic. Jonas, who labored at length only to get a very occasional fleeting flash in which reality would suddenly appear to him in a new light, had only a very vague idea of his own esthetic. His disciples, on the other hand, had several ideas, contradictory and categorical, and they would allow no joking on the subject. Jonas would have liked, at times, to resort to his whim, that humble friend of the artist. But his disciples' frowns in the face of certain pictures that strayed from their idea forced him to reflect a little more about his art, and this was all to his advantage.

Finally, the disciples helped Jonas in another way by obliging him to give his opinion about their own production. Not a day went by, in fact, without someone's bringing him a picture barely sketched in, which its author would set between Jonas and the canvas he was working on, in order to take advantage of the best light. An opinion was expected. Until then Jonas had always been secretly ashamed at his fundamental inability to judge a work of art. Except for a handful of pictures that carried him away, and for the obviously coarse daubs, everything seemed to him equally interesting and indifferent. Consequently he was obliged to build up a stock of judgments, which had to be varied because his disciples, like all the artists of the capital, after all had a measure of talent and, when they were around, he had to draw rather fine lines of distinction to satisfy each. Hence that happy obligation forced him to amass a vocabulary and opinions about his art. Yet his natural kindness was not embittered by the effort. He soon realized that his disciples were not asking him for criticisms, for which they had no use, but only for encouragement and, if possible, praise. The praises merely had to be different. Jonas was not satisfied to be his usual agreeable self. He showed ingenuity in his ways of being so.

Thus the time went by for Jonas, who painted amidst friends and pupils seated on chairs that were now arranged in concentric circles around his easel. Often, in addition, neighbors would appear at the windows across the way and swell his public. He would discuss, exchange views, examine the paintings submitted to him, smile as Louise went by, soothe the children, and enthusiastically answer telephone calls, without ever setting down his brushes with which he would from time to time add a stroke to a half-finished painting. In a way, his life was very full, not an hour was wasted, and he gave thanks to fate that spared him boredom. In another way, it took many brush-strokes to finish a picture and it occasionally occurred to him that boredom had the one advantage that it could be avoided through strenuous work. But Jonas's production slowed down in proportion to his friends' becoming more interesting. Even in the rare moments when he was altogether alone, he felt too tired to catch up. And at such moments he could but dream of a new regime that would reconcile the pleasures of friendship with the virtues of boredom.

He broached the subject to Louise, who was independently beginning to worry about the growth of the two older children and the smallness of their room. She suggested putting them in the big room with their bed hidden by a screen and moving the baby into the small room where he would not be wakened by the telephone. As the baby took up no room, Jonas could turn the little room into his studio. Then the big one would serve for the daytime gatherings, and Jonas could wander back and forth, either chat with his friends or work, since he was sure of being understood in his need for isolation. Furthermore, the necessity of putting the older children to bed would allow them to cut the evenings short. "Wonderful," Jonas said after a moment's reflection. "Besides," said Louise, "if your friends leave early, we'll see a little more of each other." Jonas looked at her. A suggestion of melancholy passed over Louise's face. Touched, he put his arms around her and kissed her in his most affectionate way. She surrendered to him and for a moment they were happy as they had been in the beginning of their marriage. But she shook herself free; the room was perhaps too small for Jonas. Louise got a folding rule and they discovered that because of the congestion caused by his canvases and those of his pupils, by far the more numerous, he generally worked in a space hardly any larger than the one that was about to be assigned to him. Jonas hastened to move the furniture.

Luckily, the less he worked, the more his reputation grew. Each exhibit was eagerly awaited and extolled in advance. To be sure, a small number of critics, among whom were two regular visitors to the studio, tempered the warmth of their reviews with some reservations. But the disciples' indignation more than made up for this little misfortune. Of course, the latter would emphatically assert, they ranked the pictures of the first period above everything else, but the present experiments foreshadowed a real revolution. Jonas would rather reproach himself for the slight annoyance he felt every time his first works were glorified and would thank them effusively. Only Rateau would grumble: "Weird ones . . . They like you inert, like a statue. And they deny you the right to live!" But Jonas would defend his disciples: "You can't understand," he told Rateau, "because you like everything I do." Rateau laughed: "Of course! It's not your pictures I like; it's your painting."

The pictures continued to be popular in any event and, after an exhibit that was enthusiastically received, the dealer suggested, on his own, an increase in the monthly remittance. Jonas accepted, declaring how grateful he was. "Anyone who heard you now," the dealer said, "would think money meant something to you." Such goodheartedness disarmed the painter. However, when he asked the dealer's permission to give a canvas to a charity sale, the dealer wanted to know whether or not it was a "paying charity." Jonas didn't know. The dealer therefore suggested sticking squarely to the terms of the contract which granted him the exclusive right of sale. "A contract's a contract," he said. In theirs, there was no provision for charity. "Just as you say," the painter said.

The new arrangement was a source of constant satisfaction to Jonas. He could, in fact, get off by himself often enough to answer the many letters he now received, which his courtesy could not leave unanswered. Some concerned Jonas's art, while others, far more plentiful, concerned the correspondent, who either wanted to be encouraged in his artistic vocation or else needed advice or financial aid. The more Jonas's name appeared in the press, the more he was solicited, like everyone, to take an active part in exposing most revolting injustices. Jonas would reply, write about art, thank people, give his advice, go without a necktie in order to send a small financial contribution, finally sign the just protests that were sent him. "You're indulging in politics now? Leave that to writers and ugly old maids," said Rateau. No, he would sign only the protests that insisted they had no connection with any particular party line. But they all laid claim to such beautiful independence. For weeks on end, Jonas would go about with his pockets stuffed with correspondence, constantly neglected and renewed. He would answer the most urgent, which generally came from unknowns, and keep for a better moment those that called for a more leisurely reply—in other words, his friends' letters. So many obligations at least kept him from dawdling and from yielding to a carefree spirit. He always felt behindhand, and always guilty, even when he was working, as he was from time to time.

Louise was ever more mobilized by the children and wore herself out doing everything that, in other circumstances, he could have done in the home. This made him suffer. After all, *he* was working for his pleasure whereas she had the worst end of the bargain. He became well aware of this when she was out marketing. "The telephone!" the eldest child would shout, and Jonas would drop his picture right there, only to return to it, beaming, with another invitation. "Gasman!" the meter-reader would shout from the door one of the children had opened for him. "Coming! Coming!" And when Jonas would leave the telephone or the door, a friend or a disciple, sometimes both, would follow him to the little room to finish the interrupted conversation. Gradually they all became regular frequenters of the hallway. They would stand there, chat among themselves, ask Jonas's opinion from a distance, or else overflow briefly into the little room. "Here at least," those who entered would exclaim, "a fellow can see you a bit, and without interruption." This touched Jonas. "You're right," he would say. "After all, we never get a chance to see each other." At the same time he was well aware that he disappointed those he didn't see, and this saddened him. Often they were friends he would have preferred to meet. But he didn't have time, he couldn't accept everything. Consequently, his reputation suffered. "He's become proud," people said, "now that he's a success. He doesn't see anyone any more." Or else: "He doesn't love anyone, except himself." No, he loved Louise, and his children, and Rateau, and a few others, and he had a liking for all. But life is short, time races by, and his own energy had limits. It was hard to paint the world and men and, at the same time, to live with them. On the other hand, he couldn't complain, or explain the things that stood in his way. For, if he did, people slapped him on the back, saying: "Lucky fellow! That's the price of fame!"

Consequently, his mail piled up, the disciples would allow no falling off, and society people now thronged around him. It must be added that Jonas admired them for being interested in painting when, like everyone else, they might have got excited about the English Royal Family or gastronomic tours. In truth, they were mostly society women, all very simple in manner. They didn't buy any pictures themselves and introduced their friends to the artist only in the hope, often groundless, that *they* would buy in their place. On the other hand, they helped Louise, especially in serving tea to the visitors. The cups passed from hand to hand, traveled along the hallway from the kitchen to the big room, and then came back to roost in the little studio, where Jonas, in the center of a handful of friends and visitors, enough to fill the room, went on painting until he had to lay down his brushes to take, gratefully, the cup that a fascinating lady had poured especially for him.

He would drink his tea, look at the sketch that a disciple had just put on his easel, laugh with his friends, interrupt himself to ask one of them to please mail the pile of letters he had written during the night, pick up the second child, who had stumbled over his feet, pose for a photograph, and then at "Jonas, the telephone!" he would wave his cup in the air, thread his way with many an excuse through the crowd standing in the hall, come back, fill in a corner of the picture, stop to answer the fascinating lady that certainly he would be happy to paint her portrait, and would get back to his easel. He worked, but "Jonas! A signature!" "What is it, a registered letter?" "No, the Kashmir prisoners." "Coming! Coming!" Then he would run to the door to receive a young friend of the prisoners and listen to his protest, worry briefly as to whether politics were involved, and sign after receiving complete assurance on that score, together with expostulations about the duties inseparable from his privileges as an artist, and at last he would reappear only to meet, without being able to catch their names, a recently victorious boxer or the greatest dramatist of some foreign country. The dramatist would stand facing him for five minutes, expressing through the emotion in his eyes what his ignorance of French would not allow him to state more clearly, while Jonas would nod his head with a real feeling of brotherhood. Fortunately, he would

suddenly be saved from that dead-end situation by
the bursting-in of the latest spellbinder of the pulpit who wanted to be introduced to the great
painter. Jonas would say that he was delighted,
which he was, feel the packet of unanswered letters in his pocket, take up his brushes, get ready
to go on with a passage, but would first have to
thank someone for the pair of setters that had just
been brought him, go and close them in the master
bedroom, come back to accept the lady donor's
invitation to lunch, rush out again in answer to
Louise's call to see for himself without a shadow
of doubt that the setters had not been broken in
to apartment life, and lead them into the shower-
room, where they would bark so persistently that
eventually no one would even hear them. Every
once in a while, over the visitors' heads, Jonas
would catch a glimpse of the look in Louise's eyes
and it seemed to him that that look was sad. Finally
the day would end, the visitors would take leave,
others would tarry in the big room and wax emotional as they watched Louise put the children to
bed, obligingly aided by an elegant, overdressed
lady who would complain of having to return to
her luxurious home where life, spread out over

two floors, was so much less close and homey than at the Jonases'.

One Saturday afternoon Rateau came to bring an ingenious clothes-drier that could be screwed onto the kitchen ceiling. He found the apartment packed and, in the little room, surrounded by art-lovers, Jonas painting the lady who had given the dogs, while he was being painted himself by an official artist. According to Louise, the latter was working on order from the Government. "It will be called *The Artist at Work*." Rateau withdrew to a corner of the room to watch his friend, obviously absorbed in his effort. One of the art-lovers, who had never seen Rateau, leaned over toward him and said: "He looks well, doesn't he?" Rateau didn't reply. "You paint, I suppose," he continued. "So do I. Well, take my word for it, he's on the decline." "Already?" Rateau asked. "Yes. It's success. You can't resist success. He's finished." "He's on the decline or he's finished?" "An artist who is on the decline is finished. Just see, he has nothing in him to paint any more. He's being painted himself and will be hung in a museum."

Later on, in the middle of the night, Louise, Rateau, and Jonas, the latter standing and the other two seated on a corner of the bed, were silent. The children were asleep, the dogs were boarding in the country, Louise had just washed, and Jonas and Rateau had dried, the many dishes, and their fatigue felt good. "Why don't you get a servant?" Rateau had asked when he saw the stack of dishes. But Louise had answered sadly: "Where would we put her?" So they were silent. "Are you happy?" Rateau had suddenly asked. Jonas smiled, but he looked tired. "Yes. Everybody is kind to me." "No," said Rateau. "Watch out. They're not all good." "Who isn't?" "Your painter friends, for instance." "I know," Jonas said. "But many artists are that way. They're not sure of existing, not even the greatest. So they look for proofs; they judge and condemn. That strengthens them; it's a beginning of existence. They're so lonely!" Rateau shook his head. "Take my word for it," Jonas said; "I know them. You have to love them." "And what about you?" Rateau said. "Do you exist? You never say anything bad about anyone." Jonas began to laugh. "Oh! I often think bad of them. But then I forget." He became serious. "No, I'm not sure of existing. But someday I'll exist, I'm sure."

Rateau asked Louise her opinion. Shaking off her fatigue, she said she thought Jonas was right: their visitors' opinion was of no importance. Only Jonas's work mattered. And she was aware that the child got in his way. He was growing anyway, and they would have to buy a couch that would take up space. What could they do until they got a bigger apartment? Jonas looked at the master bedroom. Of course, it was not the ideal; the bed was very wide. But the room was empty all day long. He said this to Louise, who reflected. In the bedroom, at least, Jonas would not be bothered; after all, people wouldn't dare lie down on their bed. "What do you think of it?" Louise in turn asked Rateau. He looked at Jonas. Jonas was looking at the windows across the way. Then he raised his eyes to the starless sky, and went and pulled the curtains. When he returned, he smiled at Rateau and sat down beside him on the bed without saying a word. Louise, obviously done in, declared that she was going to take her shower. When the two friends were alone, Jonas felt Rateau's shoulder touch his. He didn't look at him, but said: "I love to paint. I'd like to paint all my life, day and night. Isn't that lucky?" Rateau looked at him affectionately: "Yes," he said, "it's lucky."

The children were growing and Jonas was glad to see them happy and healthy. They were now in school and came home at four o'clock. Jonas could still enjoy them Saturday afternoons, Thursdays, and also for whole days during their frequent and prolonged vacations. They were not yet big enough to play quietly but were hardy enough to fill the apartment with their squabbles and their laughter. He had to quiet them, threaten them, sometimes even pretend to hit them. There was also the laundry to be done, the buttons to be sewed on. Louise couldn't do it all. Since they couldn't house a servant, nor even bring one into the close intimacy in which they lived, Jonas suggested calling on the help of Louise's sister, Rose, who had been left a widow with a grown daughter. "Yes," Louise said, "with Rose we'll not have to stand on ceremony. We can put her out when we want to." Jonas was delighted with this solution, which would relieve Louise at the same time that it relieved his conscience, embarrassed by his wife's fatigue. The relief was even greater since the sister often brought along her daughter as a reinforcement. Both were as good as gold; virtue and unselfishness predominated in their honest natures. They did everything possible to help out and didn't begrudge their time. They were helped in this by the boredom of their solitary lives and their delight in the easy circumstances prevailing at Louise's. As it was foreseen, no one stood on ceremony and the two relatives, from the very beginning, felt at home. The big room became a common room, at once dining-room, linen closet, and nursery. The little room, in which the last-born slept, served as a storeroom for the paintings and a folding bed on which Rose sometimes slept, when she happened to come without her daughter.

Jonas occupied the master bedroom and worked in the space separating the bed from the window. He merely had to wait until the room was made up in the morning, after the children's room. From then on, no one came to bother him except to get a sheet or towel, for the only cupboard in the house happened to be in that room. As for the visitors, though rather less numerous, they had developed certain habits and, contrary to Louise's hope, they didn't hesitate to lie down on the double bed to be more comfortable when chatting with Jonas. The children would also come in to greet their father. "Let's see the picture." Jonas would show them the picture he was painting and would kiss them affectionately. As he sent them away, he felt that they filled his heart fully, without any reservation. Deprived of them, he would have merely an empty solitude. He loved them as much as his painting because they were the only things in the world as alive as it was.

Nevertheless Jonas was working less, without really knowing why. He was always diligent, but he now had trouble painting, even in the moments of solitude. He would spend such moments looking at the sky. He had always been absent-minded, easily lost in thought, but now he became a dreamer. He would think of painting, of his vocation, instead of painting. "I love to paint," he still said to himself, and the hand holding the brush would hang at his side as he listened to a distant radio.

At the same time, his reputation declined. He was brought articles full of reservations, others frankly unfriendly, and some so nasty that they deeply distressed him. But he told himself that he could get some good out of such attacks that would force him to work better. Those who continued to come treated him more familiarly, like an old friend with whom you don't have to put yourself out. When he wanted to go back to his work, they would say: "Aw, go on! There's plenty of time." Jonas realized that in a certain way they were already identifying him with their own fail-

ure. But, in another way, there was something salu-
tary about this new solidarity. Rateau shrugged his
shoulders, saying: "You're a fool. They don't care
about you at all!" "They love me a little now,"
Jonas replied. "A little love is wonderful. Does it
matter how you get it?" He therefore went on
talking, writing letters, and painting as best he
could. Now and then he really would paint, especially Sunday afternoons when the children went
out with Louise and Rose. In the evening he would
rejoice at having made a little progress on the picture under way. At that time he was painting skies.

The day when the dealer told him that, because
of the considerable falling-off in sales, he was re-
gretfully obliged to reduce the remittance, Jonas
approved, but Louise was worried. It was Septem-
ber and the children had to be outfitted for school.
She set to work herself with her customary courage
and was soon swamped. Rose, who could mend
and sew on buttons, could not make things. But
her husband's cousin could; she came to help Louise. From time to time she would settle in Jonas's
room on a corner chair, where the silent woman
would sit still for hours. So still that Louise suggested to Jonas painting a *Seamstress*. "Good idea,"
Jonas said. He tried, spoiled two canvases, then

went back to a half-finished sky. The next day, he walked up and down in the apartment for some time and meditated instead of painting. A disciple, all excited, came to show him a long article he would not have seen otherwise, from which he learned that his painting was not only overrated but out of date. The dealer phoned him to tell him again how worried he was by the decline in sales. Yet he continued to dream and meditate. He told the disciple that there was some truth in the article, but that he, Jonas, could still count on many good working years. To the dealer he replied that he understood his worry without sharing it. He had a big work, really new, to create; everything was going to begin all over again. As he was talking, he felt that he was telling the truth and that his star was there. All he needed was a good system.

During the ensuing days he tried to work in the hall, two days later in the shower-room with electric light, and the following day in the kitchen. But, for the first time, he was bothered by the people he kept bumping into everywhere, those he hardly knew and his own family, whom he loved. For a little while he stopped working and meditated. He would have painted landscapes out of doors if the weather had been propitious. Unfortunately, it was just the beginning of winter and it was hard to do landscapes before spring. He tried, however, and gave up; the cold pierced him to the marrow. He lived several days with his canvases, most often seated beside them or else planted in front of the window; he didn't paint any more. Then he got in the habit of going out in the morning. He would give himself the assignment of sketching a detail, a tree, a lopsided house, a profile as it went by. At the end of the day, he had done nothing. The least temptation—the newspapers, an encounter, shopwindows, the warmth of a café— would lead him astray. Each evening he would keep providing good excuses to a bad conscience that never left him. He was going to paint, that was certain, and paint better, after this period of apparent waste. It was all just working within him, and the star would come out newly washed and sparkling from behind these black clouds. Meanwhile he never left the cafés. He had discovered that alcohol gave him the same exaltation as a day of good productive work at the time when he used to think of his picture with the affection and warmth that he had never felt except toward his children. With the second cognac he recovered that poignant emotion that made him at one and the same time master and servant of the whole world. The only difference was that he enjoyed it in a vacuum, with idle hands, without communicating it to a work. Still, this was closest to the joy for which he lived, and he now spent long hours sitting and dreaming in smoke-filled, noisy places.

Yet he fled the places and sections frequented by artists. Whenever he met an acquaintance who spoke to him of his painting, he would be seized with panic. He wanted to get away, that was obvious, and he did get away. He knew what was said behind his back: "He thinks he's Rembrandt," and his discomfort increased. In any event, he never smiled any more, and his former friends drew an odd and inevitable conclusion from this: "If he has given up smiling, this is because he's very satisfied with himself." Knowing that, he became more and more elusive and skittish. It was enough for him, on entering a café, to have the feeling that someone there recognized him for everything to cloud over within him. For a second, he would stand there, powerless and filled with a strange sadness, his inscrutable face hiding both his uneasiness and his avid and sudden need for friendship. He would think of Rateau's cheering look and would rush out in a hurry. "Just look at that guy's hangover!" he heard someone say close to him one day as he was disappearing.

He now frequented only the outlying sections, where no one knew him. There he could talk and smile and his kindliness came back, for no one expected anything of him. He made a few friends, who were not very hard to please. He particularly enjoyed the company of one of them, who used to serve him in a station buffet where he often went. That fellow had asked him "what he did in life." "Painter," Jonas had replied. "Picture-painter or house-painter?" "Picture." "Well," said the fellow, "that's not easy." And they had never broached the subject again. No, it was not easy, but Jonas would manage all right, as soon as he had found how to organize his work.

Day after day and drink after drink, he had many encounters, and women helped him. He could talk to them, before or after the love-making, and especially boast a little, for they would understand him even if they weren't convinced. At times it seemed to him that his old strength was returning. One day when he had been encouraged by one of his female acquaintances, he made up his mind. He returned home, tried to work again in the bedroom, the seamstress being absent. But after an hour

of it he put his canvas away, smiled at Louise without seeing her, and went out. He drank all day
long and spent the night with his acquaintance,
though without being in any condition to desire
her. In the morning, the image of suffering with
its tortured face received him in the person of Louise. She wanted to know if he had taken that
woman. Jonas said that, being drunk, he had not,
but that he had taken others before. And for the
first time, his heart torn within him, he saw that
Louise suddenly had the look of a drowned woman,
that look that comes from surprise and an excess
of pain. It dawned upon him that he had not
thought of Louise during this whole time, and he
was ashamed. He begged her forgiveness, it was
all over, tomorrow everything would begin again
as it had been in the past. Louise could not speak
and turned away to hide her tears.

The following day Jonas went out very early.
It was raining. When he returned, wet to the skin,
he was loaded down with boards. At home, two
old friends, come to ask after him, were drinking
coffee in the big room. "Jonas is changing his technique. He's going to paint on wood!" they said.
Jonas smiled. "That's not it. But I am beginning
something new." He went into the little hall lead-

ing to the shower-room, the toilet, and the kitchen. In the right angle where the two halls joined, he stopped and studied at length the high walls rising to the dark ceiling. He needed a stepladder, which he went down and got from the concierge.

When he came back up, there were several additional people in the apartment, and he had to struggle against the affection of his visitors, delighted to find him again, and against his family's questions in order to reach the end of the hall. At that moment his wife came out of the kitchen. Setting down his ladder, Jonas hugged her against him. Louise looked at him. "Please," she said, "never do it again." "No, no," Jonas said, "I'm going to paint. I must paint." But he seemed to be talking to himself, for he was looking elsewhere. He got to work. Halfway up the walls he built a flooring to get a sort of narrow, but high and deep, loft. By the late afternoon, all was finished. With the help of the ladder, Jonas hung from the floor of the loft and, to test the solidity of his work, chinned himself several times. Then he mingled with the others and everyone was delighted to find him so friendly again. In the evening, when the apartment was relatively empty, Jonas got an oil lamp, a chair, a stool, and a frame. He took them all up into the loft before the puzzled gaze of the three women and the children. "Now," he said from his lofty perch, "I'll be able to work without being in anyone's way." Louise asked him if he were sure of it. "Of course," he replied. "I don't need much room. I'll be freer. There have been great painters who painted by candlelight, and . . ." "Is the floor solid enough?" It was. "Don't worry," Jonas said, "it's a very good solution." And he came back down.

Very early the next day he climbed into the loft, sat down, set the frame on the stool against the wall, and waited without lighting the lamp. The only direct sounds he heard came from the kitchen or the toilet. The other noises seemed distant, and the visits, the ringing of the doorbell and the telephone, the comings and goings, the conversations, reached him half muffled, as if they came from out on the street or from the farther court. Besides, although the whole apartment was overflowing with blinding sunlight, the darkness here was restful. From time to time a friend would come and plant himself under the loft. "What are you doing up there, Jonas?" "I'm working." "Without light?" "Yes, for the moment." He was not painting, but he was meditating. In the darkness and this half-silence which, by contrast with what he had known

before, seemed to him the silence of the desert or
of the tomb, he listened to his own heart. The
sounds that reached the loft seemed not to concern him any more, even when addressed to him.
He was like those men who die alone at home in
their sleep, and in the morning the telephone rings,
feverish and insistent, in the deserted house, over
a body forever deaf. But he was alive, he listened
to this silence within himself, he was waiting for
his star, still hidden but ready to rise again, to burst
forth at last, unchanged and unchanging, above the
disorder of these empty days. "Shine, shine," he
said. "Don't deprive me of your light." It would
shine again, of that he was sure. But he would have
to meditate still longer, since at last the chance
was given him to be alone without separating from
his family. He still had to discover what he had
not yet clearly understood, although he had always
known it and had always painted as if he knew it.
He had to grasp at last that secret which was not
merely the secret of art, as he could now see. That
is why he didn't light the lamp.

Every day now Jonas would climb back into
his loft. The visitors became less numerous because
Louise, preoccupied, paid little attention to the conversation. Jonas would come down for meals and

then climb back to his perch. He would sit motionless in the darkness all day long. At night he would go to his wife, who was already in bed. After a few days he asked Louise to hand up his lunch, which she did with such pains that Jonas was stirred. In order not to disturb her on other occasions, he suggested her preparing some supplies that he could store in the loft. Little by little he got to the point of not coming down all day long. But he hardly touched his supplies.

One evening he called Louise and asked for some blankets. "I'll spend the night up here." Louise looked at him with her head bent backward. She opened her mouth and then said nothing. She was merely scrutinizing Jonas with a worried and sad expression. He suddenly saw how much she had aged and how deeply the trials of their life had marked her too. It occurred to him that he had never really helped her. But before he could say a word, she smiled at him with an affection that wrung his heart. "Just as you say, dear," she said.

Henceforth he spent his nights in the loft, almost never coming down any more. As a result, the apartment was emptied of visitors since Jonas couldn't be seen any more either by day or night. Some were told that he was in the country; others, when lying became an effort, that he had found a studio. Rateau alone came faithfully. He would climb up on the ladder until his big, friendly head was just over the level of the flooring. "How goes it?" he would ask. "Wonderfully." "Are you working?" "It comes to the same thing." "But you have no canvas!" "I'm working just the same." It was hard to prolong this dialogue from ladder to loft. Rateau would shake his head, come back down, help Louise replace fuses or repair a lock, then, without climbing onto the ladder, say good night to Jonas, who would reply in the darkness: "So long, old boy." One evening Jonas added thanks to his good-night. "Why thanks?" "Because you love me." "That's really news!" Rateau said as he left.

Another evening Jonas called Rateau, who came running. The lamp was lighted for the first time. Jonas was leaning, with a tense look, out of the loft. "Hand me a canvas," he said. "But what's the matter with you? You're so much thinner; you look like a ghost." "I've hardly eaten for the last two days. But that doesn't matter. I must work." "Eat first." "No, I'm not hungry." Rateau brought a canvas. On the point of disappearing into the loft, Jonas asked him: "How are they?" "Who?"

"Louise and the children." "They're all right. They'd be better if you were with them." "I'm still with them. Tell them above all that I'm still with them." And he disappeared. Rateau came and told Louise how worried he was. She admitted that she herself had been anxious for several days. "What can we do? Oh, if only I could work in his place!" Wretched, she faced Rateau. "I can't live without him," she said. She looked like the girl she had been, and this surprised Rateau. He suddenly realized that she had blushed.

The lamp stayed lighted all night and all the next morning. To those who came, Rateau or Louise, Jonas answered merely: "Forget it, I'm working." At noon he asked for some kerosene. The lamp, which had been smoking, again shone brightly until evening. Rateau stayed to dinner with Louise and the children. At midnight he went to say goodnight to Jonas. Under the still lighted loft he waited a moment, then went away without saying a word. On the morning of the second day, when Louise got up, the lamp was still lighted.

A beautiful day was beginning, but Jonas was not aware of it. He had turned the canvas against the wall. Exhausted, he was sitting there waiting, with his hands, palms up, on his knees. He told himself that now he would never again work, he was happy. He heard his children grumbling, water running, and the dishes clinking together. Louise was talking. The huge windows rattled as a truck passed on the boulevard. The world was still there, young and lovable. Jonas listened to the welcome murmur rising from mankind. From such a distance, it did not run counter to that joyful strength within him, his art, these forever silent thoughts he could not express but which set him above all things, in a free and crisp air. The children were running through the apartment, the little girl was laughing, Louise too now, and he hadn't heard her laugh for so long. He loved them! How he loved them! He put out the lamp and, in the darkness that suddenly returned, right there! wasn't that his star still shining? It was the star, he recognized it with his heart full of gratitude, and he was still watching it when he fell, without a sound.

"It's nothing," the doctor they had called declared a little later. "He is working too much. In a week he will be on his feet again." "You are sure he will get well?" asked Louise with distorted face. "He will get well." In the other room Rateau was looking at the canvas, completely blank, in the center of which Jonas had merely written in very small letters a word that could be made out, but without any certainty as to whether it should be read *solitary* or *solidary*.

THE
GROWING
STONE

T HE AUTOMOBILE swung clumsily around
the curve in the red sandstone trail, now a mass of
mud. The headlights suddenly picked out in the
night—first on one side of the road, then on the
other—two wooden huts with sheet-metal roofs.
On the right near the second one, a tower of coarse
beams could be made out in the light fog. From
the top of the tower a metal cable, invisible at its
starting-point, shone as it sloped down into the light
from the car before disappearing behind the em-

bankment that blocked the road. The car slowed down and stopped a few yards from the huts.

The man who emerged from the seat to the right of the driver labored to extricate himself from the car. As he stood up, his huge, broad frame lurched a little. In the shadow beside the car, solidly planted on the ground and weighed down by fatigue, he seemed to be listening to the idling motor. Then he walked in the direction of the embankment and entered the cone of light from the headlights. He stopped at the top of the slope, his broad back outlined against the darkness. After a moment he turned around. In the light from the dashboard he could see the chauffeur's black face, smiling. The man signaled and the chauffeur turned off the motor. At once a vast cool silence fell over the trail and the forest. Then the sound of the water could be heard.

The man looked at the river below him, visible solely as a broad dark motion, flecked with occasional shimmers. A denser motionless darkness, far beyond, must be the other bank. By looking fixedly, however, one could see on that still bank a yellowish light like an oil lamp in the distance. The big man turned back toward the car and nodded. The chauffeur switched off the lights, turned them on again, then blinked them regularly. On the embankment the man appeared and disappeared, taller and more massive each time he came back to life. Suddenly, on the other bank of the river, a lantern held up by an invisible arm swung back and forth several times. At a final signal from the lookout, the chauffeur turned off his lights once and for all. The car and the man disappeared into the night. With the lights out, the river was almost visible—or at least a few of its long liquid muscles shining intermittently. On each side of the road, the dark masses of forest foliage stood out against the sky and seemed very near. The fine rain that had soaked the trail an hour earlier was still hovering in the warm air, intensifying the silence and immobility of this broad clearing in the virgin forest. In the black sky misty stars flickered.

But from the other bank rose sounds of chains and muffled plashings. Above the hut on the right of the man still waiting there, the cable stretched taut. A dull creaking began to run along it, just as there rose from the river a faint yet quite audible sound of stirred-up water. The creaking became more regular, the sound of water spread farther and then became localized, as the lantern grew larger. Now its yellowish halo could be clearly seen. The halo gradually expanded and again contracted while the lantern shone through the mist and began to light up from beneath a sort of square roof of dried palms supported by thick bamboos. This crude shelter, around which vague shadows were moving, was slowly approaching the bank. When it was about in the middle of the river, three little men, almost black, were distinctly outlined in the yellow light, naked from the waist up and wearing conical hats. They stood still with feet apart, leaning somewhat to offset the strong drift of the river pressing with all its invisible water against the side of a big crude raft that eventually emerged from the darkness. When the ferry came still closer, the man could see behind the shelter on the downstream side two tall Negroes likewise wearing nothing but broad straw hats and cotton trousers. Side by side they weighed with all their might on long poles that sank slowly into the river toward the stern while the Negroes, with the same slow motion, bent over the water as far as their balance would allow. In the bow the three mulattoes, still and silent, watched the bank approach without raising their eyes toward the man waiting for them.

The ferry suddenly bumped against something.

And the lantern swaying from the shock lighted up a pier jutting into the water. The tall Negroes stood still with hands above their heads gripping the ends of the poles, which were barely stuck in the bottom, but their taut muscles rippled constantly with a motion that seemed to come from the very thrust of the water. The other ferrymen looped chains over the posts on the dock, leaped onto the boards, and lowered a sort of gangplank that covered the bow of the raft with its inclined plane.

The man returned to the car and slid in while the chauffeur stepped on the starter. The car slowly climbed the embankment, pointed its hood toward the sky, and then lowered it toward the river as it tackled the downward slope. With brakes on, it rolled forward, slipped somewhat on the mud, stopped, started up again. It rolled onto the pier with a noise of bouncing planks, reached the end, where the mulattoes, still silent, were standing on either side, and plunged slowly toward the raft. The raft ducked its nose in the water as soon as the front wheels struck it and almost immediately bobbed back to receive the car's full weight. Then the chauffeur ran the vehicle to the stern, in front of the square roof where the lantern

was hanging. At once the mulattoes swung the inclined plane back onto the pier and jumped simultaneously onto the ferry, pushing it off from the
muddy bank. The river strained under the raft and
raised it on the surface of the water, where it
drifted slowly at the end of the long drawbar running along the cable overhead. The tall Negroes
relaxed their effort and drew in their poles. The
man and the chauffeur got out of the car and came
over to stand on the edge of the raft facing upstream. No one had spoken during the maneuver,
and even now each remained in his place, motionless and quiet except for one of the tall Negroes
who was rolling a cigarette in coarse paper.

The man was looking at the gap through which
the river sprang from the vast Brazilian forest and
swept down toward them. Several hundred yards
wide at that point, the muddy, silky waters of the
river pressed against the side of the ferry and then,
unimpeded at the two ends of the raft, sheered off
and again spread out in a single powerful flood
gently flowing through the dark forest toward the
sea and the night. A stale smell, come from the water or the spongy sky, hung in the air. Now the
slapping of the water under the ferry could be
heard, and at intervals the calls of bullfrogs from

the two banks or the strange cries of birds. The big man approached the small, thin chauffeur, who was leaning against one of the bamboos with his hands in the pockets of his dungarees, once blue but now covered with the same red dust that had been blowing in their faces all day long. A smile spread over his face, all wrinkled in spite of his youth. Without really seeing them, he was staring at the faint stars still swimming in the damp sky.

But the birds' cries became sharper, unfamiliar chatterings mingled with them, and almost at once the cable began to creak. The tall Negroes plunged their poles into the water and groped blindly for the bottom. The man turned around toward the shore they had just left. Now that shore was obscured by the darkness and the water, vast and savage like the continent of trees stretching beyond it for thousands of kilometers. Between the near-by ocean and this sea of vegetation, the handful of men drifting at that moment on a wild river seemed lost. When the raft bumped the new pier it was as if, having cast off all moorings, they were landing on an island in the darkness after days of frightened sailing.

Once on land, the men's voices were at last heard. The chauffeur had just paid them and, with

voices that sounded strangely gay in the heavy
night, they were saying farewell in Portuguese as
the car started up again.

"They said sixty, the kilometers to Iguape.
Three hours more and it'll be over. Socrates is
happy," the chauffeur announced.

The man laughed with a warm, hearty laugh
that resembled him.

"Me too, Socrates, I'm happy too. The trail is
hard."

"Too heavy, Mr. D'Arrast, you too heavy," and
the chauffeur laughed too as if he would never
stop.

The car had taken on a little speed. It was advancing between high walls of trees and inextrica-
ble vegetation, amidst a soft, sweetish smell. Fire-
flies on the wing constantly crisscrossed in the
darkness of the forest, and every once in a while
red-eyed birds would bump against the windshield.
At times a strange, savage sound would reach them
from the depths of the night and the chauffeur
would roll his eyes comically as he looked at his
passenger.

The road kept turning and crossed little streams
on bridges of wobbly boards. After an hour the
fog began to thicken. A fine drizzle began to fall,

dimming the car's lights. Despite the jolts, D'Arrast was half asleep. He was no longer riding in the damp forest but on the roads of the Serra that they had taken in the morning as they left São Paulo. From those dirt trails constantly rose the red dust which they could still taste, and on both sides, as far as the eye could see, it covered the sparse vegetation of the plains. The harsh sun, the pale mountains full of ravines, the starved zebus encountered along the roads, with a tired flight of ragged urubus as their only escort, the long, endless crossing of an endless desert . . . He gave a start. The car had stopped. Now they were in Japan: fragile houses on both sides of the road and, in the houses, furtive kimonos. The chauffeur was talking to a Japanese wearing soiled dungarees and a Brazilian straw hat. Then the car started up again.

"He said only forty kilometers."

"Where were we? In Tokyo?"

"No. Registro. In Brazil all the Japanese come here."

"Why?"

"Don't know. They're yellow, you know, Mr. D'Arrast."

But the forest was gradually thinning out, and the road was becoming easier, though slippery.

The car was skidding on sand. The window let in a warm, damp breeze that was rather sour.

"You smell it?" the chauffeur asked, smacking his lips. "That's the good old sea. Soon, Iguape."

"If we have enough gas," D'Arrast said. And he went back to sleep peacefully.

Sitting up in bed early in the morning, D'Arrast looked in amazement at the huge room in which he had just awakened. The lower half of the big walls was newly painted brown. Higher up, they had once been painted white, and patches of yellowish paint covered them up to the ceiling. Two rows of beds faced each other. D'Arrast saw only one bed unmade at the end of his row and that bed was empty. But he heard a noise on his left and turned toward the door, where Socrates, a bottle of mineral water in each hand, stood laughing, "Happy memory!" he said. D'Arrast shook himself. Yes, the hospital in which the Mayor had lodged them the night before was named "Happy Memory." "Sure memory," Socrates continued. "They told me first build hospital, later build water. Meanwhile, happy memory, take fizz water to wash." He disappeared, laughing and singing, not at all exhausted apparently by the cataclysmic

sneezes that had shaken him all night long and kept
D'Arrast from closing an eye.

Now D'Arrast was completely awake. Through
the iron-latticed window he could see a little red-
earth courtyard soaked by the rain that was noiselessly pouring down on a clump of tall aloes. A
woman passed holding a yellow scarf over her
head. D'Arrast lay back in bed, then sat up at once
and got out of the bed, which creaked under his
weight. Socrates came in at that moment: "For
you, Mr. D'Arrast. The Mayor is waiting outside."
But, seeing the look on D'Arrast's face, he added:
"Don't worry; he never in a hurry."

After shaving with the mineral water, D'Arrast
went out under the portico of the building. The
Mayor—who had the proportions and, under his
gold-rimmed glasses, the look of a nice little weasel
—seemed lost in dull contemplation of the rain.
But a charming smile transfigured him as soon as
he saw D'Arrast. Holding his little body erect, he
rushed up and tried to stretch his arms around the
engineer. At that moment an automobile drove up
in front of them on the other side of the low wall,
skidded in the wet clay, and came to a stop on an
angle. "The Judge!" said the Mayor. Like the
Mayor, the Judge was dressed in navy blue. But he

was much younger, or at least seemed so because of his elegant figure and his look of a startled adolescent. Now he was crossing the courtyard in their direction, gracefully avoiding the puddles. A few steps from D'Arrast, he was already holding out his arms and welcoming him. He was proud to greet the noble engineer who was honoring their poor village; he was delighted by the priceless service the noble engineer was going to do Iguape by building that little jetty to prevent the periodic flooding of the lower quarters of town. What a noble profession, to command the waters and dominate rivers! Ah, surely the poor people of Iguape would long remember the noble engineer's name and many years from now would still mention it in their prayers. D'Arrast, captivated by such charm and eloquence, thanked him and didn't dare wonder what possible connection a judge could have with a jetty. Besides, according to the Mayor, it was time to go to the club, where the leading citizens wanted to receive the noble engineer appropriately before going to inspect the poorer quarters. Who were the leading citizens?

"Well," the Mayor said, "myself as Mayor, Mr. Carvalho here, the Harbor Captain, and a few others less important. Besides, you won't have to pay much attention to them, for they don't speak French."

D'Arrast called Socrates and told him he would meet him when the morning was over.

"All right," Socrates said, "I'll go to the Garden of the Fountain."

"The Garden?"

"Yes, everybody knows. Have no fear, Mr. D'Arrast."

The hospital, D'Arrast noticed as he left it, was built on the edge of the forest, and the heavy foliage almost hung over the roofs. Over the whole surface of the trees was falling a sheet of fine rain which the dense forest was noiselessly absorbing like a huge sponge. The town, some hundred houses roofed with faded tiles, extended between the forest and the river, and the water's distant murmur reached the hospital. The car entered drenched streets and almost at once came out on a rather large rectangular square which showed, among numerous puddles in its red clay, the marks of tires, iron wheels, and horseshoes. All around, brightly plastered low houses closed off the square, behind which could be seen the two round towers of a blue-and-white church of colonial style. A smell of salt water coming from the estuary dominated this bare setting. In the center of the square a few wet silhouettes were wandering. Along the houses a motley crowd of gauchos, Japanese, half-breed Indians, and elegant leading citizens, whose dark suits looked exotic here, were sauntering with slow gestures. They stepped aside with dignity to make way for the car, then stopped and watched it. When the car stopped in front of one of the houses on the square, a circle of wet gauchos silently formed around it.

At the club—a sort of small bar on the second floor furnished with a bamboo counter and iron café tables—the leading citizens were numerous. Sugar-cane alcohol was drunk in honor of D'Arrast after the Mayor, glass in hand, had wished him welcome and all the happiness in the world. But while D'Arrast was drinking near the window, a huge lout of a fellow in riding-breeches and leggings came over and, staggering somewhat, delivered himself of a rapid and obscure speech in which the engineer recognized solely the word "passport." He hesitated and then took out the document, which the fellow seized greedily. After having thumbed through the passport, he manifested obvious displeasure. He resumed his speech, shaking the document under the nose of the engineer, who, without getting excited, merely looked at the angry man. Whereupon the Judge, with a smile, came over and asked what was the matter. For a moment the drunk scrutinized the frail creature who dared to interrupt him and then, staggering even more dangerously, shook the passport in the face of his new interlocutor. D'Arrast sat peacefully beside a café table and waited. The dialogue became very lively, and suddenly the Judge broke out in a deafening voice that one would never have suspected in him. Without any forewarning, the lout suddenly backed down like a child caught in the act. At a final order from the Judge, he sidled toward the door like a punished schoolboy and disappeared.

The Judge immediately came over to explain to D'Arrast, in a voice that had become harmonious again, that the uncouth individual who had just left was the Chief of Police, that he had dared to claim the passport was not in order, and that he would be punished for his outburst. Judge Carvalho then addressed himself to the leading citizens, who stood in a circle around him, and seemed to be questioning them. After a brief discussion, the Judge expressed solemn excuses to D'Arrast, asked him to agree that nothing but drunkenness could explain such forgetfulness of the sentiments of respect and gratitude that the whole town of Iguape owed him, and, finally, asked him to decide himself on the punishment to be inflicted on the wretched individual. D'Arrast said that he didn't want any punishment, that it was a trivial incident, and that he was particularly eager to go to the river. Then the Mayor spoke up to assert with much simple good-humor that a punishment was really mandatory, that the guilty man would remain incarcerated, and that they would all wait until their distinguished visitor decided on his fate. No protest could soften that smiling severity, and D'Arrast had to promise that he would think the matter over. Then they agreed to visit the poorer quarters of the town.

The river was already spreading its yellowish waters over the low, slippery banks. They had left behind them the last houses of Iguape and stood between the river and a high, steep embankment to which clung huts made of clay and branches. In front of them, at the end of the embankment, the forest began again abruptly, as on the other bank. But the gap made by the water rapidly widened between the trees until reaching a vague grayish line that marked the beginning of the sea. Without saying a word, D'Arrast walked toward the slope, where the various flood levels had left marks that were still fresh. A muddy path climbed toward the huts. In front of them, Negroes stood silently staring at the newcomers. Several couples were holding hands, and on the edge of the mound, in front of the adults, a row of black children with bulging bellies and spindly legs were gaping with round eyes.

When he arrived in front of the huts, D'Arrast beckoned to the Harbor Captain. He was a fat, laughing Negro wearing a white uniform. D'Arrast asked him in Spanish if it were possible to visit a hut. The Captain was sure it was, he even thought it a good idea, and the noble engineer would see very interesting things. He harangued the Negroes at length, pointing to D'Arrast and to the river. They listened without saying a word. When the Captain had finished, no one stirred. He spoke again, in an impatient voice. Then he called upon one of the men, who shook his head. Whereupon the Captain said a few brief words in a tone of command. The man stepped forth from the group, faced D'Arrast, and with a gesture showed him the way. But his look was hostile. He was an elderly man with short, graying hair and a thin, wizened face; yet his body was still young, with hard wiry shoulders and muscles visible through his cotton pants and torn shirt. They went ahead, followed by the Captain and the crowd of Negroes, and climbed a new, steeper embankment where the huts made of clay, tin, and reeds clung to the ground with such difficulty that they had to be strengthened at the base with heavy stones. They met a woman going down the path, sometimes slipping in her bare feet, who was carrying on her head an iron drum full of water. Then they reached a small irregular square bordered by three huts. The man walked toward one of them and pushed open a bamboo door on hinges made of tropical liana. He stood aside without saying a word, staring at the engineer with the same impassive look. In the hut, D'Arrast saw nothing at first but a dying fire built right on the ground in the exact center of the room. Then in a back corner he made out a brass bed with a bare, broken mattress, a table in the other corner covered with earthenware dishes, and, between the two, a sort of stand supporting a color print representing Saint George. Nothing else but a pile of rags to the right of the entrance and, hanging from the ceiling, a few loincloths of various colors drying over the fire. Standing still, D'Arrast breathed in the smell of smoke and poverty that rose from the ground and choked him. Behind him, the Captain clapped his hands. The engineer turned around and, against the light, saw the graceful silhouette of a black girl approach and hold out something to him. He took a glass and drank the thick sugar-cane alcohol. The girl held out her tray to receive the empty glass and went out with such a supple motion that D'Arrast suddenly wanted to hold her back.

But on following her out he didn't recognize her in the crowd of Negroes and leading citizens gathered around the hut. He thanked the old man, who bowed without a word. Then he left. The Captain, behind him, resumed his explanations and asked when the French company from Rio could begin work and whether or not the jetty could be built before the rainy season. D'Arrast didn't know; to tell the truth, he wasn't thinking of that. He went down toward the cool river under the fine mist. He was still listening to that great pervasive sound he had been hearing continually since his arrival, which might have been made by the rustling of either the water or the trees, he could not tell. Having reached the bank, he looked out in the distance at the vague line of the sea, the thousands of kilometers of solitary waters leading to Africa and, beyond, his native Europe.

"Captain," he asked, "what do these people we have just seen live on?"

"They work when they're needed," the Captain said. "We are poor."

"Are they the poorest?"

"They are the poorest."

The Judge, who arrived at that moment, slipping somewhat in his best shoes, said they already loved the noble engineer who was going to give them work.

"And, you know, they dance and sing every day."

Then, without transition, he asked D'Arrast if he had thought of the punishment.

"What punishment?"

"Why, our Chief of Police."

"Let him go." The Judge said that this was not possible; there had to be a punishment. D'Arrast was already walking toward Iguape.

In the little Garden of the Fountain, mysterious and pleasant under the fine rain, clusters of exotic flowers hung down along the lianas among the banana trees and pandanus. Piles of wet stones marked the intersection of paths on which a motley crowd was strolling. Half-breeds, mulattoes, a few gauchos were chatting in low voices or sauntering along the bamboo paths to the point where groves and bush became thicker and more impenetrable. There, the forest began abruptly.

D'Arrast was looking for Socrates in the crowd when Socrates suddenly bumped him from behind.

"It's holiday," he said, laughing, and clung to D'Arrast's tall shoulders to jump up and down.

"What holiday?"

"Why, you not know?" Socrates said in surprise as he faced D'Arrast. "The feast of good Jesus. Each year they all come to the grotto with a hammer."

Socrates pointed out, not a grotto, but a group that seemed to be waiting in a corner of the garden.

"You see? One day the good statue of Jesus, it came upstream from the sea. Some fishermen found it. How beautiful! How beautiful! Then they washed it here in the grotto. And now a stone grew up in the grotto. Every year it's the feast. With the hammer you break, you break off pieces for blessed happiness. And then it keeps growing and you keep breaking. It's the miracle!"

They had reached the grotto and could see its low entrance beyond the waiting men. Inside, in the darkness studded with the flickering flames of candles, a squatting figure was pounding with a hammer. The man, a thin gaucho with a long mustache, got up and came out holding in his open palm, so that all might see, a small piece of moist schist, over which he soon closed his hand carefully before going away. Another man then stooped down and entered the grotto.

D'Arrast turned around. On all sides pilgrims were waiting, without looking at him, impassive under the water dripping from the trees in thin sheets. He too was waiting in front of the grotto under the same film of water, and he didn't know for what. He had been waiting constantly, to tell the truth, for a month since he had arrived in this country. He had been waiting—in the red heat of humid days, under the little stars of night, despite the tasks to be accomplished, the jetties to be built, the roads to be cut through—as if the work he had come to do here were merely a pretext for a surprise or for an encounter he did not even imagine but which had been waiting patiently for him at the end of the world. He shook himself, walked away without anyone in the little group paying attention to him, and went toward the exit. He had to go back to the river and go to work.

But Socrates was waiting for him at the gate, lost in voluble conversation with a short, fat, strapping man whose skin was yellow rather than black. His head, completely shaved, gave even more sweep to a considerable forehead. On the other hand, his broad, smooth face was adorned with a very black beard, trimmed square.

"He's champion!" Socrates said by way of introduction. "Tomorrow he's in the procession."

The man, wearing a sailor's outfit of heavy serge, a blue-and-white jersey under the pea jacket, was examining D'Arrast attentively with his calm black eyes. At the same time he was smiling, showing all his very white teeth between his full, shiny lips.

"He speaks Spanish," Socrates said and, turning toward the stranger, added: "Tell Mr. D'Arrast." Then he danced off toward another group. The man ceased to smile and looked at D'Arrast with outright curiosity.

"You are interested, Captain?"

"I'm not a captain," D'Arrast said.

"That doesn't matter. But you're a noble. Socrates told me."

"Not I. But my grandfather was. His father too and all those before his father. Now there is no more nobility in our country."

"Ah!" the Negro said, laughing. "I understand; everybody is a noble."

"No, that's not it. There are neither noblemen nor common people."

The fellow reflected; then he made up his mind.

"No one works? No one suffers?"

"Yes, millions of men."

"Then that's the common people."

"In that way, yes, there is a common people. But the masters are policemen or merchants."

The mulatto's kindly face closed in a frown. Then he grumbled: "Humph! Buying and selling, eh! What filth! And with the police, dogs command."

Suddenly, he burst out laughing.

"You, you don't sell?"

"Hardly at all. I make bridges, roads."

"That's good. Me, I'm a ship's cook. If you wish, I'll make you our dish of black beans."

"All right."

330

The cook came closer to D'Arrast and took his arm.

"Listen, I like what you tell. I'm going to tell you too. Maybe you will like."

He drew him over near the gate to a damp wooden bench beneath a clump of bamboos.

"I was at sea, off Iguape, on a small coastwise tanker that supplies the harbors along here. It caught fire on board. Not by my fault! I know my job! No, just bad luck. We were able to launch the lifeboats. During the night, the sea got rough; it capsized the boat and I went down. When I came up, I hit the boat with my head. I drifted. The night was dark, the waters are vast, and, besides, I don't swim well; I was afraid. Just then I saw a light in the distance and recognized the church of the good Jesus in Iguape. So I told the good Jesus that at his procession I would carry a hundred-pound stone on my head if he saved me. You don't have to believe me, but the waters became calm and my heart too. I swam slowly, I was happy, and I reached the shore. Tomorrow I'll keep my promise."

He looked at D'Arrast in a suddenly suspicious manner.

331

"You're not laughing?"

"No, I'm not laughing. A man has to do what he has promised."

The fellow clapped him on the back.

"Now, come to my brother's, near the river. I'll cook you some beans."

"No," D'Arrast said, "I have things to do. This evening, if you wish."

"Good. But tonight there's dancing and praying in the big hut. It's the feast for Saint George." D'Arrast asked him if he danced too. The cook's face hardened suddenly; for the first time his eyes became shifty.

"No, no, I won't dance. Tomorrow I must carry the stone. It is heavy. I'll go this evening to celebrate the saint. And then I'll leave early."

"Does it last long?"

"All night and a little into the morning."

He looked at D'Arrast with a vaguely shameful look.

"Come to the dance. You can take me home afterward. Otherwise, I'll stay and dance. I probably won't be able to keep from it."

"You like to dance?"

"Oh, yes! I like. Besides, there are cigars, saints,

women. You forget everything and you don't obey
any more."

"There are women too? All the women of the
town?"

"Not of the town, but of the huts."

The ship's cook resumed his smile. "Come. The
Captain I'll obey. And you will help me keep my
promise tomorrow."

D'Arrast felt slightly annoyed. What did that
absurd promise mean to him? But he looked at the
handsome frank face smiling trustingly at him, its
dark skin gleaming with health and vitality.

"I'll come," he said. "Now I'll walk along with
you a little."

Without knowing why, he had a vision at the
same time of the black girl offering him the drink
of welcome.

They went out of the garden, walked along several muddy streets, and reached the bumpy square,
which looked even larger because of the low
structures surrounding it. The humidity was now
dripping down the plastered walls, although the
rain had not increased. Through the spongy expanse of the sky, the sound of the river and of the
trees reached them somewhat muted. They were

walking in step, D'Arrast heavily and the cook with elastic tread. From time to time the latter would raise his head and smile at his companion. They went in the direction of the church, which could be seen above the houses, reached the end of the square, walked along other muddy streets now filled with aggressive smells of cooking. From time to time a woman, holding a plate or kitchen utensil, would peer out inquisitively from one of the doors and then disappear at once. They passed in front of the church, plunged into an old section of similar low houses, and suddenly came out on the sound of the invisible river behind the area of the huts that D'Arrast recognized.

"Good. I'll leave you. See you this evening," he said.

"Yes, in front of the church."

But the cook did not let go of D'Arrast's hand. He hesitated. Finally he made up his mind.

"And you, have you never called out, made a promise?"

"Yes, once, I believe."

"In a shipwreck?"

"If you wish." And D'Arrast pulled his hand away roughly. But as he was about to turn on his

334

heels, he met the cook's eyes. He hesitated, and then smiled.

"I can tell you, although it was unimportant. Someone was about to die through my fault. It seems to me that I called out."

"Did you promise?"

"No. I should have liked to promise."

"Long ago?"

"Not long before coming here."

The cook seized his beard with both hands. His eyes were shining.

"You are a captain," he said. "My house is yours. Besides, you are going to help me keep my promise, and it's as if you had made it yourself. That will help you too."

D'Arrast smiled, saying: "I don't think so."

"You are proud, Captain."

"I used to be proud; now I'm alone. But just tell me: has your good Jesus always answered you?"

"Always . . . no, Captain!"

"Well, then?"

The cook burst out with a gay, childlike laugh.

"Well," he said, "he's free, isn't he?"

At the club, where D'Arrast lunched with the leading citizens, the Mayor told him he must sign

the town's guest-book so that some trace would
remain of the great event of his coming to Iguape.
The Judge found two or three new expressions to
praise, besides their guest's virtues and talents, the
simplicity with which he represented among them
the great country to which he had the honor to belong. D'Arrast simply said that it was indeed an
honor to him and an advantage to his firm to have
been awarded the allocation of this long construction job. Whereupon the Judge expressed his admiration for such humility. "By the way," he
asked, "have you thought of what should be done
to the Chief of Police?" D'Arrast smiled at him
and said: "Yes, I have a solution." He would consider it a personal favor and an exceptional grace
if the foolish man could be forgiven in his name so
that his stay here in Iguape, where he so much enjoyed knowing the beautiful town and generous
inhabitants, could begin in a climate of peace and
friendship. The Judge, attentive and smiling,
nodded his head. For a moment he meditated on
the wording as an expert, then called on those present to applaud the magnanimous traditions of the
great French nation and, turning again toward
D'Arrast, declared himself satisfied. "Since that's
the way it is," he concluded, "we shall dine this

evening with the Chief." But D'Arrast said that he was invited by friends to the ceremony of the dances in the huts. "Ah, yes!" said the Judge. "I am glad you are going. You'll see, one can't resist loving our people."

That evening, D'Arrast, the ship's cook, and his brother were seated around the ashes of a fire in the center of the hut the engineer had already visited in the morning. The brother had not seemed surprised to see him return. He spoke Spanish hardly at all and most of the time merely nodded his head. As for the cook, he had shown interest in cathedrals and then had expatiated at length on the black bean soup. Now night had almost fallen and, although D'Arrast could still see the cook and his brother, he could scarcely make out in the back of the hut the squatting figures of an old woman and of the same girl who had served him. Down below, he could hear the monotonous river.

The cook rose, saying: "It's time." They got up, but the women did not stir. The men went out alone. D'Arrast hesitated, then joined the others. Night had now fallen and the rain had stopped. The pale-black sky still seemed liquid. In its transparent dark water, stars began to light up, low on the horizon. Almost at once they flickered out, falling one by one into the river as if the last lights were trickling from the sky. The heavy air smelled of water and smoke. Near by the sound of the huge forest could be heard too, though it was motionless. Suddenly drums and singing broke out in the distance, at first muffled and then distinct, approaching closer and closer and finally stopping. Soon after, one could see a procession of black girls wearing low-waisted white dresses of coarse silk. In a tight-fitting red jacket adorned with a necklace of varicolored teeth, a tall Negro followed them and, behind him, a disorderly crowd of men in white pajamas and musicians carrying triangles and broad, short drums. The cook said they should follow the men.

The hut, which they reached by following the river a few hundred yards beyond the last huts, was large, empty, and relatively comfortable, with plastered walls. It had a dirt floor, a roof of thatch and reeds supported by a central pole, and bare walls. On a little palm-clad altar at the end, covered with candles that scarcely lighted half the hall, there was a magnificent colored print in which Saint George, with alluring grace, was getting the better of a bewhiskered dragon. Under the altar a sort of niche decorated with rococo paper sheltered a little statue of red-painted clay representing a horned god, standing between a candle and a bowl of water. With a fierce look the god was brandishing an oversized knife made of silver paper.

The cook led D'Arrast to a corner, where they stood against the wall near the door. "This way," he whispered, "we can leave without disturbing." Indeed, the hut was packed tight with men and women. Already the heat was rising. The musicians took their places on both sides of the little altar. The men and women dancers separated into two concentric circles with the men inside. In the very center the black leader in the red jacket took his stand. D'Arrast leaned against the wall, folding his arms.

But the leader, elbowing his way through the circle of dancers, came toward them and, in a solemn way, said a few words to the cook. "Unfold your arms, Captain," the cook said. "You are hugging yourself and keeping the saint's spirit from descending." Obediently D'Arrast let his arms fall to his sides. Still leaning against the wall, with his long, heavy limbs and his big face already shiny with sweat, D'Arrast himself looked like some bestial and kindly god. The tall Negro looked at them and, satisfied, went back to his place. At once, in a resounding voice, he intoned the opening notes of a song that all picked up in chorus, accompanied by the drums. Then the circles began to turn in opposite directions in a sort of heavy, insistent dance rather like stamping, slightly emphasized by the double line of swaying hips.

The heat had increased. Yet the pauses gradually diminished, the stops became less frequent, and the dance speeded up. Without any slowing of the others' rhythm, without ceasing to dance himself, the tall Negro again elbowed his way through the circles to go toward the altar. He came back with a glass of water and a lighted candle that he stuck in the ground in the center of the hut. He poured the water around the candle in two concentric circles and, again erect, turned maddened eyes toward the roof. His whole body taut and still, he was waiting. "Saint George is coming. Look! Look!" whispered the cook, whose eyes were popping.

Indeed, some dancers now showed signs of being in a trance, but a rigid trance with hands on hips, step stiff, eyes staring and vacant. Others quickened their rhythm, bent convulsively backward, and began to utter inarticulate cries. The cries gradually rose higher, and when they fused in a collective shriek, the leader, with eyes still raised, uttered a long, barely phrased outcry at the top of his lungs. In it the same words kept recurring. "You see," said the cook, "he says he is the god's field of battle." Struck by the change in his voice, D'Arrast looked at the cook, who, leaning forward with fists clenched and eyes staring, was mimicking the others' measured stamping without moving from his place. Then he noticed that he himself, though without moving his feet, had for some little time been dancing with his whole weight.

But all at once the drums began to beat violently and suddenly the big devil in red broke loose. His eyes flashing, his four limbs whirling around him, he hopped with bent knee on one leg after the other, speeding up his rhythm until it seemed that he must eventually fly to pieces. But abruptly he stopped on the verge of one leap to stare at those around him with a proud and terrible look while the drums thundered on. Immediately a dancer sprang from a dark corner, knelt down, and held out a short saber to the man possessed of the spirit. The tall Negro took the saber without ceasing to look around him and then whirled it above his head. At that moment D'Arrast noticed the cook dancing among the others. The engineer had not seen him leave his side.

In the reddish, uncertain light a stifling dust rose from the ground, making the air even thicker and sticking to one's skin. D'Arrast felt gradually overcome by fatigue and breathed with ever greater difficulty. He did not even see how the dancers had got hold of the huge cigars they were now smoking while still dancing; their strange smell filled the hut and rather made his head swim. He merely saw the cook passing near him, still dancing and puffing on a cigar. "Don't smoke," he said. The cook grunted without losing the beat, staring at the central pole with the expression of a boxer about to collapse, his spine constantly twitching in a long shudder. Beside him a heavy Negress, rolling her animal face from side to side, kept barking. But the young Negresses especially went into the most frightful trance, their feet glued to the floor and their bodies shaken from feet to head by convulsive motions that became more violent upon reaching the shoulders. Their heads would wag backward and forward, literally separated from a decapitated body. At the same time all began to howl incessantly with a long collective and toneless howl, apparently not pausing to breathe or to introduce modulations—as if the bodies were tightly knotted, muscles and nerves, in a single exhausting outburst, at last giving voice in each of them to a creature that had until then been absolutely silent. And, still howling, the women began to fall one by one. The black leader knelt by each one and quickly and convulsively pressed her temples with his huge, black-muscled hand. Then they would get up, staggering, return to the dance, and resume their howls, at first feebly and then louder and faster, before falling again, and getting up again, and beginning over again, and for a long time more, until the general howl decreased, changed, and degenerated into a sort of coarse barking which shook them with gasps. D'Arrast, exhausted, his muscles taut from his long dance as he stood still, choked by his own silence, felt himself stagger. The heat, the dust, the smoke of the cigars, the smell of bodies now made the air almost unbreathable. He looked for the cook, who had disappeared. D'Arrast let himself slide down along the wall and squatted, holding back his nausea.

When he opened his eyes, the air was still as stifling but the noise had stopped. The drums alone were beating out a figured bass, and groups in every corner of the hut, covered with whitish cloths, were marking time by stamping. But in the center of the room, from which the glass and candle had now been removed, a group of black girls in a semi-hypnotic state were dancing slowly, always on the point of letting the beat get ahead of them. Their eyes closed and yet standing erect, they were swaying lightly on their toes, almost in the same spot. Two of them, fat ones, had their faces covered with a curtain of raffia. They surrounded another girl, tall, thin, and wearing a fancy costume. D'Arrast suddenly recognized her as the daughter of his host. In a green dress and a huntress's hat of blue gauze turned up in front and adorned with plumes, she held in her hand a green-and-yellow bow with an arrow on the tip of which was spitted a multicolored bird. On her slim body her pretty head swayed slowly, tipped backward a little, and her sleeping face reflected an innocent melancholy. At the pauses in the music she staggered as if only half awake. Yet the intensified beat of the drums provided her with a sort of invisible support around which to entwine her languid arabesques until, stopping again together with the music, tottering on the edge of equilibrium, she uttered a strange bird cry, shrill and yet melodious.

344

D'Arrast, bewitched by the slow dance, was watching the black Diana when the cook suddenly loomed up before him, his smooth face now distorted. The kindness had disappeared from his eyes, revealing nothing but a sort of unsuspected avidity. Coldly, as if speaking to a stranger, he said: "It's late, Captain. They are going to dance all night long, but they don't want you to stay now." With head heavy, D'Arrast got up and followed the cook, who went along the wall toward the door. On the threshold the cook stood aside, holding the bamboo door, and D'Arrast went out. He turned back and looked at the cook, who had not moved. "Come. In a little while you'll have to carry the stone."

"I'm staying," the cook said with a set expression.

"And your promise?"

Without replying, the cook gradually pushed against the door that D'Arrast was holding open with one hand. They remained this way for a second until D'Arrast gave in, shrugging his shoulders. He went away.

The night was full of fresh aromatic scents. Above the forest the few stars in the austral sky, blurred by an invisible haze, were shining dimly.

The humid air was heavy. Yet it seemed delightfully cool on coming out of the hut. D'Arrast climbed the slippery slope, staggering like a drunken man in the potholes. The forest, near by, rumbled slightly. The sound of the river increased. The whole continent was emerging from the night, and loathing overcame D'Arrast. It seemed to him that he would have liked to spew forth this whole country, the melancholy of its vast expanses, the glaucous light of its forests, and the nocturnal lapping of its big deserted rivers. This land was too vast, blood and seasons mingled here, and time liquefied. Life here was flush with the soil, and, to identify with it, one had to lie down and sleep for years on the muddy or dried-up ground itself. Yonder, in Europe, there was shame and wrath. Here, exile or solitude, among these listless and convulsive madmen who danced to die. But through the humid night, heavy with vegetable scents, the wounded bird's outlandish cry, uttered by the beautiful sleeping girl, still reached his ears.

When D'Arrast, his head in the vise of a crushing migraine, had awakened after a bad sleep, a humid heat was weighing upon the town and the still forest. He was waiting now under the hospital

346

portico, looking at his watch, which had stopped, uncertain of the time, surprised by the broad daylight and the silence of the town. The almost clear blue sky hung low over the first dull roofs. Yellowish urubus, transfixed by the heat, were sleeping on the house across from the hospital. One of them suddenly fluttered, opened his beak, ostensibly got ready to fly away, flapped his dusty wings twice against his body, rose a few inches above the roof, fell back, and went to sleep almost at once.

The engineer went down toward the town. The main square was empty, like the streets through which he had just walked. In the distance, and on both sides of the river, a low mist hung over the forest. The heat fell vertically, and D'Arrast looked for a shady spot. At that moment, under the overhang on one of the houses, he saw a little man gesturing to him. As he came closer, he recognized Socrates.

"Well, Mr. D'Arrast, you like the ceremony?"

D'Arrast said that it was too hot in the hut and that he preferred the sky and the night air.

"Yes," Socrates said, "in your country there's only the Mass. No one dances." He rubbed his hands, jumped on one foot, whirled about, laughed uproariously. "Not possible, they're not possible."

Then he looked at D'Arrast inquisitively. "And you, are you going to Mass?"

"No."

"Then, where are you going?"

"Nowhere. I don't know."

Socrates laughed again. "Not possible! A noble without a church, without anything!"

D'Arrast laughed likewise. "Yes, you see, I never found my place. So I left."

"Stay with us, Mr. D'Arrast, I love you."

"I'd like to, Socrates, but I don't know how to dance." Their laughter echoed in the silence of the empty town.

"Ah," Socrates said, "I forget. The Mayor wants to see you. He is lunching at the club." And without warning he started off in the direction of the hospital.

"Where are you going?" D'Arrast shouted.

Socrates imitated a snore. "Sleep. Soon the procession." And, half running, he resumed his snores.

The Mayor simply wanted to give D'Arrast a place of honor to see the procession. He explained it to the engineer while sharing with him a dish of meat and rice such as would miraculously cure a paralytic. First they would take their places on a balcony of the Judge's house, opposite the church, to see the procession come out. Then they would go to the town hall in the main street leading to the church, which the penitents would take on their way back. The Judge and the Chief of Police would accompany D'Arrast, the Mayor being obliged to take part in the ceremony. The Chief of Police was in fact in the clubroom and kept paying court to D'Arrast with an indefatigable smile, lavishing upon him incomprehensible but obviously well-meaning speeches. When D'Arrast left, the Chief of Police hastened to make a way for him, holding all the doors open before him.

Under the burning sun, in the still empty town, the two men walked toward the Judge's house. Their steps were the only sound heard in the silence. But all of a sudden a firecracker exploded in a neighboring street and flushed on every roof the heavy, awkward flocks of bald-necked urubus. Almost at once dozens of firecrackers went off in all directions, doors opened, and people began to emerge from the houses and fill the narrow streets.

The Judge told D'Arrast how proud he was to receive him in his unworthy house and led him up a handsome baroque staircase painted chalky blue. On the landing, as D'Arrast passed, doors opened and children's dark heads popped out and disappeared at once with smothered laughter. The main room, beautiful in architecture, contained nothing but rattan furniture and large cages filled with squawking birds. The balcony on which the Judge and D'Arrast settled overlooked the little square in front of the church. The crowd was now beginning to fill it, strangely silent, motionless under the heat that came down from the sky in almost visible waves. Only the children ran around the square, stopping abruptly to light firecrackers, and sharp reports followed one another in rapid succession. Seen from the balcony, the church with its plaster walls, its dozen blue steps, its blue-and-gold towers, looked smaller.

Suddenly the organ burst forth within the church. The crowd, turned toward the portico, drew over to the sides of the square. The men took off their hats and the women knelt down. The distant organ played at length something like marches. Then an odd sound of wings came from the forest. A tiny airplane with transparent wings and frail fuselage, out of place in this ageless world, came in sight over the trees, swooped a little above the square, and, with the clacking of a big rattle, passed over the heads raised toward it. Then the plane turned and disappeared in the direction of the estuary.

But in the shadow of the church a vague bustle again attracted attention. The organ had stopped, replaced now by brasses and drums, invisible under the portico. Black-surpliced penitents came out of the church one by one, formed groups outside the doors, and began to descend the steps. Behind them came white penitents bearing red-and-blue banners, then a little group of boys dressed up as angels, sodalities of Children of Mary with little black and serious faces. Finally, on a multicolored shrine borne by leading citizens sweating in their dark suits, came the effigy of the good Jesus himself, a reed in his hand and his head crowned with thorns, bleeding and tottering above the crowd that lined the steps.

When the shrine reached the bottom of the steps, there was a pause during which the penitents tried to line up in a semblance of order. Then it was that D'Arrast saw the ship's cook. Bare from the waist up, he had just come out under the portico carrying on his bearded head an enormous rectangular block set on a cork mat. With steady tread he came down the church steps, the stone perfectly balanced in the arch formed by his short, muscular arms. As soon as he fell in behind the shrine, the procession moved. From the portico burst the musicians, wearing bright-colored coats and blowing into beribboned brasses. To the beat of a quick march, the penitents hastened their step and reached one of the streets opening off the square. When the shrine had disappeared behind them, nothing could be seen but the cook and the last of the musicians. Behind them, the crowd got in motion amidst exploding firecrackers, while the plane, with a great rattle of its engine, flew back over the groups trailing behind. D'Arrast was looking exclusively at the cook, who was disappearing into the street now and whose shoulders he suddenly thought he saw sag. But at that distance he couldn't see well.

Through the empty streets, between closed shops and bolted doors, the Judge, the Chief of Police, and D'Arrast reached the town hall. As they got away from the band and the firecrackers, silence again enveloped the town and already a few urubus returned to the places on the roofs that they seemed to have occupied for all time. The town hall stood in a long, narrow street leading from one of the outlying sections to the church square.

For the moment, the street was empty. From the balcony could be seen, as far as the eye could reach, nothing but a pavement full of potholes, in which the recent rain had left puddles. The sun, now slightly lower, was still nibbling at the windowless façades of the houses across the street.

They waited a long time, so long that D'Arrast, from staring at the reverberation of the sun on the opposite wall, felt his fatigue and dizziness returning. The empty street with its deserted houses attracted and repelled him at one and the same time. Once again he wanted to get away from this country; at the same time he thought of that huge stone; he would have liked that trial to be over. He was about to suggest going down to find out something when the church bells began to peal forth loudly. Simultaneously, from the other end of the street on their left, a clamor burst out and a seething crowd appeared. From a distance the people could be seen swarming around the shrine, pilgrims and penitents mingled, and they were advancing, amidst firecrackers and shouts of joy, along the narrow street. In a few seconds they filled it to the edges, advancing toward the town hall in an indescribable disorder—ages, races, and costumes fused in a motley mass full of gaping eyes and yelling mouths. From the crowd emerged an army of tapers like lances with flames fading into the burning sunlight. But when they were close and the crowd was so thick under the balcony that it seemed to rise up along the walls, D'Arrast saw that the ship's cook was not there.

Quick as lightning, without excusing himself, he left the balcony and the room, dashed down the staircase, and stood in the street under the deafening sound of the bells and firecrackers. There he had to struggle against the crowd of merrymakers, the taper-bearers, the shocked penitents. But, bucking the human tide with all his weight, he cut a path in such an impetuous way that he staggered and almost fell when he was eventually free, beyond the crowd, at the end of the street. Leaning against the burning-hot wall, he waited until he had caught his breath. Then he resumed his way. At that moment a group of men emerged into the street. The ones in front were walking backward, and D'Arrast saw that they surrounded the cook.

He was obviously dead tired. He would stop, then, bent under the huge stone, run a little with the hasty step of stevedores and coolies—the rapid, flat-footed trot of drudgery. Gathered about him, penitents in surplices soiled with dust and candle-drippings encouraged him when he stopped. On his left his brother was walking or running in silence. It seemed to D'Arrast that they took an interminable time to cover the space separating them from him. Having almost reached him, the cook stopped again and glanced around with dull eyes. When he saw D'Arrast—yet without appearing to recognize him—he stood still, turned toward him. An oily, dirty sweat covered his face, which had gone gray; his beard was full of threads of saliva; and a brown, dry froth glued his lips together. He tried to smile. But, motionless under his load, his whole body was trembling except for the shoulders, where the muscles were obviously caught in a sort of cramp. The brother, who had recognized D'Arrast, said to him simply: "He already fell." And Socrates, popping up from nowhere, whispered in his ear: "Dance too much, Mr. D'Arrast, all night long. He's tired."

The cook advanced again with his jerky trot, not like a man who wants to progress but as if he were fleeing the crushing load, as if he hoped to lighten it through motion. Without knowing how, D'Arrast found himself at his right. He laid his hand lightly on the cook's back and walked beside him with hasty, heavy steps. At the other end of the street the shrine had disappeared, and the crowd, which probably now filled the square, did not seem to advance any more. For several seconds, the cook, between his brother and D'Arrast, made progress. Soon a mere space of some twenty yards separated him from the group gathered in front of the town hall to see him pass. Again, however, he stopped. D'Arrast's hand became heavier. "Come on, cook, just a little more," he said. The man trembled; the saliva began to trickle from his mouth again, while the sweat literally spurted from all over his body. He tried to breathe deeply and stopped short. He started off again, took three steps, and tottered. And suddenly the stone slipped onto his shoulder, gashing it, and then forward onto the ground, while the cook, losing his balance, toppled over on his side. Those who were preceding him and urging him on jumped back with loud shouts. One of them seized the cork mat while the others took hold of the stone to load it on him again.

Leaning over him, D'Arrast with his bare hand wiped the blood and dust from his shoulder, while the little man, his face against the ground, panted. He heard nothing and did not stir. His mouth opened avidly as if each breath were his last.

D'Arrast grasped him around the waist and raised him up as easily as if he had been a child. Holding him upright in a tight clasp with his full height leaning over him, D'Arrast spoke into his face as if to breathe his own strength into him. After a moment, the cook, bloody and caked with earth, detached himself with a haggard expression on his face. He staggered toward the stone, which the others were raising a little. But he stopped, looked at the stone with a vacant stare, and shook his head. Then he let his arms fall at his sides and turned toward D'Arrast. Huge tears flowed silently down his ravaged face. He wanted to speak, he was speaking, but his mouth hardly formed the syllables. "I promised," he was saying. And then: "Oh, Captain! Oh, Captain!" and the tears drowned his voice. His brother suddenly appeared behind him, threw his arms around him, and the cook, weeping, collapsed against him, defeated, with his head thrown back.

D'Arrast looked at him, not knowing what to say. He turned toward the crowd in the distance, now shouting again. Suddenly he tore the cork mat from the hands holding it and walked toward the stone. He gestured to the others to hold it up and then he loaded it almost effortlessly. His head pressed down under the weight of the stone, his shoulders hunched, and breathing rather hard, he looked down at his feet as he listened to the cook's sobs. Then with vigorous tread he started off on his own, without flagging covered the space separating him from the crowd at the end of the street, and energetically forced his way through the first rows, which stood aside as he approached. In the hubbub of bells and firecrackers he entered the square between two solid masses of onlookers, suddenly silent and gaping at him in amazement. He advanced with the same impetuous pace, and the crowd opened a path for him to the church. Despite the weight which was beginning to crush his head and neck, he saw the church and the shrine, which seemed to be waiting for him at the door. He had already gone beyond the center of the square in that direction when brutally, without knowing why, he veered off to the left and turned away from the church, forcing the pilgrims to face him. Behind him, he heard someone running. In front of him mouths opened on all sides. He didn't understand what they were shouting, although he seemed to recognize the one Portuguese word that was being constantly hurled at him. Suddenly Soc-

358

rates appeared before him, rolling startled eyes, speaking incoherently and pointing out the way to the church behind him. "To the church! To the church!" was what Socrates and the crowd were shouting at him. Yet D'Arrast continued in the direction in which he was launched. And Socrates stood aside, his arms raised in the air comically, while the crowd gradually fell silent. When D'Arrast entered the first street, which he had already taken with the cook and therefore knew it led to the river section, the square had become but a confused murmur behind him.

The stone weighed painfully on his head now and he needed all the strength of his long arms to lighten it. His shoulders were already stiffening when he reached the first streets on the slippery slope. He stopped and listened. He was alone. He settled the stone firmly on its cork base and went down with a cautious but still steady tread toward the huts. When he reached them, his breath was beginning to fail, his arms were trembling under the stone. He hastened his pace, finally reached the little square where the cook's hut stood, ran to it, kicked the door open, and brusquely hurled the stone onto the still glowing fire in the center of the room. And there, straightening up until he was suddenly enormous, drinking in with desperate gulps the familiar smell of poverty and ashes, he felt rising within him a surge of obscure and panting joy that he was powerless to name.

When the inhabitants of the hut arrived, they found D'Arrast standing with his shoulders against the back wall and eyes closed. In the center of the room, in the place of the hearth, the stone was half buried in ashes and earth. They stood in the doorway without advancing and looked at D'Arrast in silence as if questioning him. But he didn't speak. Whereupon the brother led the cook up to the stone, where he dropped on the ground. The brother sat down too, beckoning to the others. The old woman joined him, then the girl of the night before, but no one looked at D'Arrast. They were squatting in a silent circle around the stone. No sound but the murmur of the river reached them through the heavy air. Standing in the darkness, D'Arrast listened without seeing anything, and the sound of the waters filled him with a tumultuous happiness. With eyes closed, he joyfully acclaimed his own strength; he acclaimed, once again, a fresh beginning in life. At that moment, a firecracker went off that seemed very close. The brother moved a little away from the cook and, half turning toward D'Arrast but without looking at him, pointed to the empty place and said: "Sit down with us."

The Best of the World's Best Books
COMPLETE LIST OF TITLES IN
THE MODERN LIBRARY

MISCELLANEOUS

MODERN LIBRARY GIANTS

A series of sturdily bound and handsomely printed, full-sized library editions of books formerly available only in expensive sets. These volumes contain from 600 to 1,400 pages each.

THE MODERN LIBRARY GIANTS REPRESENT A SELECTION OF THE WORLD'S GREATEST BOOKS